MICHAEL MUHAMMAD KNIGHT

Soft Skull
Brooklyn

DEDICATION

for Mom first, Allah second

Library of Congress Cataloging-in-Publication Data
is available upon request.

ISBN 10: 1-59376-229-1
ISBN 13: 978-1-59376-229-2

Cover design by Goodloe Byron
Printed in the United States of America

Soft Skull Press
An Imprint of Counterpoint LLC
2117 Fourth Street
Suite D
Berkeley, CA 94710

www.softskull.com
www.counterpointpress.com

Distributed by Publishers Group West

10 9 8 7 6 5 4 3 2 1

MUHAMMAD WAS A PUNK ROCKER

I SEE MUHAMMAD
DOWN AT THE CORNER STORE
ROCKING ON GALAGA
GETTING THE HIGH SCORE
WHEN HE DELIVERS SERMONS
THE KIDS THINK HE'S A BORE
BUT WHEN HE SMASHES IDOLS
EVERYONE CHEERS FOR MORE

MUHAMMAD WAS A PUNK ROCKER
HE TORE EVERYTHING DOWN
MUHAMMAD WAS A PUNK ROCKER
AND HE ROCKED THAT TOWN

ALL THE PEOPLE IN MECCA
KNEW MUHAMMAD'S NAME
THEY KNEW HIM BY HIS FUCKED-UP HAIR
AND DANGLING WALLET CHAIN
THE KNEW HIM BY HIS SPIKES
AND SAID HE WAS INSANE
BUT ALI KNEW BETTER
UNCLE WOULDN'T PLAY THEIR GAME

MUHAMMAD WAS A PUNK ROCKER
YOU KNOW HE TORE SHIT UP
MUHAMMAD WAS A PUNK ROCKER
RANCID STICKER ON HIS PICKUP TRUCK

WHEN HE WAS IN A DUMPSTER BY HIMSELF
ALLAH TOLD HIM CRAZY THINGS
FOR MUHAMMAD TO SHARE WITH ALL OF US
ON HIS SIX HOLY STRINGS

CHAPTER I

Bismillahir, Rahmanir *and so on—*

"He lost his right index finger in a bet."

"Are you fuckin' kidding? What was the bet?"

"That he wouldn't chop off his finger."

"So he won the bet."

"Yeah, but he lost his finger. And he never went to the hospital or anything. Ended up with a massive infection in his hand—like a swollen abscess the size of a golfball that would have killed him if he didn't drain it."

"Is he okay now?"

"Yeah but when he's in salat and it comes time for the Tashahud, instead of the index he has to bob his *middle* finger up and down. It's like he flips himself off every time he prays."

In a few hours they were both unconscious.

It seemed like there was always at least one person awake in that punk house every hour of the day, as though it needed someone on alert at all times. Quietly descending the stairwell after another of Jehangir's parties, I assumed myself the sole bearer of that unofficial role for this shift. But turning into the lightless living room I encountered a scene that I believe, insha'Allah, will be forever subject to reevaluation in my mind. Even now I cannot say if it struck me as tragic, comedic or beautiful in a way that our imams would never fathom.

In the center of the floor, surrounded by wasted corpses of consciousness slumped into couches, passed out over each other and one who had thrown up on himself, flanked by littered armies of brown glass bottles and caved-in cans, an anonymous punk with dozens of hair antennas extending far from his head sat on the white cardboard of a pizza box. It was too dark to identify him but I probably would not have known the kid anyway. But I watched him for a moment; sitting on his feet, hands on his knees, facing the hole Umar had smashed in the cheap plaster with a baseball bat to indicate qiblah.

The kid bent forward in sujdah and came up with his forehead most likely wearing the chalky gray confetti of someone's tipped-over ashtray but he went down again, and I could hear the movements of his mouth if not the words he said. Then he stood up for another rakat, hands folded across his stomach. With a glance out the window I surmised that it was probably Fajr time—staghfir'Allah—and I should have joined him, increasing the rewards of his prayer by twenty-seven times; but instead I leaned at the living room doorway and watched as though this salaat had been executed on all our behalf. When he sat up again, I made sure to dip down the hall before he turned his head my way in salaams.

One thing I have faithfully observed and noted about punks: they're all legends, each and every last one of them, in one circle or another. Even if you never see them in the elements of their renown, even in a mere courtesy-handshake between friends of friends in a parking lot, you cannot help but feel an immortal vibrancy, a comic-book kind of costumed exuberance like that parking lot is host to a historic summit or a scene in ten thousand movies we're living right now. At least that's what I felt; but what's a punk anyway? I'm not going to open that can of worms here but I will say that in the story of myself and this house I ran through many conceptions of the word, and grew confident speaking of rude boys, riot grrrls, crust, Oi! and straightedge, and by knowing enough lingo to move comfortably in the culture, well, at one point seemed to make me punk myself; that is, if there are punks who major in engineering because their parents told them to.

Inevitably I reached the understanding that this word 'punk' does not mean anything tangible like 'tree' or 'car.' Rather, *punk* is like a flag; an open symbol, it only means what people believe it means. There was a time in China when red traffic lights meant 'go.' How would you begin to argue?

I stopped trying to define Punk around the same time I stopped trying to define Islam. They aren't so far removed as you'd think. Both began in tremendous bursts of truth and vitality but seem to have lost something along the way—the energy, perhaps, that comes with knowing the world has never seen such positive force and fury and never would again. Both have suffered from sell-outs and hypocrites, but also from true believers whose devotion had crippled their creative drive. Both are viewed by outsiders as unified, cohesive communities when nothing can be further from the truth.

I could go on but the most important similarity is that like Punk as mentioned above, Islam is itself a flag, an open symbol representing not *things*, but *ideas*. You cannot hold Punk or Islam in your hands. So what could they mean besides what you want them to?

I crept through the darkness until finding the kitchen, lest that praying kid detect my presence. Turned the light on and the place looked like W. had bombed the hell out if it looking for evildoers. I made my way past an obstacle course of tipped-over chairs, empty bottles and miscellaneous garbage around the table to get to the fridge, finding it completely empty except for a carton from the Chinese place—of what or how old, Allahu Alim—and a case of beer. There was always beer.

"Salaam-alaik," said a girl's voice behind me and I turned to find a baggy ninja with various band patches on her flowing burqa. You couldn't even see her eyes behind the fabric grid but I looked to the grungy kitchen floor anyway.

"Wa-alaikum as-salaam," I replied, "wa Rahmatullahi wa barakatuh. I was just looking for something to drink."

"There's plenty to drink."

"I was thinking, something *halal*."

"Ah, halal. You need to be specific in this place." She navigated around the table, grabbed a dirty glass, washed it out at the sink, let it fill and handed it to me.

"Jazakullah khair," I said. She picked up the chair I had climbed over, stood it up and sat down.

"Have a seat."

"Uh, I kind of have to get going, get ready for school in a couple hours."

"Oh right," she laughed. "Every time a man and woman are alone, Shaytan is the third present."

"Yeah—I mean no, it's not that or anything, it's, you know, I don't know if Umar would—"

"Umar straightedged himself into a sober stupor, don't worry about it. He'll wake up at noon, get all pissy that he missed Fajr and punch the TV."

"If it's just the TV," I replied, focusing on the grid where her eyes would be, "it's an improvement from last night."

"I thought he was going to kill that kid. Fuckin' macho pricks." There was something about Rabeya's language, or the fact that it came from *her*, that never ceased to unsettle me. And she knew it.

"Uh, did you make Fajr? Because I haven't yet, and I don't think the sun is up so if—"

"Sorry y'akhi, I'm raggin' it."

"Oh." I looked at my feet. Wa'Allah, what a filthy floor. "Well, I guess I'm going to." I went over to the sink, took off my shoes and then my socks while standing on my shoes, rolled up my sleeves and proceeded with wudhu while the water ran over empty green Heinekens in the sink. Rabeya sat content knowing that none of my existing scripts for male-female interaction, mumin or kafr, gave me any frame of reference for dealing with her.

We never saw her face, which I think empowered Rabeya with a certain psychological leverage. However, not everything she did with said benefit would find such easy encouragement from tradition. While Rabeya was as staunch a Muslim as anyone there, it remained her own Islam as she saw fit to live it. This was the girl who jumped in front of the microphone at last night's party decked out in full purdah to cover the Stooges' "Nazi Girlfriend" through her niqab singing slow and spooky like Iggy Pop's withered Old Man Mortality voice—"I want to fuck her on the floor, among my books of ancient lore"—the same girl who stood in front of our baseball-bat-through-the-wall-mihrab on Fridays to give khutbah and circulated handwritten rants on the sexism of both hemispheres in her self-published zine *Ayesha's Hymen.*

I went back down the hall and into the living room. Noted the pizza box that had been a prayer rug—the praying kid was gone and the sky outside those windows was just light enough for me to see fully all the filth and ruin of the room, including the living ruin on the couches. The scene was enclosed in walls covered with punk posters, 8 1/2 x 11 fliers for local shows, stains, scuffs and around the smashed-in mihrab, various plaques and posters of Arabic calligraphy: Qur'anic ayats, 99 Names of Allah, a green Saudi flag wearing the anarchy symbol in black spray paint and so on—all of it mantled in that grayness which occurs just before the sun's really out and hurts your eyes; those last gasps of night as it shuffles on out for a new day and McDonald's prepares for the seniors with their coffees and newspapers. Had the sun technically risen? Was it too late for Fajr? I had forgotten how the whole thing worked.

Came back in the afternoon and collapsed in a smelly beat-up recliner on the front porch. Hanging lifeless my right hand brushed against an empty bottle left standing by the chair. I half-wondered about Umar's mood but was too tired to care. A pack of cigarettes rested on the porch railing. My eyelids pulled themselves down without any help from me; I was on my way out. Then Sham 69's "Hey Little Rich Boy" came blaring from inside the house, meaning that someone had detected my presence. It was a daily joke as reliable as Zuhr's adhan in Masjid Haram.

The screen door swung open and out lunged Amazing Ayyub the bone-thin Iranian smack-head in tight blue jeans and no shirt and a huge KARBALA tattooed in Old English letters just below his collarbone, dancing like a bald idiot on the porch and hollering along:

"HEY, LITTLE RICH BOY! TAKE A GOOD LOOK AT ME! HEY, LITTLE RICH BOY—"

"I don't *want* to look at you," I replied. "I want to die for like, a week and then I'll be set, insha'Allah." Amazing Ayyub kept on stomping and thrusting his fists in the air.

"HEY, LITTLE RICH BOY! TAKE A GOOD LOOK AT ME!"

I closed my eyes knowing the song would eventually have to end. Amazing Ayyub went inside.

Then the song started again.

"Ayyub, man!" He flew back out as though thrown and stomped the porch for one more round.

"HEY, LITTLE RICH BOY! TAKE A GOOD LOOK AT

ME! HEY, LITTLE RICH BOY! TAKE A GOOD LOOK AT ME!"

"Al-hamdulilah, Ayyub. Please, man, come on—my eyes are—"

"HEY, LITTLE RICH BOY! TAKE A GOOD LOOK AT ME! HEY, LITTLE RICH BOY! TAKE A GOOD LOOK AT ME!"

Then he went back in, the statement finally made to his own satisfaction.

With the porch to myself, I drifted through varying states of consciousness; it was that kind of tired where you're not sure if you were ever really asleep but you couldn't remember something that had happened five minutes ago, so you must have been.

The familiar refrain of *don't drink-don't smoke-don't fuck* from Minor Threat's "Out of Step" came cacophoning round the corner, accompanied by the static and pops of speakers pushed beyond their means. I knew I'd see, if I had the strength to turn my head, a charismatically war-torn pickup truck with the tailgate covered by stickers of various bands and a green one reading "ISLAM is the way." Umar pulled up in front of the house and hopped out in all his Umar-ness, the details communicating his conviction which came forth as both admirable and irritating: the plain white tee stretched around thick biceps and a barrel chest, the shaved head of assumed militancy, the rhetoric of tattoos—big black "X" on the back of each hand, star-and-crescent on outer right forearm, Muhammad's name—*sallallaho alayhe wa salaam*—in Arabic on outer left forearm, and then there was the kicker that I found myself studying intently no matter how hard I tried to avoid it: right across the front of his neck, right on his throat, a green 2:219.

"As-salaamu alaikum," I called, frozen in the recliner as Umar walked up the steps.

"Brother Yusef Ali! Wa-alaikum as-salaam. Kay fallahukum,

y'akhi?"

"Ana bikail," I replied, heaving myself up to shake his hand. The little I knew of Arabic beyond what served a religious purpose, I learned from him. To make it fair, he got some Urdu. "Key ali?" I asked.

"Teek hai, achha." He reached into his khaki pocket and pulled out two thin siwaks, offering one to me. As I took it I noticed the broken skin on his knuckles but chose not to bring up the previous night. If Umar were in a bad mood I failed to see it. Perhaps he felt a special bond between us, being the only two in the house who had no idea what beer tasted like. I jerked the siwak between my teeth while Umar's hung from his lips like a cigarette. He always stood as though anxiously prepared for some assailant to jump out at him from behind a tree. Kept trying not to but still stared at the 2:219 and cringed at the idea of a needle driving ink into my neck, but that summed up Umar. He wore his struggles like a badge. Our eyes met and I looked away quick.

"Did that hurt?" I asked, though we had talked about it before, most likely on other occasions that he caught me gawking.

"Al-hamdulilah," he replied, holding the siwak between his index and middle fingers with the same cocky coolness of a cigarette.

Then we were both startled by a shrill whine whose source was unknowable because its sudden volume consumed the whole world, sounding like some outer-space animal as the pitch climbed until our ears hurt and kept going, kept going, reaching higher still until finally descending in a familiar melody.

It was an electric-guitar adhan.

With the second *Allahu Akbar* I realized it came from the roof.

I went inside and upstairs on a mission, straight to the bathroom past barefooted Amazing Ayyub making his wudhu in the sink. Following a coiled black cord that must have began at the amp down the hall, I climbed out the window onto the roof where

Jehangir Tabari stood statuesque with foot-high yellow mohawk thick and bristly like the brush on an old Roman soldier's helmet, guitar hanging off his lean but urgently powerful frame. The house's other mohawk, molded into four or five long orange points, belonged to an Indonesian called Fasiq Abasa who sat close to the roof's edge with a blunt in hand and the Qur'an in his lap. Neither of them saw me. Jehangir kept to his role as muezzin with utmost seriousness. Fasiq inhaled again and lowered his head, though I couldn't tell if he was reading Qur'an or just silently mouthing the adhan. I felt the chill in my spine as calls to prayer have often provided, but there came with Jehangir Tabari's a sensation entirely new: a surging resonance of hope, a vibrant six-stringed promise that Islam's glory days were not the sole property of Abbasids and Fatimids but could be our days here, now, if we had the spirit to claim them.

His fingers lingered on the final *la ilaha illa Allah*, hitting every note of a man in Badshahi's minaret. Like the adhan as traditionally performed, that last line hit me as vaguely sorrowful in its tone, almost a little death. Jehangir stood staring out over the roofs across the street, past them, past those, forward on to *something*, I don't know what and I would have looked that way to see but my eyes were frozen on *him*. There's no word for me but *taqwa* to call what beamed from his empyreal profile: the hair reaching for heaven, black leather vest crowded with spikes reflecting the sun, guitar dangling freely on its strap as he let go. I just looked at him, my body charged with a kind of holy nervousness until he turned and saw me.

"Fuck," he said smiling, returning us to Earth with that raspy, scratchy voice like he had spent all night chain-smoking in the freezing rain—imagine Tim Armstrong with a Punjabi accent. "As-salaams, man, what's up."

That made Fasiq turn around.

"Shit! Yusef Ali, what's the good word?"

"Wa-alaikum as-salaam," I replied to Jehangir, shaking his hand and embracing delicately with the hanging guitar between us. Then I leaned just enough towards the roof edge to reach Fasiq's offered hand.

"Yusef, you—?" asked Fasiq, gesturing to me with the blunt.

"I'm straight." How long had that psychotic hashishiyyun known me and how many times had he offered? If I had been as harsh in my declines as Umar, the kid would have learned by now.

"Mash'Allah," Fasiq replied. With a big suck on the blunt he looked back down at his Qur'an.

And there we were, three idiots out on the roof: Jehangir with guitar hanging off him, Fasiq with his weed and kitab and me with my hands in my pockets.

"That's bid'ah," said a voice from inside the house. Umar stood leaning on the bathroom windowsill, peeling off some chipped paint in full hero pose. Everything that guy did, he just looked *tough* doing it.

"Okay," Jehangir replied, "so it's bid'ah." Umar was then distracted by the sight of Fasiq Abasa at the roof's edge reading the Qur'an as he puffed. Fasiq looked back at Umar. My eyes darted from one to the other as though watching a game of telepathic tennis. Umar with 2:219 carved into his neck, Fasiq with lips pursed holding in the smoke. "You know," said Jehangir, breaking the silence, "it's only *Muslims* who use the term 'innovation' to mean something bad."

"Don't forget that you're Muslim too," said Umar, turning from Fasiq. "Aren't you?"

"La ilaha illa Allah," Jehangir replied. "Time for Asr." Fasiq exhaled his smoke and we climbed back in the window.

I made wudhu in the same sink that Amazing Ayyub had just used. When I came downstairs Umar and Jehangir had cleared most of the living room floor and laid out the prayer rugs, a line of four with one up in front facing the big hole in the wall. While in different colors with a variety of border designs, the rugs looked more or less uniform when laid out one next to the other. Green and gold with al-Aqsa, tan and red with the Prophet's Masjid, green and gold with the Ka'ba, another green-and-gold al-Aqsa. Some of them had tags revealing where they had come from. Turkey, Egypt, Saudi, Pakistan. The imam rug was blue and gold with al-Aqsa. We had a five-man jamaat: me, Jehangir, Umar, Fasiq and Amazing Ayyub, all standing around with our discarded shoes scattered around the rugs.

"Who's going to lead?" I asked.

"Fasiq?" asked Jehangir though I knew it was only to get a rise from Umar.

"He's fuckin' intoxicated," Umar snapped. "I'm not praying behind him."

"Fuck you, Umar," said Fasiq, turning then to the Amazing One. "Ayyub?" Amazing Ayyub, still shirtless, threw his fists and knees in the air and did a dumb frenzied punk dance almost shaking the house with his stomps.

"Who knows the most Qur'an?" I asked. Fasiq looked at the carpet, its beer stains and cigarette burns partially veiled by our rugs.

"That'd be Umar," Jehangir conceded, still in his spike-covered jacket.

"It smells like shit in here," said Amazing Ayyub. "Shit and puke and… fuckin' beer and shit."

"Staghfir'Allah," Umar replied, whipping out a bottle of rosewood or sandalwood or Egyptian musk or something—you never knew what with him and his sophistication when it came to that stuff—and spilled it around the room. I'm not sure of the effect.

"Allahu Akbar, Allahu Akbar," said Jehangir, to which we

assembled behind Umar. "Allahu Akbar, Allahu Akbar, ashadu an la ilaha illa Allah, ashadu anna Muhammadu rasullullah, hayyal as-salat, hayyal al-falah, qad iqama tis-salat, qad iqama..."

Umar turned his back on the big hole in the wall, Qur'anic plaques and posters and the Saudi flag with spray-painted anarchy-A and looked at us.

"Straighten out your lines," he said before turning back around. Umar was annoying at times but remained the right guy to pray behind. He took it seriously and approached the manner with a firm holiness that immediately put me in the proper mode.

Umar made a silent du'a, building up the tense anticipation as I waited for him to finally lift his hands to his ears and begin the prayer. The underlying hostility between Umar and Jehangir or Umar and Fasiq died before our first sujdah. By the time Imam Umar greeted those angels on his left, we were all brothers again.

I had moved in little over a year before. Telling Ummi and Abu back in Syracuse that it'd be a house full of Muslims, they were more than happy to send the rent every month.

"It'd be better for you than living in the dorms," Abu told me. "There are the very bad things there."

"You live with Muslims," said Ummi, "and stay focused."

"As-salaamu alaikum," Umar answered when I called the number on the flier. After a brief rundown on the rent, utilities and such he made sure to check whether I knew it was a *Muslim* house. Said my room's previous occupant had been gone at least a year. His name was Mustafa and he lived firmly by Islamic principles, Umar explained, at such a level that no other resident attained in his time and none since have even approached. I discovered this upon my first inspection of the room as Mustafa had left some books behind: all nine volumes of Sahih Bukhari bound in green leather, a copy of *The Spectacle of Death* and a cardboard box filled with gorgeously ornamented Qur'ans. "He used to get them free from the Saudi embassy all the time," Umar explained. A flap on the box bore Mustafa's name and the house's address.

Along with unofficial tenant Fasiq Abasa, who crashed on one of our couches and occasionally put in for groceries, I constituted the third generation in the house's Islamic history. The previous wave had seen the appearances of Jehangir Tabari and Amazing Ayyub. Originally, in what Umar would impress upon me as a primordial golden age, it was Mustafa, Umar, Rabeya and Rude Dawud (who back then was only Dawud).

"That was when we really had it," Umar once told me in his truck. It, I assumed, meant *Islam*. "That's why Rabeya's room is downstairs," he explained. "Back then we didn't even want to live with a female, you know, but Mustafa said we could give her the room downstairs that went right to the back door so she could go in through the back. No males were allowed to use the downstairs bathroom, that was just for her. And we had curtains hanging over the doorway to the kitchen, you had to knock if you needed something. If she wasn't in there you could go in but you had to announce yourself in case she was on her way to the kitchen, and if she was in there already she would slide you what you needed under the curtain."

"Mash'Allah," I replied. "So she wore full purdah even back then?"

"Al-hamdulilah, of course she did and back then she didn't have patches on it or anything. Back then we prayed together, and we did it *right*. Right times, right ways. That was before Rabeya started demanding to lead salat, and before all these haram influences came in—khamr, zina, before all these parties." More or less, Umar was saying *before Jehangir Tabari*. "Even me," he said to my surprise. "Even me, brother."

"What?"

"I had something back then I might not have now. You know..." He looked at his truck's tape player running Youth of Today's "Disengage." "You know, y'akhi, they say the stringed instruments are not actually halal, they count as *ma'aazif*—"

"Insha'Allah," I replied.

"Yeah," said Umar. "Insha'Allah, that's what the scholars say. Back when Mustafa had your room, we didn't listen to haram things. We didn't talk about haram things. We weren't consuming haram things and we didn't have kafrs in our house mixing males and females together, singing, swearing, doing such-and-such."

I knew it was not Umar's intention but somehow I felt as though it were all my fault—or at least that my presence symbolized the declining state of affairs. *Back when Mustafa had your room.* If Mustafa were still there Umar would have felt better about himself.

I confess that in the time I had that room, I barely cracked any of Mustafa's books. The Bukharis gathered dust on his old bookshelf—if I needed anything of the good Imam it was easier to just look through hadith databases online. I took one of the Saudi Embassy's Qur'ans and put it by my bed, where it stayed more or less untouched besides the occasional bedtime reading of *Ya Sin.* Fasiq Abasa wanted the rest and I gladly parted with the obtrusive box. As for *The Spectacle of Death*, that went to Amazing Ayyub and gave him a steady supply of conversation starters. *Hey y'akhi, you know what happens in Jehennam to women who wear perfume?* Thus-and-so.

On Fridays the living room doubled as a masjid, mostly for kids from the campus who couldn't identify with the MSA. They were nowhere near being ersatz mumins of Fasiq's level, but you still had girls who didn't cover their hair, guys who went to clubs down on Chippewa and so forth. Our house with its punk posters and vandalized Saudi flag was the closest thing they had to a comfortable Islamic experience in which they could pray and embrace their culture without having to feel inadequate. It took awhile for some to really adjust to that atmosphere in which it was okay to admit you did not pray five times daily, or that you once had an ice-cream dessert containing rum, or you dated and went to *kafr* parties.

Umar had been the original impetus behind holding jumaa in our house, but the feeling of the place easily surrendered itself to Jehangir. He'd stand up there by the hole in our wall with brilliant high stripe of hair down the middle of his head, the sides often dark with stubble and whip up something about the life of Rasullullah, *sallallaho alayhe wa salaam*, that would send us charging out the door feeling like we could be all the secret heroes who lurked as fantasies in our chests, the Super Mumins, MegaMujahids and Laser-Eyed Shaheeds. And Jehangir did it, Jehangir in his brown qurtab with gold trim and big yellow mohawk, Jehangir did it.

Rabeya's khutbahs, though lacking the gleaming punk melodrama promise of Jehangir's, hit me with the feeling that we had done a great deal for Islam just by sitting there to hear her. She knew her stuff more than any of us, used books for furniture in her room—guests sitting on stacks of Betty Freidan and Adrienne Rich and Simone de Beauvoir, and Fatima Mernissi and Leila Ahmed and Amina Wadud and what-not—and gave everything she had, every stupid second of her life, to that Islam. But I felt like there was nowhere else in the world that she could give a khutbah to men, and for that maybe we would be the vanguard of something new.

When it came Umar's turn to play imam, he did it all Sunna. Gave the proper du'as, recited ayats in perfect Arabiyya, told us to make our lines straight. Once while leading, Umar had us do an extra sujdah. I asked him about it after prayer.

"It's a sujdah-e-sahw," Umar explained. "I had forgotten to straighten up after the second ruku; you didn't notice?"

"Oh," I replied. "Oh yeah, yeah I remember that, I just didn't know you were doing, you know, a sujdah-e-sahw. That's cool, though."

Didn't even realize Rabeya was in the house until I heard Tori Amos' "Muhammad My Friend" blaring from her room. I went out to the porch and leaned back in the recliner ready to pass out again. The two mohawks came out and chilled. Jehangir's eyes stayed glazed to the street in front of our house, as though if he looked at it long enough the road would just reach out, grab his neck and take him somewhere. Fasiq seemed focused on his feet. Nobody said anything for awhile.

Then came a dread-headed white girl jogging around the corner, dreads flopping around with her bounces. Hoped Umar wouldn't come out and see her gym shorts and sportsbra or he'd complain about it when she was gone. Lynn, the Muslimah-gone-wrong; maybe it was Islam-done-*her*-wrong. She had converted to Islam, or *re*-verted to Islam or *embraced* Islam or however they say, from a Catholic upbringing. Somebody had turned her onto Rumi which led her to read up a little on the deen and she liked the general idea of it—you know, One God who doesn't beget children, remembering your Creator five times a day, the whole racial-unity Malcolm sense and *theoretical* lack of a priesthood. So she went to a masjid in the suburb of Amherst and took shahadah. They gave her a hejab but were nice about it. They were nice about everything—those guys could say the meanest, most ignorant things but still use a gentle voice and try to sound rational and loving through it all. Told her she had to break up with her then-boyfriend, get rid of her dog, throw away old kafr clothes and cover it all except the face and hands, take a nice Arabic name, stop listening to her favorite artists, give dawah to her family or else their brains would burn and boil like Abu Talib, the whole nine. Eventually Lynn gave up on it, kept to her Rumi and stopped going there. We constituted the last vestige of her abusive relationship with the *umma.*

"Peace," she said, slowing down to a walk.

"Peace," Jehangir replied.

"Wasalaam," I replied.

"Lynn, man," said Fasiq. "What's the good word?"

"Oh, just out for a jog. You know, won't be long before I can't anymore."

"Yeah," Fasiq replied. "Fuckin' Buffalo. We have like five good months, maybe."

"Can never tell," she said. "Can't wait for the summer to get here, though. Finish up school—"

"You're graduating?" I asked.

"I mean, just for the year," she replied. "Just to not be stressin' shit."

"Oh."

"I still have a ways to go."

"Mash'Allah."

"I like the hair," said Fasiq.

"Really? Thanks. It's getting kind of itchy."

"You should show it to Rude Dawud," said Jehangir.

"Have you noticed his accent changing?" noted Fasiq. "It's like, this weird hybrid of Sudanese and Jamaican."

"I think it's the guys he's hanging out with all the time," Jehangir replied. "The whole Caribbean thing, it's rubbing off on him."

"Is he still in that band?" Lynn asked.

"Which one?"

"What were they called… Save Me the Skank, I think."

"No, they broke up," Fasiq replied. "Then he had another one called Skallahu Akbar."

"Oh," said Lynn, smiling. "I like that."

"They broke up too."

"Oh."

"Only two ska bands in Buffalo history," said Jehangir with a laugh.

Just then Umar shoved the screen door hard out of his way and went stomping down the steps.

"Where are you off to?" asked Fasiq.

"I gotta go get 'em," answered Umar.

"Who?"

"Rude Dawud. He's down at the Jamaican store on Main Street, needs a ride." Umar climbed into his truck and drove off, Minor Threat playing where they had left off.

Rude Dawud was one of *those* guys, you know, the automatic and necessary legends. He never said much, did not really do much to impose his personality on the place the way somebody like Umar would, but there was something about him that made you love the idea that he was there, to some extent a participant in your life and you'd relish his role because he was the only one who could fill it. Nobody could step into that house and take Rude Dawud's spot any more than I could have taken Mustafa's.

Fasiq, Jehangir and Lynn had gone inside and I had almost fallen asleep in the recliner when Umar's truck returned, this time blaring Desmond Dekker's "It's a Shame" which I received as comedic simply for Umar's usual diet of straightedge fare. When he pulled up to the curb, out climbed Rude Dawud—skinny Sudanese guy in sharp black suit, tie, shades and pork-pie hat—and a chubby dreadlocked character in red, yellow and green shirt looking like the flag of some country, but which one I had no idea. Umar looked pissed when he got out—maybe not pissed, at least not any more pissed than usual, but vaguely *wary*.

"As-salaamu alaikum," Dawud said to me with big warm smile.

"Wa alaikum as-salaam," I sent back at him. I pulled myself up for a genuine handshake and embrace.

"This here is Albert," said Dawud.

"What's up," I said to Albert upon casually taking his hand.

"Chillin'," Albert replied.

"Where's brother Fasiq?" asked Rude Dawud.

"He's in there," I replied. "Lynn stopped by too."

"Mash'Allah," said Dawud, and they went inside. I could have gone upstairs to my room but it was too easy to just sink in that recliner and sleep. When I woke up the sky was a different color and I felt as though twenty years had passed. I sat silently appreciating the time-travel of a heavy nap. Then Umar crashed out the door with a small bat in his hand.

"The screen door, be careful," I said wimpishly.

"Fuckin' kids," snarled Umar. "Fuckin', fuckin' *kids*, that's fuckin' bullshit."

"What?"

"Oh, please forgive the language, y'akhi."

"No, no it's cool, what's—"

"Those fuckin' kids!" Umar went over to his truck at the curb and banged on the side once with his little bat, giving a loud *clang* that reverberated through the neighborhood. Then he turned and walked toward the house looking like he was about to tear it down with his weapon, but stopped at the sidewalk. "You know what they're doing up there?" I automatically assumed it had something to do with *khamr* or *zina*. "They're smoking up!" he exclaimed. "But you know, whatever they want to do, fine. If they want to poison their bodies and their minds and destroy themselves, *al-hamdulilah*, let 'em at it. That's not what it is. What it is, is... fuckin' Rude Dawud, man... he had that shit in *my* truck. Him or his man, whichever, one of them had that shit in *my* truck. When Rude Dawud called for a ride, he knew they would be bringing that shit in *my* truck, over here to *my* home, to smoke with Fasiq. That's just disrespect, man. That is total fucking lack of respect. All of them, man. Fuckin' Dawud, fuckin' whats-his-name Rasta Man, fuckin' Fasiq, and fuck it, that bitch too man. Fuck all 'em. Man, I am sorry for cursing right now, but I am heated. I am real mad, y'akhi. They just completely disrespected me man, and I'm pissed."

"I understand," I said.

"Man, if we were pulled over with weed in my truck? That'd be it. I would be busted for that too. That would go on *my* record. I'd have drugs on my fuckin' record. Wouldn't that be something."

"Fasiq thinks that shit's halal," I said for no real purpose.

"Yeah, little hashishiyyun," Umar replied. "That's because of all these characters the King of Ska's bringing by. He thinks he has some fuckin' spiritual basis for it, too."

"Well," I said, though I had no real place in the argument, "he says the Qur'an only specifically forbids alcohol."

"That's fuckin' bullshit," Umar snapped back. "That is fucking bullshit. 5:90, man. That shit is fuckin' as *khamr* as anything else." Umar always seemed to pronounce Arabic terms with a certain tonal emphasis. I realized what a stupid scene it was, me half-out in the recliner and Umar storming up and down the sidewalk in front of our house. "2:219," he added for good measure, making me wince with a hard slap to his own tattooed neck. "Is Dawud even Muslim anymore?"

"Sure he is."

"Mash'Allah," he replied with sarcastic relief.

"Was Jehangir in there with them?" I asked.

"I don't know. I don't think so." Umar looked at me quizzically, as though confused or even annoyed by my interest. Sometimes I did approach Jehangir Tabari with a sort of childish hero-worship; and while I knew he was no straightedger, hearing of his occasional abstinence gave me a strange comfort.

"I got to get out of here, y'akhi. I'll check you later." While walking back to his truck Umar turned and said "insha'Allah" as an afterthought.

CHAPTER II

Jehangir Tabari had come from California and would often speak of the Muslim punk scene out there—"taqwacore" as he called it, pointing to various patches on his spiked leather jacket and red plaid DogPile pants as he told stories about the bands. Taqwacore bands ran the gamut in attitude and ideology; there were groups like the Bin Qarmats and the Zaqqums whose lyrics and behavior lurked somewhere between social protest and juvenile disesteem, but also bands such as Bilal's Boulder that wouldn't even allow girls into their shows. Some bands had high political content and others veered more toward the aloof Sufi end of the spectrum. Jehangir seemed equally proud of them all, as though nothing in the world could pin him down to an intellectual commitment.

"You should see it, y'akhi," he told me once, sitting on the back of his car in a parking lot while we waited for Fasiq to buy rolling papers. "I was at this fuckin' Mutaweens show in Sacramento and—"

"Who?" I asked.

"The Mutaweens," he replied, pointing to a sticker on his car. "Great fuckin' band, I have one of their records up here, you should check them out. Anyway, I'm at this Mutaweens show and I'm in the pit, getting tossed around n' whatever, and then the music just *stops*—bam, just like that, it stops and we stop slamming into each other, everything just freezes and all you hear is the singer up there reciting *ar-Rahman* as beautiful as I'd ever heard, and he just keeps going with it—the whole sura, you know, all the *fabi-ayyi ala irabbikuma tukazibans* and shit, and all these hard-ass punks just stand there listening and by the time he's done, half of us are in fuckin' tears, bro."

"Mash'Allah," I replied gravely.

"Yeah, y'akhi. It's an amazing scene of people out there." Sitting on the trunk of his car, I looked down at all the stickers, a few representing bands I'd never heard of. Jehangir had since gotten New York plates for his car, but the stickers still bore witness to his voyage; he had really been out *there*, out *West*; he had stood at the very edge of this continent, soaking in the future of American Islam, and then came out here to share the good news. Actually, I never found out why he had come out here. Once I thought he said it had something to do with his brother, but Jehangir didn't have any brothers.

"How did you get to Buffalo?" I asked, realizing as soon as I said it that the question had nothing to do with anything.

"The I-90," he replied.

"The whole way?"

"I actually left from Seattle," he explained. "I had some friends up there, I drove up for a big show and crashed at their house. You should see their place, y'akhi—it's the ultimate taqwacore house. Had a fuckin' cupola on the side that they used as a minaret. My boy Uthman climbed up on the roof, put a gold fuckin' crescent right on the top of it. Unbelievable, y'akhi. You should've seen that fucker shining in the sun. Made you really feel something, you know? Had a sound-system in there, the whole neighborhood heard their fuckin' adhan." Just then I noticed that faraway gleaming gaze that Jehangir got sometimes, as though he were right in Seattle looking at it. Made me almost feel like *I* could see it, cupola-minaret with sun bouncing off a golden crescent, before Jehangir came back to the world. "But yeah, mash'Allah, I went up to Seattle for a show, had my car all packed, left the next morning. Did you know the I-90's the longest interstate in the country?"

"No."

"It is. In fuckin' Montana there's spots where it's not even a divided highway, it's just a regular road."

"Really?"

"We should go out West sometime, Yusef Ali. Get a van, make like an interstate jam'aat. Fuck, if we did it this summer we could stop at the ISNA convention in Chicago." I laughed at that knowing how taqwacores felt about ISNA scenes, or how such scenes felt about *them.* "Fuckin' A, Yusef. We should do that. Hit 'em all, make a tour of it. ISNA, ICNA, CAIR, AMC, MPAC, shit, what else do they have now? We'll get thrown out of all of 'em. And along the way we'd round up all the queer alims, drunk imams, punk ayatollahs, masochistic muftis, junkie shaykhs, retarded mullahs and gutter-mouthed maulanas we can find, just load up a van 'til we can't fit no more and then have guys hangin' off the side like in Rawal-fuckin'pindi! Shit, man, down the I-90. And it all ends in Khalifornia."

"*Khalif*-ornia?"

"Yeah, y'akhi, Khalifornia. There's a group out there, they're trying to establish the Khilafah out there. Call themselves fuckin' Khalifornia."

We laughed and then Fasiq came out of the cigar store with his big dumb mohawk and rolling papers. "What took you so long?" yelled Jehangir across the parking lot.

"You wouldn't believe it," Fasiq yelled back. "Fuckin' Sayyed was in there."

"What? What the shit is Sayyed doing in there? Is he hashishiyyun now?"

"Nah, he was going out and his kafr friend asked him to pick up papers so we were just in there shooting the shit."

"We'll wait for him, see if he needs a ride."

Sayyed was a good Muslim—at least less likely than Jehangir and crew to get thrown out of an ISNA convention. I sat in the back seat with him as Jehangir peeled out of the parking lot, Fasiq riding shotgun, Screeching Weasel's "Anthem for a New Tomorrow" emanating from Jehangir's cheap old tape player. We all tried coming up with things to talk about with Sayyed—*how are classes, how's your family* and so forth. It all seemed somehow awkward; but I fear that I might have been in his place once before learning to coolly interact with guys like Fasiq Abasa. We dropped him off at the campus with the usual pleasantries and then swung back to our awful house.

Amazing Ayyub was out on the porch with big KARBALA you could read on his chest a mile away, saw us and ran inside to put on Sham 69's "Hey Little Rich Boy." Then he burst back out, flew over the porch steps and leaped onto the roof of Jehangir's car to dance above my head. When I stepped out he met me with a flying plancha off the car. We rolled around on the front lawn for awhile. I've learned from experience not to wear my nicer clothes around these guys.

I'm not sure how Amazing Ayyub got that appellation or even how he ended up a permanent pseudo-resident of our house, but I remember the first time I met him. I was down in the living room trying to troubleshoot my laptop, fairly new to the house myself. Jehangir introduced us. Ayyub was shirtless, bringing my eyes immediately to his tattoo.

"Do you know anything about computers?" I asked. "My sound-chip is giving me a hassle, but it worked fine upstairs—"

Ayyub leaned over me as though he would assess the situation, but then—with no kleenex or even his hand to block it—he blew his nose with such violent energy it sent a long yellow-green projectile right at my screen. We both just looked at it, contemplating the sparkly rainbow-dots its accompanying spray made of my pixels.

Then I looked at the Amazing One. "What are you studying?" I asked. "What's, uh, what's your major? Or do you not, uh, do you go to school, or…"

After examining the grass stains from our impromptu wrestling match, I went inside to see what the guys were up to though I should have figured since Fasiq had just bought rolling papers. They were up in Rude Dawud's room with the door closed and the Specials' "Rudy Ska" coming through the walls.

I opened the door to a blast of smoke and Rude Dawud explaining to Fasiq that "whether you say 'Allah' or you say 'Jah,' brother, what does it matter?" Dawud—Rude, priceless Dawud in an almost-Hawaiian shirt but still with the sunglasses and pork-pie hat—saw me and smiled. "Hey, brother Yusef, how are you doing man?"

"Al-hamdulilah," I replied, shaking Dawud's hand and sitting on his bed by Jehangir. He had the weed in his left and passed it to Fasiq. The room smelled rotten. Dawud's walls were covered with pictures of Haile Selassie and two three-foot by five-foot flags—one for his homeland, the other a fashion statement. He saw me looking at them.

"The Sudan," he explained, pointing to the one with green triangle against red, white and black stripes. "Jamaica," he added, pointing to the yellow X dividing green top-bottom from black left-right.

"Mash'Allah," I replied. Fasiq inhaled and then motioned to me. I raised my hand in silent but polite refusal and he passed the ganja to Jehangir.

"In the Sudan, brother, that is where you see Islam, the way it really is, the way Islam is supposed to be," he said, struggling to get his words together. "I mean, brother, the government there is very bad, they are very very bad—but the *people*, y'akhi, they are the good people. They are good Muslim people."

"Al-hamdulilah," I replied.

"And Jamaica, brother, you know, it is the same way—spiritual people, brother, good people. I was just saying to brother Fasiq here, brother, you know? Whether you say 'Allah' or if you say 'Jah' what does it matter? We are all brothers, right?"

"Right."

"We all come from single pair, right?"

"Subhana'Allah," I said smiling.

"Yes, brother! Subhana *Jah!* It is same, right?"

"We're all brothers," said Fasiq. Jehangir leaned back taking it all in.

"Brother," said Rude Dawud, "we all come from the Earth, you know? We all come from the Earth, and we all go back to the Earth—"

He said 'Earth' with a slight discarding of the *h*—almost *ert*, but not quite.

As Fasiq stood up I noticed he had a Qur'an with him, one of the copies I had given him from Mustafa's legacy. He gave his salaams to everyone and left the room, closing Dawud's door behind him. I knew he'd climb out the bathroom window to the roof. With Fasiq gone, it suddenly seemed unnatural for me to sit in a room clouded with marijuana smoke, so I gave my salaams and followed him.

Standing by the bathroom sink, I looked out the window at that mohawked Malaysian hashishiyyun in black zip-up Operation Ivy hoodie, his back to me bearing the faceless image of Ska Man. I looked at the character who was really only an outline, a ragged hat-wearing silhouette against the backdrop of a full moon as he lunged forward in frozen leap from some urban rooftop, perhaps, as he pounced down on muggers and evil-doers. Then I felt self-conscious about studying a cartoon on the back of my friend's sweatshirt, especially since Fasiq was unaware of my presence. I left him and his Qur'an, wondering if maybe I should have just stayed there in case he took a chemically-impaired fall off the roof. Staghfir'Allah.

I walked back to Dawud's room, opened the door and just kind of stood there awkwardly watching them smoke and laugh.

"Al-hamdulilah," said Jehangir, leaning back, his eyes red. "Al-hamdulilahi rabbil'Alameen, yeah yeah, ar-Rahmanir Raheem, maliki yawmi-deen! Yusef, I'm just an innocent poor heart, that's all. And maybe I'm just an innocent poor heart because my Abu kicked off when I was seven and left me surrounded by women who only wanted me to be *happy* and didn't give a fuck how I ended up otherwise. Did you ever think of that?"

"No," I replied, half-wondering if this had anything to do with my parents instructing me to take engineering for a major. "I never thought of that, y'akhi."

"Fuck," he said, sitting up straight on the bed, eyes off to nowhere, keeping his mouth open long after saying the word. "Me neither."

I never approached my eternal sobriety with the same militancy as Umar; nor have I ever identified with his straightedge punk scene, mainly because I don't care for the music. Straightedge bands are just mad and noisy; I happen to prefer melody and at least *somewhat* coherent lyrics. There have been times, however, that I conceded to others' placement of me in the straightedge category, because with the label came a validation of my own coolness; without it I would simply be a guy who didn't drink, smoke or have sex. So I may have attended at least one of Jehangir's parties with black-marker X's across my hands and requesting Minor Threat from whoever was manning the CD player at the time.

Strangely, however, for as many punks who replied with "oh, you're straightedge?" when I turned down weed or beer, almost as many have told me that I'm as far from edge as Fasiq Abasa. As the movement evolved it lent itself to a variety of interpretations and criteria as to what exactly *straightedge* meant. Some hard-liners have taken the "poison-free" ideology so far as to say that I could not call myself straightedge if I used Tylenol for a headache. Many others have added eating meat to the straightedge *fard*, some of whom require complete veganism.

It is also worth noting that the man credited as founding father and patron saint of the culture, former Minor Threat singer Ian MacKaye—while still abstaining from alcohol, drugs and meat—does not call himself straightedge or identify with the movement. It had swelled into something outlandishly removed from anything he intended with that simple song back in 1981.

Jehangir told me that many taqwacore bands in California were straightedge, forming amongst themselves a unique sub-scene amalgam from the existing straightedge culture and traditional Islamic practice—the local equivalent of which, I imagine, was our own Umar, who had fashioned his own Islamo-Punk identity completely unaware of the taqwacores out West. X's on his hands, 2:219 on his neck—straightedge offered Umar not only an endorsement of Muslim abstinence but also the heroic stand-tall toughness that he personally craved.

When he came home I was in the kitchen, waiting for my tea to cool.

"Don't blow on it," he said firmly.

"What?"

"Don't blow on it. It's not Sunnah."

"Oh," I replied. "I had never heard that before."

"Prophet Rasullullah *sallallaho alayhe wa salaam* said not to blow on hot food or drink. It's been proven by modern science too, the wisdom in that."

"Subhana'Allah," I said.

"But you know, y'akhi, it's not a good idea to be drinking tea anyway."

"Why not?"

"Caffeine's a stimulant. I wouldn't go so far as to call tea haram, but it's at least makrooh."

"Tea's makrooh?" I asked.

"It's a plague on the Muslim world, is what it is."

Then Rabeya came in from her bedroom adjacent to the kitchen, in full burqa as always. Umar gave salaams and walked out.

"It's great," she said with tone suggesting a sarcastic smile under that cloth; "all you need to get rid of Umar is a vagina." I laughed cautiously. "So how's life, Yusef? How's engineering treating you?"

"Oh, it's alright," I replied. "Finals coming up, and stuff. Can't wait for this semester to be over."

"How do you think you're doing?"

"Pretty good, mash'Allah."

"That's good, Yusef. So have you decided yet, Xerox or Kodak?" It was a joke. Rabeya originally hailed from Rochester, maybe an hour away on the I-90 East and home to the world headquarters of both.

"Insha'Allah," I replied smiling, thankful for all the handy Islamic phrases I could draw from when there was nothing else to say.

"Rochester's Muslim community is overwhelmingly Pakistani," she added.

"Really?"

"Sure."

"That's cool." Just then I wondered of Rabeya's heritage. She had no accent, was never heard speaking another language and the ethnically ambiguous shade of her hands did little to help. Somehow, the topic never came up and it made sense not to ask.

"The Islamic Center down on Westfall," she continued, "that's like the main masjid in town—the one the local news always goes to during Ramadan or to clear up the whole Islam and Terrorism thing. It's like eighty percent Pakistani but there's over thirty groups represented in the leftovers."

"Wow."

"Yeah, and then there's also a Turkish mosque and an NOI one, and I think one that used to be NOI but isn't—like maybe they're one of Warith Deen Mohammed's—"

"Acha," I replied.

Amazing Ayyub stormed the kitchen looking for a rematch, knocking my tea over and sending me to the floor.

"Oh my gawd!" he shrieked in imitation of a TV wrestling announcer. "Amazing Ayyub has 'em! Oh my gawd folks, we've never seen anything like *this* before!

"Yusef Ali's gonna tap, folks! Yusef Ali cannot withstand this punishment!" The primary punishment, of course, was the smell of a dirty shirtless Amazing Ayyub on top of me. I freed my left arm and wrapped it around his head, clinching my hands together and squeezing. Then Rabeya came over, jumped up and did a mock-elbow in the center of Ayyub's back. In enough cumbersome fabric to clothe a family, she grabbed hold of Ayyub's waist and tried to pull up while my chinlock anchored him to the floor. "AHHHHHH!" he screamed comically. "YOU'RE GONNA PULL OFF MY FUCKIN' HEAD!" Then Jehangir came in, black suspenders hanging at the sides of his red plaid pants, and of course he jumped on too with an effortless tackle on top of Rabeya, who still had Ayyub by the waist, who was still on top of me, and I still had my hold on Ayyub, and Ayyub pulled at Jehangir's stray suspenders and there we were, me at the bottom of a crazy pile of goofy laughing mumins and it might not have made sense anywhere but on that dirty kitchen floor.

It was Fasiq's turn to give khutbah that week, which I think inspired Umar's particular gruffness on Friday, as though he were preparing to be offended hours in advance. About two dozen people came in through the front door, causing Umar to remark that in the old days women used the back.

As the worshippers filtered through to make sunna salaats in the crowded living room and neighboring family room, one kid I recognized from my classes asked Jehangir about the spray-painted flag.

"It just means 'anarchy,' y'akhi," Jehangir half-whispered.

"But Saudi is where Islam is practiced the most purely," the kid replied. "Anywhere in the world you go, they will say look to Saudi for the real Islam."

"Al-hamdulilah, brother," said Jehangir, never one to argue such points. "But the Saudi government, you know, they—"

"But it's still Allah's Name on that flag," the kid interrupted. "You spray-painted on the shahadahtain."

"Staghfir'Allah," said Jehangir. "I'm sorry bro, I didn't realize.

It wasn't meant in that way."

"Mash'Allah," replied the kid. "You know, I am not trying to cause trouble—"

"Mash'Allah," said Jehangir.

"But you know, it is just a good thing, a good practice to, you know, respect the Name of Allah."

"Of course," Jehangir replied.

The living and family rooms—which had no door or wall dividing them so only a difference in carpeting distinguished them as separate—were packed to the point of physical discomfort where sujdahs jammed your elbows into your ribs and you strained to keep your forehead from brushing against someone else's feet. Our jamaat smelled of oils from at least twenty countries combined with those spilled-beer, body-odor and stale-hashish scents that never completely left the house. Fasiq stood by the hole in the wall in his Operation Ivy hoodie, mohawk tucked away under black Yankee ski hat. His khutbah, only a few minutes long, revolved around ayats 19 and 20 from *Suratul-Hijr* about how Allah sent 'suitable things' to grow on the earth and with Him were the treasures of everything in the world and He only sent them down in a known measure. To Fasiq Abasa this meant that all things from nature were a blessing from Allah and He only gave us what we could handle. While Fasiq's talk gave no specific mention of marijuana, I knew that would be Umar's angry interpretation. It often seemed as though Umar thought about drugs more than anyone in the house.

The jamaat was an almost silly mish-mash of people: Rude Dawud's pork-pie hat poking up here, a jalab-and-turban type there, Jehangir's big mohawk rising from a sea of kufis, Amazing Ayyub still with no shirt, girls scattered throughout—some in hejab, some not and Rabeya in punk-patched burqa doing her thing. But in its randomness it was gorgeous, reflecting an Islam I felt could not happen anywhere else despite Jehangir's traveler's-tales of California taqwacore. With every Friday hearing khutbahs and standing alongside brothers and sisters together yelling AAAAAMEEEEEEEEN after *Fatiha* with enough force to knock you down flanked at every wall by dumb band posters and stains and peeling paint, I grew more and more amazed at that house and this incredible thing we had pulled off, though I cannot take much credit. I was one of the quiet ones, the boring ones, the future engineers for Xerox and Kodak. If Islam was to be saved, it would be saved by the crazy ones: Jehangir and Rabeya and Fasiq and Dawud and Ayyub and even Umar.

If Friday afternoons meant jumaa, Friday nights meant my home would play host to stupid wasted kids from all walks of life. Everyone in the house would unload their CDs by the stereo and fight for turns at DJ. Besides his beloved taqwacore bands that varied in style and sound, Jehangir Tabari liked the '77 working-class heroic drinking-buddy songs. Rude Dawud played his Desmond Dekker and Specials and Skatalites. Umar put on the expected Minor Threat and Youth of Today though he never got into the straightedge taqwacore bands that Jehangir talked about, as though he were unsure whether someone could really be Muslim and Punk simultaneously. In that way he reminded me of my father, who when I was growing up would buy nearly every animated Disney video but then say that for *me* to draw living things was haram. Fasiq Abasa liked it loud and fast in the vein of NOFX or the Descendents and even had a CD containing one hundred songs that were each approximately thirty seconds long. Amazing Ayyub went mainly for Sham 69. Rabeya would put in political bands like

Propagandhi or riot-grrrl fare like the Lunachicks. I knew enough of everyone's tastes to play along and make requests.

The diversity often led to arguments. A Jamaican-fundamentalist, Rude Dawud hated any corrupted second-wave American *punk-ska.* Ayyub called Fasiq's notion of punk misguided because there was no longer any such thing as punk, to him it died in 1980. Umar huffed and pouted when Jehangir played a Business song like "Guinness Boys" for a variety of objections. Rabeya in turn denounced punk-rock misogyny and patriarchy in maybe half the songs they played.

Sometimes the music disputes inspired theological debates. While arguing punk, Amazing Ayyub demanded that someone put on Iggy Pop and the Stooges' "I Wanna Be Your Dog" and Fasiq said the song blew his mind in a whole big Sufi way because he had been reading about the dog being a symbol for the *nafs* and had a book by Javad Nurbaksh of the Khaniqahi Nimatullahi explaining it all.

"It's like Iggy's du'a," Fasiq exclaimed. "He's fuckin' talking to Allah, you know? He wants to be Allah's dog. It's like punk Rumi."

"You're fucked up right now," Amazing Ayyub replied. I agreed and the discussion ended at that. Fasiq asked to borrow the CD, then found his headphones and disappeared for the night.

Jehangir threw his arms around everybody and raised a brown-glass bottle in the air. Umar stood tough in the corner, arms folded. He could have easily sulked in his room or gone somewhere else, but I suspect he enjoyed being The Straightedge Guy. It became almost his *thing* with his intimidating glare, white wifebeater shirt and tattoos. People expected him to be there standing at angry attention.

It seemed as though Jehangir and Umar were opposing poles, each hoping to pull the collective psyche in his direction with his own method. While Umar pulled with his unending stance, a drunken Jehangir Tabari fell in love with everyone in the world. Every guy was his best friend, every girl his little sister and he would fight to his dying breath for each of us. It was an insatiable but charismatic sentimentality that moved him. Sometimes he pulled back to stand on the fringes of the scene and observe circles forming accidentally throughout the house: conversations, introductions, debates and story-tellings, all these characters stumbling in from their respective movies which somehow took them to Buffalo or maybe had been set in Buffalo the whole time but at any rate took them to his house and his party. There they were together in a massive grab bag of lives and cultures and perspectives, an exact combination of people that would never happen again on this Earth and maybe somebody would get something out of these random interactions and maybe nobody would but *al-hamdulilah* for all of it either way, and during such a retreat I would briefly look over and he'd nod to me as if to suggest that I were the only one who understood that moment exactly as he did.

Well enough into the night for him to be completely out of his mind, Jehangir came over and put his arm around me.

"Where's Imam Fasiq?" he asked.

"He's out there," I replied with a nod toward the door, "somewhere with his headphones and CD player and 'I Wanna Be Your Dog' stuck on repeat."

"Oh really."

"He's taking it as the expression of some Sufi concept about the nafs."

"Yeah! Shit!" Jehangir shouted with a slap on my back." Make the heart a polished mirror, was that it… I know my stuff, right? I was just gonna congratulate the imam on his packed house today, there wasn't even room to piss in there—"

"Seems like every week we have more."

"Did you see all those kids here today?"

"Um, yeah." With a brief scan of the faces before us, I appreciated how far removed the afternoon's activities were from this sloshing mess.

"Bro, listen," said Jehangir. "They were Muslims, man, but not your uncles. They need a deen that's not your uncle's deen. Iman, think about it like that, *iman!* It's supposed to be all about having no fear of death, right? And we got that part down, we've done that and we have plenty of Muslims who aren't afraid to die. Mash'Allah—but now Muslims are afraid to *fuckin' live!* They fear life, y'akhi, more than they fear shaytans or shirk or fitna or bid'a or kafr or qiyamah or the torments in the grave, they fear Life, they fear *this*—" He raised his bare arm, grabbed and slapped the skin to indicate *this*. "You got all these poor kids who think they're inferior because they don't get their two Fajr in, their four Zuhr, four Asr, three Maghrib, four Isha, their fuckin' Sunna, their Witr, their Nafl, they don't wear leather socks and they don't brush their teeth with twigs, they don't have beards, they don't wear hejab, maybe they went to their fuckin' high school proms and the only masjid around was regular horseshit-horseshit-takbir-masjid and they had to pretend like they were doing everything right, wiping their asses the way Bukhari tells you to and making the proper du'a—well I say fuck that and this whole house says fuck that—even Umar, you think Umar can go in a regular masjid with all his stupid tattoos and dumb straightedge bands? Even Umar, bro, as much as he tries to Wahabbi-hard-ass his way around here, he's still one of us. He's still fuckin' taqwacore—"

That was the first time I heard Jehangir Tabari use that word in reference to anything *Buffalo*. I looked at his glazed eyes, figuring I had just been privy to the pointless ramblings of yet another dumb kid who in one plastered moment briefly imagined that he had it all figured out. He kept going. "You can run after Life," he said with a lazy look out to some distance beyond me. "You can live and fuckin' love it and still have taqwa bursting out your guts. That's all it is, bro."

The Dropkick Murphys' "Boys on the Docks" came on and a big Irish kafr put his arm around Jehangir, ripped him away from me and they sang together like stupid drunks do. I just watched, trying to see something behind Jehangir's face that really explained it all. He almost had me sold on the idea that some advanced Sufi wisdom stood as the thesis upon which these orgies were founded—that if only I'd run upstairs and dive into Mustafa's Bukharis, I might find the arcane secret to Jehangir dancing with sloppy wasted punks.

Jehangir did not *sing* songs when drunk, he *yelled* them. His new friend seemed to have been cut from the same cloth so I went out on the porch.

Lynn was in the recliner, sporting a little spaghetti-strap top and full head of dreadlocks.

"As-salaamu alaikum," she said as though trying to be cute.

"Wa alaikum as-salaam," I replied. "I don't know if sitting in that chair's a good idea, it's been through a lot."

"You here to carry out the fatwa?" she asked.

"What?"

"You know—I'm an apostate, technically you can kill me."

"Really," I replied with a half-laugh.

"Give me the Salman Rushdie Special," she said with arms outstretched and eyes closed.

"I think that's only applicable in Muslim countries."

"Oh. Phew." She ran the back of her hand along her forehead to gesture facetious relief.

"So you really consider yourself an apostate?"

"Well, when enough people tell you you're not Muslim," she replied, "eventually you start to believe it."

"Oh."

"But until you reach the point when you don't even care anymore, it's pretty painful."

"You still believe in Allah, right?"

"I believe we were created, or *came from*, Something... and that Something has a compassion for us that we are nowhere near comprehending."

"That sounds like Islam to me."

"Yeah?" she asked with raised eyebrows.

"The hadiths say, you know, Allah's Mercy overwhelms His Wrath."

"If you eat with your left hand, you're imitating the devil."

"Yeah, there's that." I nervously tried to laugh again.

"It's hard," she said. "It's like there's some things in Islam that sound so beautiful and make you just... feel it and love Allah so much... and then, then there's the stupid shit, you know?"

"Yeah," I replied, wondering if my confession of Islam having *stupid shit* made me an apostate as well. "But it sounds like you have tawhid down, that's the important thing."

"I guess."

"What about Muhammad, do you believe in Muhammad?"

"That's the thing," she said with a sudden alertness. "What's the deal with Muhammad? If they don't make him out to be the Muslim Christ, then why is belief in him so vital?"

"Well, it's not so much belief *in* Muhammad, as—"

"Besides even that, what am I supposed to believe about a guy who married a six-year-old?"

"Yes, but—"

"He did marry a six-year-old," she said.

"But he did not consummate until she was—"

"Nine, I know. That makes it all okay. It's okay Rasullullah, she's nine, she had her period so throw it in'er. What am I supposed to do with that, Yusef?"

"I don't know, Lynn."

"I'm a spiritual person," she said. "I believe in Allah, you know, though I don't always call It 'Allah' and I pray the way I want to pray. Sometimes I just look out at the stars and this love-fear thing comes over me, you know? And sometimes I might sit in a Christian church listening to them talk about Isa with a book of Hafiz in my hands instead of the hymnal. And you know what, Yusef? Sometimes, every once in a while, I get out my old rug and I pray like Muhammad prayed. I never learned the shit in Arabic and my knees are uncovered, but if Allah has a problem with that then what kind of Allah do we believe in?"

"I don't know." Her ride pulled up by the curb, just behind Umar's truck.

"I'm sorry," she said, rising out of the recliner. "I don't mean to come across like that, it's just hard sometimes."

"Oh no, no, that's okay."

"I *wanted* to be Muslim, do you know that?"

"Yes." She had her face half-turned to me as she descended the steps of our porch.

"They just had to give me so much shit about it," she said.

"I know they did."

"I'll talk to you later, Yusef."

Once the car drove out of sight I went off the porch myself and walked. Had no idea where I was going or even what time of night it was. Walked up the street and turned the corner. Looked at all the houses, the lights out in every one, wondering what it would have been like to be Umar and walk through neighborhoods in moral opposition to everything, and then wondering whether he had something beautiful that I had lost; had I really reasoned above so much of my religion, or merely sold out for the path of least resistance? It would have been a hassle to pray faithfully five times daily, but Umar did it. I could excuse myself from class for five minutes, make wudhu in the men's room sink and find somewhere quiet. I was sure that other guys did.

But if there was something beautiful in Umar, why did it block him from seeing the beauty in Lynn? She had so much love and faith that she didn't even *need* religion anymore. Or she was just lazy.

Somewhere on those streets, I imagined, Fasiq Abasa was bugging out to Shaikh Iggy Pop; while somewhere in the house Jehangir Tabari was probably passed out, the golden-drunk majesty that Allah had sprinkled on him long gone. Umar was most likely still mad and strong, refueled for the night by but one look at unconscious Jehangir. Amazing Ayyub would have decorated the bathroom floor with his stomach-lining. Rabeya had undoubtedly drawn two or three people into a heated discussion; she was almost like Umar in that way, but with more people-skills. Rude Dawud would have been floating through the party, making the rounds, shaking hands and then finally heading upstairs with his victim for the night.

It was so easy to imagine them, each in their standard costumes: spikes, mohawks, burqas, patches, tattoos, sunglasses, porkpie hats, hoodies. And then there was me. What the hell was my place in that zoo?

CHAPTER III

The next morning, my place would be *recorder*. I awoke to Jehangir Tabari tapping on my skull with an index finger while holding my digital video camera in his other hand.

"Yusef, bro, wake up," he said gently, leaning over me. "We're gonna go shred."

"Don't you get hangovers?" I asked with one eye open.

"Al-hamdulilah," he replied, handing me the camera. Jehangir commonly recruited me on skateboarding expeditions just to have someone capture his stunts and bumps on film.

"I'm sure my parents only bought me this so I could tape you breaking your neck every weekend." It had been an Eid present.

"Tell them I said *jazakullah khair*. C'mon man, get up." He slapped my blanketed leg.

"Give me a minute," I whined.

"Alright, I'll go get Fasiq." Jehangir got off the bed, almost knocking the three-inch by five-inch Pakistani flag from its stand on my headboard. I looked at the green field and white crescent, thought about Rawalpindi and adhans waking you for Fajr from neighborhood minarets. Jehangir rumbled down the stairs and yelled something. From the sounds of Fasiq's reaction I could tell that Jehangir had jumped on him.

"C'mon, man," groaned Fasiq. "Get off me, it's not even fuckin' eleven yet—"

"Get off my couch, asshole! We're shredding today!"

"Fuck," said Fasiq.

Fasiq threw some shoes on and grabbed his board from under the mess of clothes and Qur'ans that had accumulated by the couch he called a bed. We went in Jehangir's car, me in the back seat. Jehangir brought along his boom box and a handful of his skillfully arranged mix-tapes.

"Got a little something for everyone on here," he bragged, holding the tapes. "It's the philosophy of the three-ring circus. If you don't like the clowns, you'll like the elephants. If you don't like the elephants, you'll like the acrobats." There was only one component lacking.

"Why don't you have any taqwacore bands?" I asked.

"Because the fuckers put all their shit out on vinyl."

"What? Why?"

"They just do," he answered shrugging.

"But who even has a record player anymore?"

"I do," said Jehangir. "But just so I can listen to those guys. And it fuckin' sucks because it can't record from vinyl to a cassette, the shit's so old."

"I don't get the vinyl thing," I said. "Is there some kind of ideological point behind that?"

"Maybe. A lot of punks turn out to be sentimental suckers."

"Like Amazing Ayyub last night," Fasiq interjected, "when he said that there hasn't been any real punk since 1980."

"What does that have to do with vinyl?" I asked. "Do they think that they're closer to the Lost Golden Age by rejecting CDs? What does that have to do with anything?"

"Allahu Alim," Fasiq replied. Jehangir popped one of his mixtapes in the deck. "Nice," remarked Fasiq as it came on halfway through the Descendents' "Suburban Home." They both slouched to accommodate their high hair. Riding in the backseat behind two brightly dyed mohawks with my digital camcorder in a grocery bag, hearing noisy music through lousy speakers, windows down, the weather pleasant but not uncomfortably summer just yet, I realized that there were a million forms of coolness floating through the world and one of them—the zeitgeist of three guys en route to juvenile stunts on public property—had been captured successfully that day. Both Jehangir and Fasiq wore exactly the same clothes as the previous day. but I had known them too long by this point to think anything of it.

Just then I noticed a patch on the left shoulder of Fasiq's Operation Ivy hoodie. He saw me looking. "Bosnian Muslim unit," he explained. It was white with green letters reading "ALLAHU EKBER" above a yellow crescent and green star.

We arrived at a museum off Elmwood to find that we had been beaten to it by a gangly gang of kids hopping around on hundred-dollar boards with little toothpick-arms poking out of clownishly oversized outfits, everything splashed with logos: Billabong, Atticus, Quiksilver, Independent.

"We should've hit Pac-Sun and gotten the right uniforms," said Fasiq. "We coulda been friends."

"Everybody's got a sunna," replied Jehangir with his Oi-tranquility. Fasiq in his Op Ivy hoodie and reasonably baggy khakis seemed at least somewhat closer to the code than Jehangir who in spike-covered leather jacket and red plaid bondage-pants was too scary, too old school, too '77 British-style grog-shop punk. The pop-punk kids picked up their boards and left on foot.

The museum's Hellenic glory of marble columns and statues stood at the end of maybe forty steps with a long narrow railing right down the middle. The bottom of the steps met a circular drive, in the middle of which loomed a massive naked and bearded Greek astride a wild stallion, one arm wrapped around its neck and the other wielding a bow. The place supplied a variety of ledges and surfaces for a litany of maneuvers, all to be categorized within a sophisticated jargon of skater-speak that excluded outsiders such as myself. Jehangir's boom box sat on the roof of his car playing Agnostic Front's "Skate Rock." He put one foot on his board and with the other pushed himself forward. Fasiq followed and soon they both sailed passively by the products of their mass and velocity, side by side, a pair of cartoon haircuts backdropped by the museum. I imagined myself the uncool sidekick for just standing around dopey holding a camera instead of flipping and falling and flying with the men of action. But after a while of watching them experiment with physics—especially Jehangir, who could manage to *fall charismatically* if such a thing were possible—I realized that I was just as vital. For every culture-hero living out his myth, there must be a witness willing to pass the story on.

Then Jehangir removed all doubt. He looked romantically to the museum's columns atop a ziggurat-like eighty or so stone steps, picked up his board, tapped the long narrow railing once for luck and jogged up to the end. He skated around a little to gain momentum. Fasiq stopped to watch. I zoomed in on Abu and Ummi's Eid camera.

The U.S. Bombs' "Ballad of Sid" came on Jehangir's CD player. Though he couldn't have heard it up there, the song and moment seemed to coincide as though all prearranged by Rabbil-Alameen. With aggressive steps off the marble floor Jehangir gained speed. He ollied up to meet the railing and rode it all the way down—on the board itself, not the wheels, with feet working it like a delicate see-saw and arms extended like a rawk American Christ. He kept going and going, sure to eventually miscalculate his balance and fall off either right or left or slip off the board and break his neck or testicles on the rail but it never happened, he just kept going, down and down the rail perhaps even to the very bottom of the steps. I zoomed out to show more of the railing. Jehangir accelerated beyond all control and lunged off the railing's curled end as though driving off a cliff. Looked like it might have scraped a layer of skin off his hands but he was too stunned from what he just did to even care. Called a railslide or boardslide in skater circles, the trick amounts to essentially supernatural degrees of balance. I wished those poser kids had stayed to see it.

Fasiq and I ran over to him as though he had just won the World Series. With a smile of exhausted disbelief Jehangir just sat staring at his wheels-up board as though asking it for confirmation of their shared experience.

"Are you okay?" asked Fasiq with an ecstatic voice-crack, grabbing Jehangir's wrist to examine his palm.

"Al-hamdulilah," Jehangir replied.

"That was insane," I said as we helped him up.

"It was weird," said Jehangir. "The railing was so long it was like I had time to stop being nervous. I was just like, fuck, I've been up here awhile, wonder when I'm going to fall."

We huddled around my camera rewinding and re-rewinding to watch the little screen.

"I can't believe you didn't break your face," said Fasiq.

"I think I'm calling it a day," Jehangir replied. "I feel like trying anything else would be asking Allah for paralysis."

"You should send that shit in," said Fasiq. "Get in a skateboard video." We threw the skateboards and boom box and digital camcorder in the back seat. Fasiq gave me shotgun this time. Sitting behind the wheel Jehangir said his whole body was trembling, holding up his right hand as proof. I offered to drive but he replied only by starting the car.

As Fasiq and I fawned like a pair of twelve-year-old TRL groupies Jehangir kept his eyes to the road, answering praise with half-smiles and almost-whispered *mash'Allahs.* If you ever doubt his Islam, please remember that.

Jehangir Tabari was a drunk and a punk and never cared what Hanafi or Hanbali or Maliki or Shafi told him to do, but he was sincere and Allah kept him humble.

Amazing Ayyub was waiting on the porch when we got back. He had no shirt on. Instead of running inside to play Sham 69's "Hey Little Rich Boy" he just sat there with a weird expression.

"Yo!" I called out to him, climbing out with the camcorder. "You have to see what Jehangir did—"

"I got a job," said Ayyub.

"No shit," Jehangir replied. "Where?"

"The gas station."

"Doing what?"

"Pumping gas."

"That's awesome," Fasiq interjected.

"Yeah," said Amazing Ayyub. "I'm gonna fuckin' contribute to society an' shit."

"You gonna move off our couch, then?" asked Jehangir with a warm smile.

"FUCK!" yelled Ayyub, darting a finger in Fasiq's direction. "What about that fuckin' guy?"

"I put in for groceries," Fasiq countered.

"Yeah, by selling fuckin' kief," Ayyub replied.

"Yeah, by selling it to you."

"Shit, see then? I give Fasiq the money he puts in for groceries!" He then looked at me. "Right, preppy?"

"Makes sense to me," I said smiling.

"What's Umar think of that?" asked Jehangir. "Does he know that his halal meat's paid for with weed?"

"I think so," answered Ayyub with his eyes to the floor. "So what you got today?" he asked, turning to Fasiq.

"I don't know if I should let you," Fasiq replied. "I mean, you're a working man now—"

"Fuck that, I don't start 'til next week." So the two of them went in and upstairs, most likely to climb out the bathroom window and smoke on the roof.

I sat on the porch steps where Amazing Ayyub had been just moments ago, camcorder in my lap. I watched Jehangir's immortal boardslide again and then looked up to see the real Jehangir pacing the sidewalk before me, relaxed but still unsure of what to do with himself at that moment. He almost looked to have a story that he couldn't commit to tell—maybe about some taqwacore kid out West who taught him the boardslide, a punked-out mumin cheered as a legend in the circles he traveled. The story, if it was a story, stayed bottled up in him. It could have been one of his little trademarked maxims that would usually spill out spontaneously with naïve third-grader innocence like "things'll sure be different twenty years from now, y'akhi—" et cetera. Or it could have been a self-praise over the boardslide that in taqwa he kept from passing his lips.

Whatever the thought might have been, he looked like he'd handle it best alone. I stood up and went inside. First went to the living room, hung out with myself and got bored of it. Trodded upstairs, heard Amazing Ayyub and Fasiq out on the roof laughing and high.

"You know what happens to artists after they die?" Ayyub asked him.

"What?" Fasiq replied.

"If you paint or draw living things, then after you die Allah says 'give life to your creations if you can' and of course you can't, so then Allah brings them to life and they fuckin' torture you forever."

"That's bullshit," said Fasiq.

"Think about it," said Ayyub. "It's crazy, man. Those guys who fuckin' made the Looney Tunes are going to be fuckin' burned and stabbed and whipped by like, Bugs Bunny and Daffy Duck an' shit."

"There's nothing about that in the Qur'an," Fasiq retorted.

"It's in the hadiths," said Ayyub.

"Fuckin' everything's in the hadiths!" yelled Fasiq. "You can find hadiths saying Muhammad used pinecones for dildos."

"There weren't pine trees in Arabia," said Ayyub.

"Fuck off," said Fasiq.

Umar's door was open but I knocked anyway. Sitting on the floor, he looked up from his book and greeted me sunna-style.

"Wa-alaikum as-salaam," I replied. The room felt anarcho-monastic. Shelves lined with books, walls adorned with Islamic calligraphy plaques and fliers for straightedge shows and two three-foot by five-foot flags hanging on separate walls. One was green with a white circle containing red crescent and lazy squiggles of Allah's Name in some generic holy phrase. It represented the Islamic Conference, an intergovernmental organization counting fifty-six nations in its membership. The second flag looked like our own Stars and Stripes after being sucked through a black hole: the starry blue field now a solid orange, the stripes green and white, and in the upper right-hand corner a big star and crescent, white on green. "Which is that?" I asked, pointing to it.

"Kashmir and Jammu," Umar replied. "Just got it mail order."

"Cool."

"Islam enjoins solidarity with our oppressed and persecuted brothers. But I'm not a nationalist; that's why I got that one up—" He gestured to the Islamic Conference flag. "We're one community, brother; that's the umma, the only legitimate political entity on this earth."

"Mash'Allah," I said, just to aid the flow of conversation.

"Islam is actually against nationalism of all kids—not only political nationalism but cultural nationalism too. There are many people who say, 'we have to adapt Islam to American culture' or 'we have to adapt Islam to such-and-such' or whatever. But brother, we do not want 'American Muslims' here and then 'Arab Muslims' over there, you know? That's division. Islam is universal. It transcends all our petty race-and-nation questions."

"True."

"It's not even a religion, brother. Religion is games and superstition. Islam is a PERFECT SYSTEM OF LIFE."

"Right."

"Everything has a purpose and meaning."

"Totally."

"Did you know that salat is even medically beneficial to us?"

"No," I replied with tone of semi-enthusiasm.

"Brother, if you study traditional yoga—not this watered-down Bally's aerobics yoga, but the real-deal stuff in India—you can see the different movements and positions in Muslim prayer. If you breathe a certain way in each position, four-rakat prayer utilizes every muscle in your body."

"Wow," I said.

"Allah is the Planner," said Umar. "He planned it all out for us."

In the early evening I found Jehangir still out in front of the house. He had taken the boom box out of his car and popped in a Billy Bragg CD, skipping it ahead to "California Stars" and lying stomach-up on the sidewalk with his hands cradling the back of his skull. I stood out there holding the screen door open loving the way the world felt at that time of day at that time of year, not too cold or hot or bright or dark, with a little breeze sometimes but not too much, everything perfect in every way. And there was my hero on the ground. The song met its end and then began again. He must have had it on repeat.

"You ever hear of a band called Burning Books for Cat Stevens?" he asked.

"No," I replied.

"They're out West," said Jehangir, eyes up to the sky.

"Are they any good?"

"They'll be huge in six months. All over MTV, just you wait and see."

"Really?" I asked, sitting at the edge of the porch.

"No, not really."

"Oh. Haha."

"They are a pretty good band, though. I might have one of their records upstairs, but I need to buy a new needle for my player."

"I still don't get the whole vinyl thing," I said. "It makes no sense."

"Technology versus Ideology," Jehangir replied. "It's a punk thing."

"Is punk an ideology?" I asked.

"Who knows anymore. Maybe it's just wearing a wallet-chain."

"To some people, I guess."

"Some people would say punk is all about disseminating your own culture, shunning mass media conglomerates and never selling out; but the bands we look to as spiritual forbears—the Sex Pistols, the Clash, the Ramones and so forth—were all on major labels. And some people would say punk is only about loud, aggressive music; but death metal's loud and aggressive. Is that punk? What about loud, aggressive rap? Or is punk supposed to be destroying social mores and manners and taboos? If so, where are the bands doing that today?"

"So what do you think it is?" I asked.

"I think it's just about being ugly." I laughed and then realized he wasn't joking. "That's why you can't be punk," he continued. "You look good and you dress good and you'll make a great engineer someday." I thought Jehangir Tabari was an inherently handsome young man, though he deliberately rendered himself ugly with the mohawk and gear. He had the face if he wanted to sing in emo pop Newfound Glory bands but he snarled too much and never had his teeth fixed—to spot the real punks, he used to say, examine their teeth. "But yeah, man... I think that's where it's at... *ugly*..."

"What's taqwacore then? Ugly Muslims?"

"Kind of."

I stayed plopped on the porch, Jehangir stayed stretched out on the sidewalk and we went awhile without speaking. In the silence I lost myself daydreaming of an Ugly Muslim Parade marching single-file down our street with every Ugly Muslim included: the women who traveled without their walis, the painters who painted people, beardless qazis, the dog owners in their angel-free houses, hashishiyyuns like Fasiq Abasa, liwats and sihaqs, Ahmadiyyas, believers who stopped reading in Arabic because they didn't know what it said, the left-handers, the beer swillers, the Kuwaiti sentenced to death for singing Qur'an, the guys who snuck off with girls to make out and undo generations of cerebral clitorectomy, the girls who stopped blaming themselves every time a man had dirty thoughts, the mumins who stopped their clock-punching, the kids who had pepperoni on their pizzas, on and on down the line.

So many failed believers, I nearly suspected they were the majority.

"Taqwacore," I said for no reason.

"The irresistible force against the immovable object," Jehangir replied.

"What?"

"The irresistible force against the immovable object. That's what they always used to say on the Saturday-morning wrestling shows."

"Oh."

"So who wins it, Captain Physics?"

"I don't know."

"It's like a NASCAR driver going three hundred miles an hour and just crashing head-on into the Ka'ba."

"Okay."

"Irresistible force against immovable object."

"Well, in that case," I replied, "before the NASCAR driver hit the Bayt, birds would come and drop clay on him." We both laughed.

A week later we were driving around Buffalo yelling things at pedestrians, just stupid nonsense stuff that seemed somehow funny to us.

"HELP ME!" yelled Jehangir in his goofiest voice while stopped at a red light. The couple walking nearby looked at him without stopping. "HELP ME!" he repeated. "HELP ME! I HAVE LOST MY BANANA!" They looked away and kept going. The light turned green and I saw an old man on my side of the street.

"GIVE ME BACK MY SHIRT!" I screamed. Jehangir laughed so hard I thought he'd die.

"What'd the guy do?" he asked.

"I don't think he understood me."

"HEY!" shouted Jehangir with his head lunged out the window. I looked to see the mother of two on his side. "YOU ARE FRIGHTENING ME!" And just as soon as he said it we were half a mile down the street, all those characters gone and forgotten, new ones on the way.

"ROWWWWWWWWRRRRRRRR!" I yelled at some trench-coat wearing winner. "I'M A LION, ROWWWWRRRRRR!" He just looked at me.

"Look in the back seat," Jehangir commanded. "Behind me."

"All I see is an old Subway sub."

"Give it to me." As I brought it to the front seat the smell hit us hard. Jehangir took the sandwich still in its wrapper and held it at a distance, waiting for the *moment*—which turned out to be a red light with us in the straight/right-turn lane and an SUV in the left-turn-only. Jehangir quickly unwrapped his sandwich. As the light turned green he launched it at the side of the SUV and peeled out with a right turn down Forest Ave, both of us howling with ecstatic immaturity.

Eventually we hit the I-90 and went to a massive mall-sized flea market, Jehangir looking more than slightly out of place among the flea culture but it was easy to keep track of him by his high hair. Many vendors peddled artifacts from our childhoods: Star Wars figures, heavy rubber wrestling dolls, He-Man, G.I. Joe, baseball cards of guys like Jose Canseco who had their prime when I was ten years old. Jehangir Tabari spotted an old Iron Sheik figure with most of the paint worn off his pants. "Look at his pointy boots," Jehangir said with a big smile. "I need some boots like that, wouldn't that shit be hot?"

While most vendors offered miscellaneous grab bags of second-hand merchandise, some were specialized in their field. One sold only bright orange hunting clothes. Another just old music tapes. One guy's whole inventory consisted of big three-by-five flags, an example of each hanging around his booth. He had the black downtrodden silhouette POW/MIA flag, an American flag with giant Native American chief in the middle, an American flag with Harley Davidson in the middle, a regular American flag, a Don't Tread On Me, a Confederate X. "I think this is where Umar bought his Kashmiri flag," mused Jehangir sarcastically.

You can walk around a big flea market like that for what seems like hours, completely lose your concept of time, get a little dizzy and grow accustomed to an entirely new sort of air: the flea-market aromas of an enclosed environment filled with goods that had aged in thousands of households.

"Look here," I said, calling Jehangir from the stack of used VCRs he had been admiring. I pointed to a wall of Osama bin Laden t-shirts. One had him in the cross-hairs. Another had him in a toilet. Another had the top of his head resembling a penis.

"Ever hear of a band in California called Osama bin Laden's Tunnel Diggers?" Jehangir asked.

"No, I don't think so."

"Real funny guys, buncha wise asses. They're Islam's NOFX, you can say."

"Cool."

While pulling out of the flea market's parking lot Jehangir arrived at the idea to visit Amazing Ayyub at his new job.

"I bet he doesn't have a shirt on," he said over the scratching and popping of his bad speakers as GBH's "Sick Boy" came on. "I bet you five bucks."

Sure enough Ayyub had his KARBALA right out there for all to see when we swung up to the pump. Upon recognizing the car he jumped onto the hood and started dancing with loud stomps that would have had Jehangir fuming if Jehangir were the type to car about dents and scratches. Amazing Ayyub hopped off and

Jehangir reached out his window for a handshake.

"What the fuck are you crazy guys doing?" Ayyub asked, leaning on the driver's side window to peer in on us.

"Just hit the flea market," Jehangir replied.

"Oh, no shit," gasped Ayyub. "I wish I'da known that, I woulda went with you guys."

"But you're working," I answered.

"Fuck that," snapped Ayyub. "Fuck this place, man, pumping gas n' shit. I'd make more money giving handjobs in Niagara Falls."

Just then a group of high school guys pulled up to the pump opposite ours in a Jeep Grand Cherokee with obnoxious rap-metal blaring. Ayyub excused himself and walked over. Perfect skin, perfect teeth, Abercrombie shirts. The one riding shotgun inexplicably wore a golden football helmet. Amazing Ayyub pumped their gas and took the money. As they drove out and Ayyub walked back to Jehangir's car, the kid in football helmet whipped out a huge Super Soaker and blasted Ayyub from maybe twenty feet away. Unfortunately for them, oncoming traffic blocked their exit from the parking lot. Amazing Ayyub ran over as the kids yelled at their driver to hurry up and go. Ayyub came to the passenger side just as the kid began rolling up his window.

It was a beautiful thing—perhaps as skilled as Jehangir Tabari's boardslide at the art museum. In the split-second of his only chance at justice, Amazing Ayyub used every muscle in his throat to reach back and bring up an awe-inspiring glob of phlegm; then, with precision matched only by his power, he sent it in just before the window rolled up completely. Ayyub took a moment to realize what he had just accomplished, wondered where the goober ended up but it didn't matter because it had successfully gotten *in* the jeep. Hearing the sound of a door-latch Ayyub booked, ran past us out of the parking lot on the far side and into the street, stopped honking traffic and disappeared into someone's backyard while the gallant high school kid stood with back straight and shoulders out, still wearing his football helmet by the Grand Cherokee with its lousy music even louder because of the open door.

"Every day is Ashura," said Jehangir Tabari, quoting Imam Ja'far. "Every land is Karbala."

"From the gold helmet," I mused, "I think they went to Kenmore East."

"Yeah?"

"Their colors were blue and gold. They were the Bulldogs."

"Is that where you went?"

"No," I replied. "I went to Catholic high school."

We drove around awhile hoping to find Amazing Ayyub. Jehangir popped out his GBH tape and rummaged under the street while still manning the wheel, finding his Sex Pistols and putting it in. The tape came on at the beginning of "Who Killed Bambi." Neither of us said anything as we kept our eyes peeled for the Amazing One. The musical accompaniment lent a dark absurdity to everything I saw. People, houses, cars, blue mailboxes that reminded me of R2-D2, trees, porches, telephone poles and wires and little Direct-TV dishes, streets and streetlights... it was all dumb, we were all meant to die and it was just funny if you wanted it to be. I was a Muslim and my parents sent me to Catholic high school, wasn't that funny? How about Jehangir, a Muslim who drank beer and threw rotting Subway sandwiches at SUVs? Or Amazing Ayyub Shi'a spitting on high school football players? Did any of it matter? Why not laugh?

"Ayyub's the fucking Man," said Jehangir Tabari to break the silence.

"Yeah, he definitely is," I replied.

"I remember one time we were riding around in his car throwing shit at people and we ended up getting pulled over. Before the cop got out of his car I said to Ayyub 'man, he wants you to walk over there and talk to him.' So Ayyub reached to open his door and get out and walk up to the cop; I had to pull him back quick and tell him I was joking."

"He would have gotten shot," I marveled.

"Shit yeah," said Jehangir. "This is fuckin' Buffalo." Jehangir took out the Sex Pistols and put in the Swingin' Utters, rewound it to the beginning of "Next in Line."

"Didn't know he had a car," I said.

"Yeah, he used to live in it; it was his house. We used to play the UK Subs' 'I Live in a Car' and say it was his theme song. Shit, miss those days. But anyway, one day he just up and says 'Jehangir, I'm going West, I'm going to see California and all the taqwacores and turn the deen on its head' and he gets in his car and heads for the I-90 and we all thought that was the end of him. A week or so later I got a call. He was at the bus station downtown."

"What happened?"

"For some reason he decided to get off the I-90 in Montana and hop on the I-25 to Colorado. Shit broke down on the way so he took a bus back to Buffalo and crashed at our place. Him and Fasiq have been fighting over the better couch ever since."

"Why'd he get off the 90?" I asked.

"Who knows," Jehangir replied. "But it's Amazing Ayyub, you know? Nothing makes sense with that guy. He's a homeless, probably now jobless bum who makes an ass-clown of himself but it works for him. He can wipe his ass with just his bare hand and girls would say 'wow, he's so interesting, so unique!"

"How do you think he would have done out there in California?" I asked. "You know, with the taqwacores?"

"They would have eaten him up, bro. He could have been the next big thing out there."

"Why?"

"Because he's Amazing Ayyub! Look at 'im. He'd be the Taqwacore Mahdi."

Rabeya occupied the porch recliner when we got home, burqa'd up as per usual. "Salaam alaik," said Jehangir as we walked towards the house.

"Wa alaik," Rabeya replied. She had an open bag of marshmallows in her lap.

"Amazing Ayyub fuckin' spit on some jocks and deserted his job."

"Jesus," sighed Rabeya, weary and free of surprise. "Oh, Yusef—I almost forgot, when you guys were out Lynn came through looking for you."

"Really?"

"Like him, specifically?" Jehangir asked.

"Him, specifically," Rabeya replied, taking a marshmallow and slipping it under her niqab.

"Did she say what she wanted?" I asked.

"Just said to give her a call," she replied while chewing.

"That's cool."

"I think it's time for prayer," said Jehangir.

"Which one?" I asked.

"Zuhr, I think." He looked up at the sun. "Anybody got a watch?"

"It's Asr time," said Rabeya.

"Oh. Shit, if I fall asleep wake me for Maghrib." With that Jehangir went inside. Through the screen door I watched him go upstairs. Rabeya took another marshmallow and put it up to her hidden mouth.

"Did you know," I said, standing by the recliner, "supposedly—I don't know, I guess they say that, um, marshmallows are made with pork gelatin?"

She leaned over and punched me hard in the stomach.

Amazing Ayyub came home and said he didn't know if he still had a job because he never made it back to the gas station. Mentioned some upcoming medical experiments he could sell his body to for quick cash.

The sun went down. I made the du'a my father had taught me. Jehangir was knocked out in his room; I'd wait to hear his input before calling Lynn.

Sayyed had given us a prayer timetable from the local masjid to stick up on our refrigerator. When Maghrib came I went up the stairs, first to Rude Dawud's room on my immediate left. I knocked, then opened the door to see Albert standing tall waving his arms around and preaching rapidly on Babylon as Dawud sat at his desk.

"Rude Dawud," I said, "man, it's time to pray."

"I'll be right down, brother."

From there I went to Umar's room and knocked. He opened the door with salaams.

"Wa-alaikum as-salaam," I returned. "Time for Maghrib."

"Al-hamdulilah, brother." The Kashmir and Jammu flag hung in the distance behind Umar's right shoulder.

And then to Jehangir.

Knocked once, no answer. Knocked twice. Knocked three times. "That's the sunna," said Umar behind me. "Knock three times, that's it." Umar went to the bathroom to make his wudhu. I opened Jehangir's door and went in.

First thing I saw was Jehangir on his stomach, sprawled across the bed. The second thing was a three-by-five American flag on the wall behind him, right next to a cloth wall-hanging of the Masjid Haram in Makkah. Then there were the assorted expecteds: Sid Vicious poster, fliers for taqwacore shows he had collected out West, tacked-up photos of old and new friends all jumbled together in a jamaat that couldn't happen on this earth because Jehangir had traveled so much, the characters of his story were spread out too far and wide.

"Yo," I said. "Time to pray."

"I had a dream I was drinking with Johnny Cash," he said, his head hanging off the far side of the bed.

"Really."

"Yeah bro." He heaved himself up to a sitting position and I noticed his mohawk had been bent out of shape by sleeping. "You ever listen to Johnny Cash?" The question threw me off.

"I don't listen to country," I said, thinking that was the cool answer.

"Johnny Cash isn't country," Jehangir snapped. "He's bigger than country. Johnny Cash is the fucking SHIT, man. Johnny Cash rules the world."

"I didn't know that."

"If you don't know, now you know."

"So what was the dream about?"

"We were in the bar that 'A Boy Named Sue' took place in. You know, the saloon where he finds his dad and they fight all over the place, breakin' chairs and smashin' through walls. We just sat on a pair of stools downing shots and laughing and I just wished I could be him, you know… I wanted to be Johnny Cash more than anything, just sitting next to him and he was so fucking *old* and withered you could see ten thousand years of pain and life on his face… and even when we laughed and sang songs I was hurting on the inside because I wanted to be him so bad, a fuckin' Everyman Baritone Populist, fuckin' beyond Time and Place. I can't be that guy, you know, who just speaks to *everyone*… I'm too wrapped up in my mix-matching of disenfranchised subcultures."

"Damn," I said.

"I'm small," said Jehangir. "I'm fuckin' small."

"Your name means 'World Conqueror,' doesn't it?"

"Something like that. I'm named after a fuckin' Mughal king."

"I know."

"His son built the Taj Mahal."

"Yep."

"Look at that shit," he said, pointing to a small picture on his wall. I walked over to see it and found Jehangir, face a little younger and head concealed in turban, wearing a shalwar kameez in front of the Taj Mahal next to an older man in matching outfit besides his Jinnah hat.

"That's awesome," I said.

"See how my turban's wrapped?" he asked. I looked closer. "I had never worn one before and had no idea what I was doing. I fuckin' wrapped it Sikh-style."

"Oh, yeah, yeah—"

"I just wanted to cover up my hawk, you know, I didn't know there was a Sikh way and a Muslim way."

"Who's that in the Jinnah?"

"That's my uncle." I stared closer, tried to see the Jehangir-ness in him.

"Were you really close?" I asked.

"Yeah—I mean he wasn't around all the time, he traveled a lot but I did get to see some of the world because of him."

"That's cool."

"He took me to Makkah."

"Really?"

"I don't have any pictures of it because you know how they are over there." I tried to picture Jehangir in the *ihram* garb with his orange mohawk standing tall.

"How was it over there?"

"Brother," he said with each facial muscle striving to convey his conviction, "it's unbelievable. That's all I can say. I don't even know how to explain it. You don't even have thoughts there that can possibly be expressed in language."

"Wow," I said.

"You know how in those photographs it looks like the people nearest the Ka'ba are kind of swirling around?"

"Yeah."

"It really feels like that."

"Wow, you were that close?"

"Yeah," he replied.

"Did you touch it?"

"No, once you're that close people start crawling all over each other, it looks like a bunkhouse brawl. I figured if I moved out of the way and let somebody else get their blessing, maybe I got baraka too."

"That makes sense."

"I hope so."

I left him and went down the hall, into the bathroom where out the open window I saw Fasiq sitting on the roof, Qur'an in hand.

"As-salaamu alaikum," I said from the bathroom.

"Wa-alaikum as-salaam," he slowly replied.

Then Umar's adhan filled the house.

Albert sat on a couch as we lined up in front of the hole in the wall, Saudi's spray-painted flag and Imam Rabeya. Umar gave the iqamah. With a look down at his feet right of mine I wondered why in all his anal sunna he would pray behind a woman. Jehangir stood on my left. On Umar's right stood Amazing Ayyub. On Jehangir's left was Fasiq Abasa. On Ayyub's right stood Rude Dawud.

"Allahu Akbar," said Rabeya, hands to covered ears. Then came a brief silence, followed by *Fatiha* and *al-Kauthar*, shortest sura in the whole Qur'an. It's about a pond or river in Paradise where Muhammad's supposedly going to meet all of us. As she recited I was sure Amazing Ayyub had a store of hadiths about it from his Muslim death book.

I almost forgot: *sallallaho alayhe wa salaam.*

After completion of the fard, Umar shuffled back to a corner of the room and did two sunna rakats. Jehangir just let himself lean back until he was lying down with feet to the qiblah. Everybody else got up except Rabeya, who sat in silent du'a, and me, who just kind of sat. I thought about a few things, thought about nothing, looked over at Jehangir, looked back at Umar, looked at Rabeya, looked at Albert getting up from the couch to go back upstairs with Rude Dawud, looked at Amazing Ayyub when he said he had to piss and Fasiq Abasa when he walked towards the kitchen.

Umar ran his hands over his face, stood up and left the living room. Rabeya got up after awhile, leaving me still sitting and Jehangir flat on his back staring at the ceiling.

"Do you think I should call Lynn?" I asked without looking at him.

"Why shouldn't you call her?" he replied, still looking to the ceiling.

"I don't know."

"See what she wants."

"Okay." I stood up and left him there. Went to my room, looked up her number in my planner—never knew her well enough to memorize it.

"Hello?"

"Lynn?"

"Hey."

"It's Yusef Ali."

"Oh hey, what's up?"

"Nothing much, I just heard that you came through today and said to call you—"

"Oh yeah, I was just wondering how you did on your finals."

"I think I did pretty good, actually."

"Cool, cool. I could have done better than I did, but I'm just glad to be done with it for a few months."

"Yeah, definitely."

"So are you guys still having jumaa over there at the house?"

"Yep."

"Cool… I think I might make an appearance one of these days."

"Really?" I asked with overexcitement.

"Yeah, I haven't been to a jumaa in forever… not going to go back to my old masjid anytime soon."

"I hear that."

"So I guess I'll see you… this Friday?"

"Insha'Allah," I replied.

"Cool… talk to you later." Did I have a jumaa date?

Jehangir Tabari had a way with girls. Sometimes the deen even helped his efforts. He could get a girl alone, run his usual game with spirited tone and raised eyebrows—"you know, Prophet Muhammad said that when a man and woman are alone together, Shaytan is the third present but I never understood that… to me, Allah has put all of us here to learn from one another and grow with one another, and to avoid an entire gender like that just seems to be limiting your growth and almost—no, definitely—denying one of Allah's favors…" and more often than not he had it. I never doubted Jehangir's sincerity—he honestly, deeply meant every word he said—but I must confess he knew such monologues would win him sexual attention.

His Islamic angle seemed to work best with kafr girls because they usually did not know enough about the religion or culture to feel anything but intrigue and sympathy for his struggles. Muslim girls were generally no fun anyways, he explained, programmed from birth to have no sexual impulses. Rabeya supported his thinking.

"I spent my whole life hearing that it was my job not to tempt men," she told me at the kitchen table. "If you ask Muslim women why they cover up, ninety-nine percent of them will say it's to avoid arousing men. Fuck that, where's your self-accountability?" I saw the moment as an opportunity to ask *why* she wore full purdah, but passed. "For the longest time I didn't even allow myself sexual thoughts—any impulse just got shut off like a light-switch. If a woman enjoyed sex, or expressed her sexuality outwardly she was automatically a slut with no respect for herself. Sex was a favor you allowed your husband so angels wouldn't curse you until morning."

"Wow," I replied. "I had heard that hadith before, but I never imagined what it was like to be a woman and read that."

"Yeah, it sucks. You know, a few years ago I was talking to a Muslim brother about marriage; shit, I must have been sixteen, can you believe that? Sixteen with no idea who I was or what I wanted from the world, and Mom was sending me potential husbands. But we talked about sex, and it was totally like a job interview—I think he just wanted to know that I was a virgin. He asked me if I masturbated, and I said no which was true because such things honestly didn't even occur to me. Then he asked if I believed it was okay to, and I said yeah, I didn't see anything wrong with it. He answered that with some fucked up hadiths about how on the Day of Judgment I'd be resurrected with pregnant hands."

"Pregnant hands?"

"Pregnant hands."

"Yikes," I said.

"Yeah. Narrated by Attaa, *radiallaho anh*."

Just then I really wanted to ask about her philosophy behind the burqa but felt as though I had missed my window. She got up and went to the refrigerator. Jehangir Tabari came in, stood behind Rabeya and wrapped his arms around her shoulders, leaning his head against the side of hers. "Yo," she said nonchalantly as they rocked left to right to left in a weird sibling way.

"What's the good word?" he asked.

"We were just talking about the sexual issues of Muslim women."

"Sounds like a party," he replied.

"Remember that time—it was back before Yusef was here—when you hooked up with that one girl from the MSA, what was her name?"

"Shit, I don't remember."

"No, no you remember," she countered, physically struggling to hold back her laughter long enough to get the words out. "You got all drunk and stumbled down the stairs yelling MUSLIM GIRLS GIVE LOUSY HEAD!"

"Yeah," said Jehangir sarcastically, "that was great. *Fantastic.* Let's move on—"

"Yeah, let's move on to Muslim men."

"What do you mean?" I asked.

"Yusef," Rabeya replied, "you ever kiss a girl?"

"What?"

"Do you shower in your underwear?"

"BEH SHARUM!" yelled Jehangir before I could even respond. Rabeya burst out laughing, which I found easier to deal with because I couldn't see her face.

CHAPTER IV

Woke up the next morning to Johnny Cash booming down the hall.

My name is Sue—how do you DO? Now you gonna DAH!

"Salaams," said Jehangir as I stood in his doorway. It was almost noon. He sat up in his bed, propped against a pile of pillows, long mohawk laying limp over the right side of his bald head.

"Wasalaams."

"Johnny Cash," said Jehangir, pointing to his record player.

"Cool." I looked at his American flag and Makkah wall-hanging.

"I'm going to tell you a secret," he said in a whisper loud enough to be heard across the room.

"What's that?"

"Listen. Come here." I walked over to his bed. He looked me in the eyes. "Yusef Ali?"

"Yeah?"

He leaned closer to me.

"The United States can save Islam." He eased himself back after saying the words as though physically strained by their weight.

"What do you mean?" I asked.

"We're going to do it right. All the bullshit's dying slow, can you see that?"

"Bullshit?"

"Yeah bro. Because Muslims are coming here from like a thousand different countries, all of them with their own ideas about what Islam is supposed to be. Arabs, South Asians, Africans, Persians, Bosnians, Turks, Afghans, Chechens, Kazakhs, Malaysians... every culture touched by Islam has taken it and added their own ingredients. So when you get all these brothers and sisters from different backgrounds together, how can you have a community?" I stayed silent for the answer. "By leaving culture behind and sticking to what we have in common, just our *iman*, you know?"

"True."

"It'll be hard at first because you have all these Muslims who have been raised and ingrained with this shit. Out West bro when I was fifteen I volunteered at an Islamic summer camp, and some little Indian kid told me that when you wear a cross into the masjid, Isa's spirit will come and break it. But you know what? Give him some years, that shit won't stick. It'll be weaker on these kids growing up here. And that much weaker on *their* kids. It's all gonna wash away."

"Wow."

"You think America will accept Islam if it means giving up all the family dogs?"

"No."

"But that's a great thing, y'akhi; they'll have the freedom to be whatever kind of Muslims they want. And another thing: we're the minority. We don't have the numbers to go runnin' around demanding the implementation of shar'ia or any of that nonsense. Nobody's getting their hands chopped off and we won't be stoning fornicators or tossing homosexuals off minarets like Ali said to do.

And sure as shit there's no marrying nine-year-olds here, bro. And no religious police cruising the streets to make sure you're praying."

"Mash'Allah."

"No killing apostates," he added.

"That's a big one too."

"Yeah, Yusef. We have a chance here to do something great." The brief conversation rose his energy twenty levels. He earnestly believed it though I knew, with his beer and sex and punk rock, he had corrupted Islam as much as anyone anywhere else. Probably more so, though I guess that is a hard judgment call.

The way I saw it: like Saudi, Turkey, Pakistan and Indonesia, the U.S. would only end up with its own distinct flavor of Islam. But for the time being it was an Islam full of promise and vitality; still young enough to be malleable, still a long ways from growing old and stale and rigid like its cousins. I think the roundabout dream of Jehangir Tabari might have been that American Islam would forever stay that way, freely shapeless like water.

He gently lifted the needle from his Johnny Cash record, put it back in its sleeve—black and white photo of Cash, with words LIVE AT FOLSOM PRISON—and place among dozens of taqwacore bands. The Mutaweens, Bilal's Boulder, the Bin Qarmats, Osama bin Laden's Tunnel Diggers, the Zaqqums, Burning Books for Cat Stevens, a mess more. He stood them up straight on his bookshelf like nearly paper-thin volumes of Bukhari.

Sitting at the kitchen table over a bowl of Apple Jacks I wondered if there was really anything at all to Lynn coming by, asking about me, wanting me to call her and saying she'd see me at jumaa. I had never had any indication of a romantic or physical interest on her part in the whole time I knew her. Rabeya sat at the other end, smuggling a bagel to her mouth carefully so as not to get jelly on the inside of her niqab.

"Yahooda-food," said Umar with a cavalier grin. Rabeya replied with a finger.

Amazing Ayyub looked at me strangely.

"Salaam," I said upon becoming uncomfortable.

"You gonna do Lynn?" he asked. Rabeya almost choked on her bagel.

"What?" I replied. "Why would you even say that?"

"You probably shouldn't," he said.

"Thanks for the input, Amazing Ayyub."

"You know what happens to the fornicators?"

"What," I answered, not at all in the tone of a question.

"Allah's gonna hang stones from your balls in Jehennam."

"I think I heard that one."

"Save it for Jennah," said Ayyub, who I knew had seen more than his share of illegal female genitals. "In Jennah you get fuckin' five hundred houris, four thousand virgins and eight thousand non-virgins, all in little see-through dresses." Rabeya moved slightly in her seat.

"You know what's interesting," she interjected. "Muhammad gave more explicit accounts of the houris and so forth when he was only living with Khadija. After she died and Rasul started piling up all those wives and slave-girls he calmed down a little."

"Really?" I asked.

"He was in his fifties having sex like, what—eleven times a night? With wives often giving up their turns so he could go again with his favorite, the nine-year-old? I would hope that was enough ass for him."

"Wow," I remarked. Umar left the kitchen.

"He didn't need to think about houris," Rabeya added, "once he became a rock star."

"Yo," said Amazing Ayyub. "You know what? In Jennah, every orgasm lasts six hundred years."

Neither of us could find an adequate response, so the dialogue just kind of drifted away.

Rabeya went out. We never knew where she went when she left the house or what she did, or for that matter who she did it with; but that day she came back with her friend Fatima, a Bangladeshi film student. When asked about religion, Fatima specified her Islam as "progressive."

"What's 'progressive Islam?'" I once asked Umar.

"A hill of shit," he answered.

She was an attractive girl with straight jet-black hair and a little sleeveless top exposing thin brown arms and black bra straps. Juxtaposed with Rabeya the pair looked like mutually exclusive personalities, but they held warmly to a shared notion of Islamic sisterhood.

"You should see her apartment," Rabeya told me as Fatima smiled from embarrassment. "She's got stacks of reels from demonstrations all over her apartment, like thousands of hours of footage. Palestine protests, Chechnya, Bosnia, Afghanistan, W's inauguration, WTO, Iraq—"

"I gotta go through all it someday," said Fatima. "Sort out the good stuff, make a kind of video autobiography. It'll take forever.

"I'm so excited," she added on an unrelated note. "One of my good friends is going to UB in the fall, so he'll be around all the time."

"Is that Muzammil?" asked Rabeya.

"Yeah," Fatima replied. "He's the best."

"What's his story?" I asked.

"I met him out in San Francisco at the Gay Muslim Conference," she explained. "He's just graduating high school this year."

"Wow," said Rabeya. "How was the conference, by the way?"

"Pretty interesting—I went to make a documentary thinking it was going to be quite the scene—but you'd be surprised how *fundy* some of those guys are."

"Really?"

"Yeah, like they're totally strict about the prayers and everything, and a lot of them straight-up tell you that gay sex is a sin—but they're openly queer and it's like, how do you guys juggle that? I don't think I could entertain beliefs that condemned my way of life."

"That'd be really hard," said Rabeya. "But I guess you do what you have to do."

"Yeah, well, anyway Muzammil's a really cool guy. I think you'll all like him."

Rabeya went out to the kitchen and poured some chocolate soy milk she kept just for when Fatima came over. "Aww Rabby, you're the sweetest!" beamed Fatima when Rabeya returned with the glass. I then heard Amazing Ayyub rummaging through the kitchen.

"I HEARD THIS STUFF MAKES YOU SHIT YOUR BRAINS OUT!" he yelled.

"Ayyub," Fatima yelled back, "come out here." Ayyub complied, again shirtless. She asked, "have you ever tried silk?"

"Silk? Silk's for homos." I imagined Rabeya rolling her eyes under the grid. "Silk's for fuckin' fags," Ayyub continued. "You know what happens to Jehennam to men who wear silk?"

"No, no, *soy milk*," Fatima replied, completely breezing past Ayyub's offense. She offered him a sip. He took the glass and tasted cautiously.

"It's different," he said.

"It's good for you."

"So Ayyub," said Rabeya, "do you think homosexuality's haram?"

"I don't know," Ayyub replied with his eyes downcast. "But fuckin' shit, if I felt a piercing in my ass I'd fuckin' even the odds."

"What?" we all answered at different times, Fatima's eyebrows raised in polite disbelief.

"Like if some dude tried to put it in my ass, you know, I'd have to balance the see-saw." He smiled at us like a first-grader who had just farted, eventually feeling the impulse to leave.

For a moment we sat silently trying to process Amazing Ayyub in our heads.

"So," said Rabeya, "tell me what's up with you and Lynn." Inexplicably I sensed that under the burqa she smiled. At the time I was too naïve to take the question as meaning anything more than simple honest curiosity. I had no idea how people functioned in arenas of sexual courtship, how they sent out feelers through mutual friends and innocent conversation.

"I don't know," I replied.

"You like her?"

"Sure, she's cool. A cool person. Real smart." I did not know what else to say. In actuality, I was not sure if I even had interest in Lynn beyond the thrill of imagining someone with romantic or sexual feelings for me.

"Yep, she *is* cool… but do you *like* her?"

"Yeah, yeah you can say that, sure. I guess I just—I don't know, I just don't really…"

"What?" asked Fatima.

"I don't really know how to date."

"What do you mean?" asked Rabeya.

"I mean, like 'hey do you want to go to the movies with me?' type stuff. I don't have a clue how any of that works."

"People don't really do that anymore," said Rabeya.

"They don't?"

"Nobody *dates*, Yusef. Basically you just hang out with a bunch of friends and sooner or later you hook up with one of them and maybe you hook up twice… and maybe you decide just to do each other to the exclusion of all others, and bam! You're in a relationship."

"Oh."

"That's especially how it was when I lived in the dorms," added Fatima. "Everyone hangs out in each other's rooms watching movies or whatever… eventually someone's just going to get done."

"I see."

"Don't worry about it, Yusef," said Rabeya, the cloth of her niqab moving as she spoke. "Just hang out and see what happens."

"Cool."

"Oh!" snapped Fatima with an urgent turn of her head to Rabeya. "I forgot to tell you what my mom said!"

"What happened?" Rabeya asked.

"She was all weird and kept saying how she hoped I could talk to her about anything and wanted us to have this close, comfortable mother-daughter relationship… and I had no idea what she was getting at but then she just spelled it out—'like if you ever meet a boy up at school, I want you to feel like you can tell me—'"

"Shit!" yelled Rabeya. "What'd you say to that?"

"I was like 'well, what would happen then?' And she said 'then we'd meet his parents and talk about the wedding.'"

"Ohhhhhhhh maaaan," groaned Rabeya.

"Yeah… yeah."

"Jesus," said Rabeya.

"I didn't even know how to begin to react. I have like the best mom in the world but sometimes she doesn't exactly get it—"

I smiled politely as Fatima and Rabeya continued their dialogue along tracks to which I could not contribute. But as I sat there I imagined Fatima's mother and a little tidbit of information Jehangir had told me after the night he got drunk and rubbed Fatima's belly. Maybe Rabeya did not even know about it.

The tidbit was this: when Fatima first got a period, Mom refused to take her to a gynecologist on the grounds that it would destroy her virginity.

Rabeya gave the khutbah that week. The usual faces poured in through our front door. Fatima was there with her hair covered by a regular blue bandana. I deliberately chose a row towards the back to increase my chances of spotting Lynn before she spotted me. Couldn't find her.

Rabeya started off with Arabic du'as, then proceeded to read off a list of actual questions posed to fatwa-dishing scholars on Islamic websites. She offered no comment or opinion on any of the questions, leaving us to receive them as we would.

"Is covering the face for women wajib or sunna?

"Is hashish haram or only makrooh?

"Is it sunna or fard for women to put henna on their hands?

"What are the sunna for vinegar, olive oil, honey and oiling the hair?

"What is the hukum for wearing a handlace with bells for a woman?

"Is the use of lipstick considered imitating the kafrs?

"Is it permissible for a menstruating woman to recite the Holy Qur'an?

"Is it permissible for a woman to visit a relative's grave?

"When in sujdah, how are Shafi women supposed to place

their feet?

"Could a woman call her husband by his name?

"Can a female travel in a different car then her mahram more than forty-eight miles, while her mahram is in the car in front of her car?

"Is it permissible for a woman to pierce her nose for the purpose of wearing jewelry?

"Does wudhu break if you look into a mirror?

"Is it permissible to write with your left hand?

As they piled up atop each other until the final question ("Is it haram for a woman to donate blood to a non-mahram man?"), I grew embarrassed of Islam—or at least of Muslims—or at least of myself for contemplating the pork gelatin in marshmallows. Were these the essential concerns for our spiritual enhancement?

She then went into her khutbah, centering around the Necklace.

Muhammad's wife Ayesha once found herself separated from their caravan while searching for a missing necklace. Alone in the desert she was completely lost and helpless until a young soldier named Safwan bin Mu'attal Sulami Zakwani showed up on his camel. Safwan lowered the steed for Ayesha to mount and they returned to the caravan.

Seeing Muhammad's favorite wife riding alone with one of the troops aroused suspicions and scandal. Ayesha and her supposed consort flatly denied any wrongdoing. Ayesha said she heard no words from him the whole time but *we are for Allah and to Him we have to return.* Safwan would not even ride the camel but walked alongside it with rope in hand.

Muhammad did not know what to do. Ayesha went home to her parents and Muhammad ran off to the mountains where he cried and suffered and waited for an answer from Allah. Meanwhile, Ali beat Ayesha's maid.

When Allah finally proclaimed his wife's innocence, a relieved Muhammad took her back. Everyone was happy, particularly Ayesha's parents whose status among the believers had been redeemed. Ayesha's mother told her to thank Muhammad, but she refused.

It was at this point in the story that we really felt the emotion coming up through Rabeya's trembling vocal folds. "Imagine this girl—and she was no woman, she was only a girl—thirteen years old. Think about that: thirteen years old, with all the prestige and responsibility and burdens of being married to the PROPHET OF ALLAH—THIRTEEN YEARS OLD, THIRTEEN YEARS OLD! Thirteen years old in a time and place that gave no voice to women—and here was this little girl standing up strong to the Prophet... peace and blessings be upon him... and Ayesha looked Muhammad dead in the eyes as she told her mother, 'I shall not thank him and laud him, but Allah alone who has vindicated my honor.' Think about that, brothers and sisters. You think you cannot criticize Muhammad or it makes you *kafr*. You think we can't do anything to improve or evolve Islam. But little Ayesha, thirteen years old in seventh-century Arabia, did it right in Muhammad's face. *Al-hamdulilahi Rabbil'Alameen.*"

"Ayesha was a bitch though," whispered Amazing Ayyub on my immediate right. "She fuckin' had arrows shot at Hasan's coffin, what about that?" I ignored him and looked down where my forehead would soon go in sudjah.

Rabeya recited Qur'an beautifully, often getting me on the verge of tears; and, as always, the AAAAAAAMMMMEEEEEEEEEEEEN after *al-Fatiha* just overwhelmed me. At the end of two rakats, as Rabeya gave her final salaams and we likewise turned our heads, I paused and in doing so saw Lynn as she greeted the angel on her left.

Up by the front, between two men. I had been unable to recognize her from behind because she wore hejab hiding all those dreadlocks and allowing only her face. From what I could see it seemed as though she had on one of her old kameezes too. I then realized she could not have possibly attended our jumaa just for my sake, and to have assumed so entailed an arrogance bordering on *self-shirk*.

The jamaat broke up into sunna prayers, du'as and quiet socializing. In the steady stream of Muslims making their way to the door I bumped into Lynn.

"As-salaamu alaikum!" she said with a huge smile and matching hug.

"Wa-alaikum as-salaam," I replied. "Good to see you." With her face outlined in cotton hejab, a certain positive energy beamed from Lynn's expression; but it was also obvious that she had strayed from her natural character.

"Rabeya's awesome," said Lynn. "I just love her."

"Yeah, she always gives good khutbahs."

"So is Jehangir having another of his parties tonight?"

"Yeah, insha'Allah."

"I always thought it was real cool," she said, "how on Friday afternoons you'd have all these Muslims here listening to khutbahs and then at night all the punks come in for beer and ass. It's like two entirely different worlds in the same house."

"I'm not sure how *Muslim* all these Muslims are, though."

"Why do you say that?" Suddenly I felt myself backed into a corner whereas any explanation I could give would portray me as a fundamentalist.

"Well, I mean... from the traditional standpoint... I guess... with women leading the prayers or standing side by side with men in the prayers, it could be seen as... I don't know, an innovation... and sometimes the messages of the khutbahs might—"

"Personally, I'm not big on the whole 'Islam is this one way, always has been and always must be and any deviation from the norm puts you in the hellfire' approach. I think religion is supposed to be ours to do with what we want. Imams aren't God, and alims aren't God, and like Rabeya kind of said in her khutbah, Prophet Muhammad isn't even God—that's what got me into Islam in the first place, the fact that we don't have things coming between us and Allah like in Christianity. Then I found out that we do, we really do—or *they* do, I guess I should say."

"They?"

"Muslims."

"I think you're more Muslim than you know."

"You're just saying that because I've dressed the part."

"No, not at all. Reminds me of a parable I read in one of Idries Shah's books, about this dog and a guy dressed up like—"

"Mulla Nasruddin can save his pleasantries for another day. I think you're going to buy me lunch."

So I bought her lunch. Lynn's opposition to the unnecessary use of automobiles provided us with a healthy walk to the pizza place.

"So you're originally from Syracuse?" she said, the statement rendered a question with her tone on the last syllable.

"Yep."

"What's the community like there?"

"The community?"

"The Muslims."

"Oh, oh yeah. It's okay. Some jerks, you know, but that's everywhere. There's definitely nobody like these guys."

"Yeah, definitely not."

"They're good people, though."

"Look at us," she said.

"Look at what?"

"Us. I got hejab on, man, isn't that something?"

"It works," I replied cautiously.

"And you got on—what shirt is that, Abercrombie?"

"Aeropostale."

"Oh, oh yes. Now I see it. Well then."

"What's that supposed to mean?"

"Oh, nothing. Just that… well…"

"What?" I asked.

"I'm Muslim-er than youuuu," she sang in a childish taunt, grabbing my arm and almost leaning in on me. I smiled wide and toothy but lacked the comfort level to actually laugh out loud.

We got to the place, Lynn ordered vegan pizza and I got a plain cheese slice. Sat at a booth with our meals on paper plates. She set hers down, took off her scarf and shook out the dirty-blonde dreadlocks which made her look even weirder when contrasted with the kameez.

Just then a guy walked in with t-shirt exposing lean but sinewy arms completely sleeved in tattoos.

"Hey, Lynn! Salaam-alaikum!" He had a thick Spanish accent.

"Wa-alaikum as-salaam, man!" she yelled back.

"What are you up to?"

"Just got back from jumaa."

"Oh, al-hamdulilah," he said, moving forward in line. "Keep it up."

"How did you do this semester?" she asked.

"Eh, so-so. How about you?"

"Could have been better."

"I hear that." The conversation stopped abruptly when it became his turn to order.

"That's Marcos," Lynn explained in a half-whisper.

"He's Muslim?"

"Yeah. Converted this past year. I think he might have gone to a jumaa or two at your house, but I don't really see too much of him. Once he finishes school he's going to go back to Spain and win it back for y'all."

"Mash'Allah."

"You should probably go tell him," she whispered, putting her hand by her mouth so Marcos couldn't read her lips from ten feet away, "that tattoos are haram."

"I'll be sure to go do that," I replied facetiously.

"At least they're haram for women," she said. "Muhammad said Allah curses the woman who tattoos. I don't know if it's the same for men."

"I think it's considered haram for everyone."

"And of course," she said with a gentle slap on my forearm, "women who pluck their eyebrows are cursed too."

"Really?"

"Oh dear Yusef Ali, you need to study your hadiths."

"I guess so."

"I remember back in the day when I was a good sister and all, going to the masjid like every day... and one of the women who took it upon themselves to tutor me one day discreetly said 'Lynn, I've noticed you don't have very thick eyebrows and I just wanted you to know what the Prophet said about that...' I was like, 'whoa, okay, I don't pluck my eyebrows anyway but thanks for the info. Now I can go to heaven.'" I tried to laugh. "So remember that, Yusef! Keep your eyebrows as they are!"

"I'll try."

The conversation paused for us to take a few bites of our respective slices. "You know," I mentioned after swallowing, "I imagine it's a lot easier for you."

"What is?" she replied with her mouth half-full.

"Separating the good stuff from the bad. You weren't raised in a Muslim family so you can just take things on your own terms. For me it's hard because I got all of this stuff in one big lump package. Some of it's worthwhile guidance that I would like to hold on to for the rest of my life, some is just culture that's a part of who I am and then there's a lot of traditional things that I can't understand and I don't know why people follow them, but they always have. I think that's why you have something to your Islam that I don't have."

"What do you mean?" she asked with half-smile of pleasant surprise.

"I can't separate spirituality from my family, my heritage, my identity as a South Asian; it's inextricably connected. You reject an aspect of one, to some extent you're rejecting all of them."

"Yeah, my family didn't seem too disappointed when I started celebrating Christmas again."

"You celebrate Christmas?"

"Just with my family. It has nothing to do with religion."

"Well, it is *Christ*-mas."

"No, no it's not. It's *see-my-family-that-I-don't-ever-see*-mas."

"Oh."

"But who cares anyway, right? It's like Attar said, 'forget what is and is not Islam.'"

"Attar?"

"Farid ud-Din Attar. *Conference of the Birds*, ever read it?"

"Can't say that I have." Marcos walked towards the door carrying his slices in a large brown paper bag, making sure to hold it straight.

Lynn called him over.

"S'up," he said standing before our booth.

"Hey Marcos, we just wanted to get a closer look at your ink." He stiffened his green arms as though to make for easier viewing. "Didn't you get one on your stomach?" Marcos lifted up his shirt to reveal a *Fisabilillah* arched huge below his ribcage.

"Got that done a month ago," he explained.

"Nice, very nice... now Marcos, what would you say to someone who told you that was haram?"

"I would say *fuck off*, and then I would say that when my body's resurrected and Allah asks 'what's that?' I would answer, 'it's to glorify Your Name.' If He wants to throw me in Hell after that, then what kind of Allah did I believe in?"

"Exactly," said Lynn.

"Mash'Allah," I added.

"Well Lynn, good seeing you again." He turned to me. "And I didn't catch your name—"

"Yusef Ali," I replied.

"Oh, cool. Yusef, I'm Marcos." We shook hands.

"Oh I'm sorry," said Lynn. "I should have taken care of that."

"It's all good," said Marcos.

"What's your *good* name?" I asked him.

"Marcos," he replied.

"Oh. I mean, you didn't change it?"

"No, I didn't."

"That's cool though."

"Yeah. Well, nice meeting you. Lynn, take care."

"Later Marcos," she said.

"Nice meeting you," I said. And then he was gone.

"*Good* name?" asked Lynn, leaning in on the table. "What the shit is that?"

"Why does Rabeya wear the full burqa?" I asked Fasiq while sitting on the roof. Blunt hanging from his lips, he closed up the Qur'an and placed it on his right. Took a hit before replying.

"What do you mean?"

"Well, she doesn't wear it for the notion that it's sunna, we know that much… and she doesn't wear it because her family is really strict… and I don't think she wears it for some Islamo-Feminist gesture… so I don't know why—" Fasiq interrupted me only with a suddenly active, alert silence that felt as though he would say something. He looked at me and said it.

"Ever have a day when you didn't want people looking at you?"

"Yeah," I replied, "I guess so. Is that why she wears it?"

"I don't know," he said with a puff and then dramatic exhale. "But that's why *I'd* wear it."

"What the shit is this?" boomed Umar, running down the stairs. I was sitting with Rabeya in the living room.

"What?"

"This!" he held it up for us.

"Looks like a Qur'an," Rabeya replied.

"Yeah, yeah it is. It's a Qur'an. And you know where I found this Qur'an?"

"The Qur'an Store?"

"Funny, sister. But no, I found this in the bathroom, sitting right on the sink."

"And…"

"And what's it doing in there? This is the Word of Allah Subhana Wa Ta'Ala!"

"Fasiq probably left it there by mistake," Rabeya replied. "You know he uses the bathroom window to get up on the roof, that's where he reads Qur'an—"

"No, that's where he smokes his ganja!"

"Yeah but it's also where he reads. I'm sure it was an accident. He probably climbed in through the window, set the Qur'an on the sink and then forgot about it."

"The bathroom is filthy."

"This whole house is filthy."

"Yeah, yeah you're right. Back when Mustafa lived here it never could have looked like this."

"Back when Mustafa lived here," Rabeya shot back, "I could never sit in the living room."

Of course, that night all of Jehangir's kafr cronies filed in and trashed the place as he stood in a corner watching it all go down with a sly satisfaction that only hours ago our house had been a masjid and now it was a riot, as though real salvation hinged on having a little taste of everything. Then Jehangir reached the point of drunkenness at which he could talk about nothing but Allah, his tragic failures as a mumin and the promise that within the next twenty American years or so Islam would blossom into something that you could not witness anywhere else in the world.

Some guy put Billy Bragg on the stereo: "Joe DiMaggio's Done it Again." Jehangir threw his spiked-leather-jacket-arm around me and hung off my body for support. He wore red plaid pants. Seemed like he always had them on.

"Listen Yusef Ali," he said. "My grandmother used to talk about DiMaggio all the fuckin' time. She hated the Yankees, did you know that? She only fuckin' hated the Yankees because her dad liked 'em, so it was like they would give each other a hard time about it. You know what I mean? If the Yankees won or lost, one would tease the other. Father-daughter bonding."

"I see."

"So then her boys in turn *liked* the Yankees, and gave her a hard time when they won."

"And then you, the next generation—you hated the Yankees, right?"

"My dad died before he could really get that ingrained in me."

"Oh. I'm sorry."

"Eh, so it goes. I grew up in a house full of women."

"I remember you telling me that."

"It worked out, I think. It all works out." He turned his head at a girl walking by. "Gave me something, I think," he whispered to me with such disgusting alcohol-breath I could smell it through my ear.

"Did you ever get with Fatima?" I asked.

"Funny you should mention that. Fuck, I need to sit down." We went over to an empty spot on the couch that Fasiq used as a bed. Surrounded by noise and dozens of autonomous conversations and blaring Billy Bragg, he told me the story. "Listen, Yusef. I had her up in my room, right? And we're making out and whatever, and I go for her tits. And that's cool, she's cool. So I'm messing around with her tits but over the shirt. So then I think, 'well, might as well go under the shirt.' So I'm under the shirt, over the bra. Then I figure I can free the tits up completely so I yank one out of the bra and then the other and she's totally good to go. I pull up the shirt, I'm suckin' on her tits and whatever, and after that what can I do? Might as well go down for the crown. I put my hands between her legs—over the jeans, of course—and I can fuckin' feel the warm moisture, bro! Even through the fuckin' jeans. She's liking it so I go to unbutton her jeans and she puts her hand over mine and I'm thinking fuck, that's it. And she just looks at me and you know what she says?"

"What?"

"She says, 'sorry if this is a dumb question, but if you were to, to…' and she couldn't even get the words out so I'm like 'finger you?' and she goes 'yeah… would that break the hymen?'"

"Wow," I replied, not knowing how else to react.

"Yeah, bro. I couldn't believe it. So I told her that most girls lose their hymens years before that's even an issue. And she had no idea! I was like, shit, you can lose your hymen when you're eight years old riding a bike. She looked at me like I just blew her mind."

"Don't they teach you all that in health class?"

"Yeah, absolutely. That's where I heard all that, like in seventh grade. But her mom kept her out of that shit, wrote a note to the teacher saying to send Fatima to another room once they hit Sex Ed. So the girl had no clue, here I was a scumbag guy trying to get in her pants and I had to tell her shit about her own body that she didn't even know."

"So what happened after that?" I asked.

"What can you do, after that?"

"I don't know."

"Fuckin'… what can you do, after that? This girl was scared I would break her hymen. Jesus, man. If we did shit I would have felt like a child molester or something."

I looked around the room. Rabeya was arguing with some guy about war in Iraq. Rude Dawud had his arm around a girl I had never seen before. Amazing Ayyub regaled a small circle with his tale of spitting in the football players' car. Then there were self-supporting crowds of strangers. Jehangir looked up at the ceiling and said "women, y'akhi."

"Women," I repeated.

"They're better than us, bro."

"Yeah."

"There's one for you right now," he said with a slow nod. I looked where his eyes directed me and saw Lynn talking to Fatima, both of them with red plastic cups in hand. Lynn had discarded her jumaa gear for a tight little top and loose-fitting khakis. The bra straps were blue. "Go let her save you." He patted me on the back and I stood up. She saw me before I had to think of an opening.

"Hey, you!" she yelled. Gave me a hug, surprising in that it had only been a matter of hours since we last saw each other. "Glad you could make it."

"I live here," I replied smiling.

"Oh, right. Well, glad you live here then." Fatima seemed to have spontaneously disappeared.

"So what's going on?"

"Nothing, really, just chillin'. Actually I was thinking about how I haven't really seen the whole house yet."

"Really?"

"Yeah, I've only been downstairs. Care to tour me?"

"Sure." I squeezed through the people towards the stairs. Lynn had her hand on my shoulder, ostensibly to keep us from being separated. "This is Dawud's room," I said upon reaching the top of the stairs with a gesture towards the closed door at our left. "That one over there is Umar's and the other one's Jehangir's."

"Where's yours?" she asked.

"Just down the hall this way." We walked in its direction, Lynn pausing to examine various Sharpie graffiti on the walls: tags, political slogans, vulgar comedy, band names and some Arabic. "And right here's our upstairs bathroom—don't leave a Qur'an in there or Umar will snap, we kind of had an issue earlier today."

"Don't worry about that," she replied.

"And there's Fasiq," I said, pointing to the open window. Fasiq sat on the roof with a closed Qur'an at his side. He was watching traffic or squirrels or something. We stepped away without him noticing. "This is my room," I said nervously, opening the door.

"Very nice," she said. "Is everyone else's this clean?"

"Umar's pretty neat."

"Oh cool," she said, walking to my bed and taking my little white and green flag from its display stand. "That's Pakistan, right?"

"Yeah."

"You ever been there?" She was standing close to me. Turned slightly to put the flag back, then returned to full attention.

"I spent a summer there when I was ten."

"Really? How was it?"

"A different planet."

"I can imagine."

"Sometimes I don't know where I feel more out of place." I looked at the floor, slowly making my way up to her eyes. I did not know what to do with our eye contact. She crinkled her eyebrows. I clumsily leaned toward her and it happened. I could not tell you *really* how it happened—I can't remember making any conscious decision to go for it, and I have no memory of her taking the initiative. The kiss came of its own volition without asking for help from either of us.

Likewise, it continued and demanded more of us, like tongues and hands. Then her shirt was off and we cascaded onto my mattress. I opened my eyes briefly and looked at her shoulder, deciding the bra should come off and soon realizing I was out of my element tugging on the hooks. She reached behind herself and it was off.

My eyes unintentionally zeroed in on the red break-out traversing her left breast.

"It's eczema," she said plainly.

"Oh." Only thought in my head, strangely, was of Rabeya and how every inch of her body, saving the hands, could have been covered with that and I never would have known. I place no value judgment on the fact; it's merely an observation.

"Silly boy," she said, pushing me over. As I lay back she straddled me and drove our loins together, grinding in such a way that I almost found painful with the obstruction of garments. *Dry-humping*, I believe it's called. She leaned forward and buried my face in her breasts, the fleshy area between them still smooth and free of rash. As she rode I took hold of her bare shoulders and made an ineffectual attempt at having some form of control in the situation.

She swung her right leg so suddenly we were side by side. I approached her breasts almost violently, squeezing as hard as I could while my soft imbibes of her nipples gave way to hard tugs with the teeth. All this time I was fully, valorously erect, throbbing like I could rip through my pants and bore a hole through her stomach. She moved her hand down and glided over it, her fingertips noting the ridge of my head. My entire body stiffened, my legs straightening out so hard I felt the strain in my knees. Then she took my hand and smoothly brought it to her, brought it down into the recesses of jeans already somehow unbuttoned, plunged me toward what had been a dark unknown; but upon first contact of my fingertips with the threshold of curly hair I yanked back up and out.

"Are you one of those guys who hates girls?" she asked, sitting up.

"What? Why would I hate—no, not at all," I stammered, hardly prepared for her question. "Why would you think I hate girls? Does *this* seem like I hate girls?" I gestured with my hands almost pointing at her, as though my mauling of her breasts had proven the point.

"Yeah, actually," she replied, head tilted playfully toward her left shoulder, which seemed to be rising to meet it. "You could be one of those guys who wants it so much he hates the girl who makes him want it. It *is* my fault, right?"

"Is what your fault?"

"That we're up here?"

"What? No, no, totally not, it's all—"

"Because I led you astray, wearing a tight little shirt so you could see my shape, right?"

"No!"

"And I'd lean over so you could see right down…" As she said it she did just that, but almost in caricature of what the intention would have been.

"It's all me, I'm the—"

"Yeah," she sighed with the resignation of an immortal, eternal woman who had seen this time and time again over the centuries: man after man, the same old thing in a thousand different guises as scriptures and nations came and went. It sounded quite like that as she explained—*I've seen it before.* I cast my gaze down. *I've dated Mormons, Jehovah's Witnesses, the whole nine.* My eyes rose to meet her briefly in a scientific curiosity about the sexual maladjustments of those faiths, how they might have compared and contrasted to mine. *And Catholics? Don't even get me started…*

"Catholics?"

"Even if you don't hate girls exactly, you at least fear them enough for your brain to process it the same way."

I just then realized the strangeness of being on a bed with a girl who had her shirt off, her breasts big and drooping with enormous nipples and eczema on the left. At least it was strange to me. Didn't seem too strange to Lynn. "Where's the romance in Islam?"

"Romance?"

"Passion."

"Passion?" I had to think about it. "Well, you know, you date after you're married."

"Huh?"

"It's exciting, you know, being with your new spouse, and going to the movies, going to dinner, doing fun romantic things together… um…”

“Yeah.”

“It’s hard to explain.”

“But that’s the Islamic way?” she asked.

“Uh… yeah, I guess so.”

“Well, it doesn’t make sense to me.”

“That’s a cultural thing,” I replied. “You know, you have a Western background, it might be hard to understand because you were raised to—”

“So you’re saying I can’t understand Islam because I wasn’t born in the right hemisphere?”

“Well, from a certain—”

“I thought Islam was universal. I thought it was for everyone. I thought it applied to every society at every corner of the earth.”

“Right, but—”

“But *shit*,” she snapped. We were silent for awhile. Eventually I could almost hear her breath rate slowing. “So… what’s your major again?”

“Engineering,” I replied.

“Why?”

“Because… what do you mean?”

“Why engineering? Is engineering what you’re passionate about? What the fuck is engineering, anyway? Because I don’t even know.”

“Engineering is just—”

“Did your mom tell you to be an engineer?”

“No!” I almost sounded like a child.

“Bullshit,” she replied.

“What are you talking about? Don’t assume—”

“Yusef you have a dick in those pants, I know you do. You can’t hide it.”

“What does that even mean?”

"When was the last time you ever did anything remotely interesting?"

"What?"

She stood up off the bed and went through the CDs on my dresser stacked up out of their jewel cases, most of them burned off the computer and labeled in my handwriting. She shuffled through them like cards, noting each one. NOFX. Qari Abdul-Basit. Descendents. Cat Stevens.

"Question," she said, eyes still on the CDs. "Has Umar ever like, *done* it?"

"Now that's ghiba—"

"Don't spout that shit at me, neither of us speak Arabic."

"Staghfir'Allah—"

"I'm talking to the wall here." She kept going through my music. Focused on Lynn's bare back, I grew accustomed to her toplessness. "You listen to this shit?" she asked, turning around with a disc in her hand. Her breasts moved when she moved.

"Which one is that?" I asked.

"Soldiers of Allah," she replied in sarcastic deference.

"It's Umar's. They have a couple songs I like; you know, about the state of the umma and such—"

"These guys are fuckin' sociopaths!"

"The Soldiers of Allah?"

"Yeah, *they* seem like a fun bunch." She placed it delicately atop the others and sat back on the bed, breasts flopping nonchalantly. "We should go party with 'em sometime."

"I don't think they're the type who'd party with you."

"You're probably right," she replied.

"Were you ever even Muslim at all?"

I am still not sure how I failed to keep myself from blurting that out. She answered only with a desperate grab for her shirt, throwing it on haphazardly and bolting out of my room, blue bra still on the bed. I think the only thing that kept her from just running out topless was the eczema.

I sat on the bed somewhat stunned from the last five minutes or so. I had put my hands on a girl's breasts, even briefly entered the realm of pubic hair. That was something, I guess. And she was gone.

I looked over at Mustafa's old green Bukharis on the bookshelf. Went over and opened Volume Nine for no reason. Flipped the pages and a folded sheet of blue-lined notebook paper fell out. I unfolded it to see a series of handwritten ayats with the English translation underneath each corresponding word. Assuming it was Mustafa's writing, I felt as though I had come into possession of some holy relic—no less than a Prophet's Hair in terms of that house and its history. How weird, finding this and five minutes ago I had touched breasts. The world itself seemed to be spinning at a different speed. Just then my brain again registered the sounds of drunks and songs coming from downstairs and I remembered that a party was going on in my house. And a girl had been in my room. And hours before that was jumaa. I felt as though I had been upstairs for three days and that afternoon's jumaa had been ten years ago.

Was not sure if I wanted to ruin the weirdness by going downstairs, but figured checking up on Lynn would be the right thing to do. Wondered how long it had been since she ran out of my room; probably long enough for me to be incredibly rude for having stayed on my bed. I managed to get up and walk to the bathroom. Looked out the window to find nobody on the roof. I pulled the window closed and drew the curtains. Closed and locked the bathroom door. Turned on the water. Climbed in and sat down. The shower had tremendous pressure, sometimes feeling like it could knock you out. I let it all crash hot on the vertex of my skull.

Stayed under the shower's steady blast long enough to again lose my concept of time. Even after turning off the water I just sat there awhile, motionless and wet until I began to feel cold.

I toweled, dressed and walked downstairs slowly to the tune of Minor Threat's "Salad Days." Just as expected, I'd find Umar standing by the CD player with arms folded across his chest.

"As-salaamu alaikum," I said timidly.

"Wa-alaik," he replied stiffly. I wondered if he knew or at least held suspicions. A guy like Umar makes you feel defensive even when you hadn't done anything wrong. Things were dying down slow. Most of the characters had left or passed out. Jehangir sat slumped exactly where I had left him, dead to the world. "Have you made Isha yet?" Umar asked.

"No," I replied.

"You have wudhu?"

"Yeah."

"Let's go then. We'll pray in my room." So I followed Umar back upstairs. Upon opening his door Umar discovered Amazing Ayyub fucking a random wasted girl in his bed. Forgive the word—I generally don't say it and until seeing that pair I never imagined a necessary use for it. But standing there watching Ayyub pound away on a sloppy vagina, I realized that there was such a distinct act as *fucking* and no other word really meant what *fucking* meant. So yes, Ayyub fucked her. It took a second for Umar to fully process what he was witnessing. Once it registered he ran over and pulled Ayyub off her so hard Ayyub was instantly on his feet. I turned away at first glance of the girl's vaginal secretions glistening on Ayyub's sizable dong—apologies again, but *dong* seems like the only word that describes it. My back to the scene, I nonetheless heard the smack and knew it was a fist on face. I turned back around. Naked Ayyub was back-up on the floor, Umar's knee pressed into his kidneys as Umar applied some sort of ultimate-fighting hold around Ayyub's neck. I ran over and tried to pull Umar off. Feeling his arms so tense and tight intimidated me. I knew Umar was worlds stronger than me and had forgotten more about the science of violence than I would ever know. I figured my chances were better if I got off and tried talking to him.

"Umar, man," I said standing in awkward stance over a men-acing Umar and moaning Ayyub. I am not sure what the girl was even doing at this point. "Umar, man, c'mon…"

"Fuckin' junkie piece of shit," Umar growled at hapless Ayyub. "You want to fuck in my bed? You want to fuck your little slut in my fucking bed? After I let you stay in my house—how long now? How long have you been sleeping on my couch, you fucking little piece of Shi'a shit? That's right, Shi'a-shit, fuckin' Shi'it, yeah there you go, fuckin' kafr." Umar untangled one of his arms from the web of limbs around Ayyub's neck, Ayyub still secured at his mercy, and punched him right below the shoulder blade. Ayyub yelped. "I could fucking kill you right now, what the shit would you even do?" I looked around the room. The girl was gone. Umar leaned in close to Ayyub's ear. "You stupid fucking kafr bitch, you're a kafr bitch, you know that? I go to Makkah, you go to Najaf because you're a fucking kafr bitch." Umar then let go of Ayyub in such a way that it looked like even that hurt. Ayyub lay motionless on the floor. "Naked fucking kafr bitch on my floor," said Umar, "that's great." He gave Ayyub a kick in the ribs. "Get your shit and get out of my house." Umar looked at me. "I'm sick of this shit," he yelled. "You didn't see this shit when Mustafa was here! Nobody was FUCKING in my bed when Mustafa was here. Nobody was out on the fucking roof smoking weed, and when they read Qur'an no less, when MUSTAFA was here!" Umar stormed out of his room. I followed with the weak idea that perhaps I could prevent further violence better than I had between him and Ayyub. Umar tromped down the stairs and into the living room to find Fasiq Abasa rolling around the floor with a big smelly golden retriever. Fasiq looked up at us, tried dodging Umar's eyes.

"Salaams, guys. Check this shit out." With this shit he pointed at the dog.

"What the fuck is that?" grunted Umar.

"I walked down to the park and found him. His leash was tied around a tree. I waited around forever but nobody came. I figure somebody just left him or something. But I named him 'Ilm,' isn't that cool?" Umar looked at the dog. Didn't say anything. Then he kicked it. Ilm let out a higher-pitched squeal than Ayyub had and put his tail between his legs. Fasiq rushed to his feet and tried giving Umar a shoulder-block in the ribs but Umar caught him and drove an elbow in the small of his back. He shoved Fasiq off and left the house. A few wasted punks stood in silent witness. Jehangir was still passed out on the couch less than ten feet away.

CHAPTER V

"What's with that?" I asked.

"What?"

"Your shirt." Jehangir's black tee bore white stencil letters reading *Vote Hezbollah.*

"It's just the name of a band," he shrugged, slapping the football with his left hand before launching it on a graceful arc that met its conclusion in my waiting arms. There's more to playing catch than just throwing and catching: there's posture, a vibe even, that implies your right to comfortably and coolly take part. It's our inherited culture. Jehangir had the posture; after each toss he seemed frozen as though in an old Jim Kelly Topps card. And he had the vibe of a guy whose old man started him early throwing pigskins in the backyard. Jehangir's father, however, died when he was little; so I don't know where he got it. I, on the other hand, did not have the posture *or* vibe. I couldn't pass or receive—more importantly, I did not know how to at least look cool trying. Jehangir could run after an overthrown ball with no chance in hell of getting it, but he still moved with a personality that I couldn't capture.

"Sorry," I said as my throw veered across the street. Jehangir waited for a car to go by before crossing to retrieve it. Even Jehangir leaning over to scoop up the ball hit me with his coolness and charisma, the magic intangibles that he possessed as much as any man I'd known. He walked slowly back to our side and nonchalantly over-handed the ball my way.

"Umar's a cock," he said.

"Yeah, he is." I waited for him to jog back to his original spot before throwing it.

"I feel bad that I was passed out," he said, cutting himself off to focus on the descending ball. Caught it and resumed. "I was right there the whole time. I could have done something. And poor fuckin' Ayyub—"

Minutes went without either of us saying a word, the casual pat-sound of our hands stopping football flights becoming all the more apparent. Then Jehangir finally said, "Yusef Ali, I need to lay off the booze."

"Insha'Allah."

"Hope so." He caught the ball and threw it back. "Booze and girls, bro. When we're resurrected and our bodies bear witness to our deeds…" He ran to catch my stray pass. "You know the parts that'll do the most talking, right?" He waited for a response but I just nodded my head. "The mouths and dicks," he said.

"Amazing Ayyub told me that," I replied.

"I can just picture my mouth on the *yawm* telling Allah how I made it an expert on fine imported ales." I laughed. "And my dick'll say 'Ya Allah subhanahu wa ta'Ala, don't let Jehangir tell you he never mingled with the kafrs." The ball went back and forth almost rhythmically as we talked, becoming in its beats and pauses a part of the conversation. "But you know what, Yusef Ali?"

"What?"

"I don't believe in hell."

"You don't?"

"Nope."

"I think that's fairly pivotal to being a Muslim."

"Probably so."

"What does that mean?"

"I don't think it means anything."

"You don't? You don't think it means anything whether or not you're a Muslim?"

"Maybe. Maybe not, Yusef. Islam's all about knowledge, right? Muslims know everything. We seek knowledge from the cradle to the grave. We seek knowledge even if it be in China, Yusef, EVEN IN CHINA! And we've reduced our religion to fuckin' academics. The guy who knows Islam best is the one who really hits the books hard, learns his shit. Muslims brag about having no priests but we're getting molested by scholars. Yusef Ali, books are not Allah. Even a book by or from Allah is not Allah." He looked up to the clouds for support, and apparently found it. He caught my pass and held onto the ball. "And the Qur'an, bro, it wasn't even a book in Muhammad's own lifetime. It had to be collected off stones and leaves and animal ribs, revised in Uthman's khilafah… with suras shortened, parts lost or switched around, subject to faulty human memory, opposing versions destroyed, and a thousand variant readings. There's a lot of human-ness in that divine text. After all is said and done it's a tiny little book for tiny little men, and Allah is BIG. You want to be Muslim? I'm so Muslim I can take a shit on Bukhari and wipe my ass with the Muwatta. I can say that Muhammad ate a fat dick and it doesn't even matter because he's dead and Allah's alive."

"How can you—"

"Because *la ilaha illa Allah,* that's how. I'm so Muslim, fuck Islam." He did not speak in a mean or cynical way—to the contrary, *fuck Islam* danced out his lips with the same romanticism as his deep drunken spiels. "I'm so Muslim, fiqh is worthless. No madrassa of imperfect human beings can claim ownership of my deen. Allah's not entrusting the alims with shit. Let them give their jerk-off fatwas about how long a man's beard should be, fuck all of 'em."

"So what are you," I asked, "an agnostic?"

"No, I'm a Muslim. But if anything, agnosticism is the real Islam; because you're waiting for answers from Allah Herself, not Imam Siraj Dickhead."

"What the hell are you doing with Islam right now?"

"I don't know. Insha'Allah subhanahu wa ta'Ala, I think I'll put on a punk show."

Fasiq spent a week at his friend's place. I tagged along when Umar went over to apologize. My only observation of the kid's house was that its wall-poster rhetoric sent out a surprising hippie vibe—Bob Marley, world peace type stuff, R. Crumb's "Stoned Agin;" but Fasiq seemed more comfortably fitted toward the place than I would have guessed. I suppose Mathew Arnold was wrong; not literature but *weed* is our cultural cement.

"Part of being a man," said Umar with back straight and chest out, "is owning up to what you did and admitting when you're wrong. Brother, I'm sorry for kicking that dog. There are many hadiths forbidding cruelty to animals."

"Thanks Umar," Fasiq replied quietly.

"I only got mad because you know the angels won't enter a house in which there's a dog." Fasiq looked at the floor. "And besides, I guess I was already heated because of Ayyub."

"I understand," said Fasiq. "I'd be mad if he were humping in my bed; if I *had* a bed, that is."

Three weeks later, I stood by my car pumping gas when someone yelled at me from across the street; or *sang* at me, rather.

"HEYYYYY, LITTLE RICH BOY!" I looked up knowing exactly who it'd be, but was surprised to find him in a shirt.

"Ayyub!" I yelled back. His t-shirt bore the Confederate flag. Red field, blue X, seven white stars. "Where have you been, man? We all thought you were dead!" Ayyub waited for a car to pass and then darted to my side of the road. "Where have you been staying?" I asked.

"Here and there. Lately I've been at Camp Fun. Yeah bro. The City Mission."

"Oh my god, Ayyub. How is that?"

"It's a fuckin' scene, bro. You have to be in at seven o'clock and you take your dumps in front of everybody. You get no privacy 'cuz they think we're all on drugs."

"That's insane."

"Free food, though. Only thing is though you have to sit and listen to Bible Study bullshit."

"You're kidding."

"No bro. But all in all it's not a bad place. Roof over your head and interesting people."

"What's with that shirt?"

"This? It means the South. I love the South. I saw Jehangir downtown the other day and he told me all about the Masjid of Manassas."

"Manassas?"

"Manassas, Virginia. Jehangir didn't tell you he saw me?"

"No."

"Good. I kind of asked him not to, I was kind of embarrassed about where I was staying. But Manassas, bro, site of Bull Run. Two Civil War battles—the South won both—and that's where General Jackson got the name 'Stonewall.' Jehangir had gone there hearing that they had a Shi'a masjid; he had never seen one before. So he finds the place around ten-thirty on a Friday with his mohawk tucked under a pakul and tells the imam how excited he is to finally see a Shi'a masjid. The imam goes 'what do you mean, Shi'a?' Jehangir doesn't know what to say. The imam tells him there's no such thing as Sunni or Shi'a. These are the types of things that divide us and that's what the kafrs want. Do you know what the word 'Shi'a' means?"

"No," I replied.

"It means 'follower.' Follower of what? What does a Muslim follow?"

"Allah," I said without hesitation.

"Right. You see? That's what the Imam of Manassas tells Jehangir; so Jehangir looks around, checks out the books they have for sale—all shit on the Ahlul-Bayt, Fourteen Infallibles, shit like that. Jehangir gets one on the Tragedy of Karbala and one on his son Zainul-Abidin. And when he goes up to pay, the Imam of Manassas has him recite the Tashahud and stops him at the part about Rasullullah's descendents. You get it, Yusef? A Muslim just follows Allah. Sunni-Shi'a? That's *farga*, the groups—Allah discourages this in the Qur'an, you know, never ever form the groups. But you see in the prayers? *As you blessed Ibrahim's progeny.* It's all sunna."

"Makes sense."

"The... every time you connect to one thing you disconnect with another thing. You can't help it. You can't be connected to all things at all times. You, Yusef: you have your studies, your car, your family... you cannot be connected to all of them at once—then you fail at all of it! So as a Muslim, you connect with Allah. He alone is the Connecter. A Muslim submits to Allah. Allah sends you the rain, the sun, the health and sickness... and you must submit. That is all. No Sunni or Shi'a. Abu Bakr was Khalif, Ali was

Imam. Al-hamdulilah. Abu Bark was following Ali, it is right there in Bukhari and all their books. And Ali was both Khalif *and* Imam, right?"

"Right."

"But shit, the Imam of Manassas gave Jehangir something and Jehangir gave it to me. Now I want to give it to you." Amazing Ayyub dug in the back pocket of his abused and worn-out jeans, pulled out a tightly folded sheet of paper and presented it to me.

It was a photocopy of the fatwa by Shaykh Mahmud Shaltut, head of Al-Azhar Islamic University, recognizing Shi'a fiqh as valid and addressing all Muslims to "free themselves toward unrightful prejudice toward specific sects." Dated 17 Rabi' al-Awwal, 1378 A.H. I folded it back up and placed it deep in my own pocket. "Leave that around the house sometime for Umar to pick up."

"I will."

"Alright bro. Check you later." We shook hands. Amazing Ayyub crossed the street and went on his way without looking back, down a sidewalk whose end I'd never know. I watched until I couldn't make out his big Johnny Reb X anymore.

Went home to find Fasiq on the roof with Jehangir Tabari. I leaned out the bathroom window.

"What are you, again?" Jehangir asked him. I knew they were wasted.

"Indonesian, bro," Fasiq answered. "How long have you known me, again?" They laughed.

"Shit, Fasiq. Did you know out in California there's a fuckin' cave off the coast that has the word 'Allah' written on its wall?"

"No shit, really?"

"Yeah, and carbon-dating showed it to predate Columbus."

"So who put it there?" Fasiq asked.

"Indonesians. Or Malaysians. Filipinos, maybe. Some Pacific Rim Muslims. They discovered America. The big sweeping Arab conquests that inspired the whole 'Islam by the sword' stereotype never reached the Southeast Asians. They embraced the deen without ever being invaded."

"Subhana'Allah."

"Sufi merchants, bro."

It felt good to see the two mohawks out there. The house was missing something without stoned hashishiyyuns on the roof.

"Salaams," I called out. They both turned their heads to discover me resting on the bathroom windowsill. "Jehangir, what would you do if they ever built a statue of you?"

"I'd hope there was a Taliban around to blow it up."

"I saw Amazing Ayyub. He told me about the Imam of Manassas." Jehangir smiled knowingly.

"Ayyub's got a good heart," he said. "You know what really got me about Manassas?"

"What's that?"

"They had this big black-and-white framed photo of the Ka'ba completely surrounded by water like an island. There's some guy in the foreground all submerged except his head and one arm and you can't tell if he's swimming his circumambulation or drowning. This picture just totally blew my mind; I couldn't stop staring, trying real hard to let it all soak deep in my marrow. I asked the Imam of Manassas about it, and he said in 1941 the Masjid Haram was flooded by a massive rain."

Another Friday night, another hosting the usual faces and handfuls of fresh extras and America's new greatest cowboy standing in some corner flashing me the occasional look to make a moment shared. With his mohawk and '77 costume and bursting halcyon gusto people rose in their own notions of self-coolness just for standing next to him, exchanging firm handshakes, letting him throw his arms around them for off-key crooning. As always, the party constituted a sexual lottery. Each time a girl spoke to Jehangir, I wondered if she was the one for the night. Midway through flirty dialogue with a contender, he might look over to wherever I stood for my nonverbal assessment. Fasiq Abasa did fairly well in his own right, usually finding himself behind closed doors in a room full of smoke and impaired judgments. Rude Dawud had his own scene autonomous from Jehangir's punk orchestrations and never had a problem with girls. Umar was Umar, and as for Rabeya I can't honestly say that I knew anything of her personal life, but she did speak with a been-there crassness that you don't find in most virgins.

At one point Jehangir was talking to Fatima with background noise of neighboring conversations and Duane Peters and the Hunns' "Blood on the Sun," and he plainly had no intention of another run at her pants, but that's exactly why each party was a lottery: you never really knew. She listened with rapt enthusiasm as he told his tale of rolling in to DC off the I-95. "Wait, no," he added, having caught his error. "That time it wasn't the 95, it was the 81... I took the 81 to the 270 to the 70, I think... or the 70 to the 270." I picked up a great deal concerning the Eisenhower Interstate System from Jehangir: 90 from Boston to Seattle, 5 from Seattle down through California, 81 from the Thousand Islands region of New York's "North Country" to Tennessee where it becomes the 40. To go from Buffalo to Dallas you'd take the 90 to 71 to 65 to 40 to 30 to 20.

In DC Jehangir stumbled into the Islamic Center: "looks real authentic, old-school in a Hollywood way," he explained. It was right by the embassy of a Gulf state but he couldn't remember which. From there he went to the campus of Saudi-funded American University and met up with three members of a Progressive Muslim group. "One guy and two girls," he related. "Neither girl in hejab. They kept saying they were going to be the vanguard of a new Islamic Renaissance. One of the girls led our Asr prayer, too."

"That's awesome," Fatima replied. "I thought Rabeya was the only girl in the world who led men in prayer."

"The girl was cute; short with sweet eyes and a smile that makes you want to say funny things all the time and her face was framed by straight black Indian hair almost shimmery-shiny…" I wondered if he embellished only to impress on Fatima his capacity for such sentiments. "If it weren't for my clear pilgrim's head, she was pretty enough to have made me nervous in a dumb innocent sixth-grader way and nullify my prayer."

"Awww," she answered. "That's so cute." I would have hated Jehangir at that moment were it not for his irresistible sincerity. "So wait… you had a 'pilgrim's head?' What was that all about?"

"I felt like it was a pilgrimage."

"Really?"

"Sure. Just a few days before that I was down in Elmira, pouring out a bottle of Zamzam on Mark Twain's grave."

"Oh wow." I left my vantage point to let that go on wherever it was meant to go, choosing then to eavesdrop from just outside a circle of South Asians—only one of whom looked like she'd mesh in Jehangir's element. Some guy who seemed to have appointed himself the circle's leadership was chiding a girl for being Indian.

"What," he scoffed, "your parents forgot to emigrate in 1947?"

"Why do you speak Urdu with a Punjabi accent?" she countered. "And why do you play off like you're all revolutionary when you let your mom push you into medical school?"

"If you look into history," he replied, "you'd find that the core leaders of most revolutions are doctors and other… kind of, *bourgeois* people." Then he embarked on a tangent about Junoon, "the greatest rock group in Asia hands-down." As I walked away from them I floated again by Jehangir, though Fatima was nowhere to be seen. With glazed eyes he told me that from DC I could take 495 to 66 and end up in Manassas—site of two Civil War battles, Stonewall Jackson's heroics and a Shi'a masjid.

"That girl back in DC was cool," he said as though he had been telling that story to me and not Fatima. "But it's weird; even though the girl was progressive enough to serve as imam, before praying she made sure to put on hejab. But that's cool; you do what you can, take what you can get, right?"

"Right."

"American Taqwa, bro, we're not the umma's only fuck-ups."

"Exactly."

"Pretty girls write ayats, Yusef Ali; did you know that?"

"No, I didn't." He put his hand on the top of my head and just left it there. "I can see that DC girl with fancy Arabic calligraphy swirling around her bare sundressed legs like tangles of string in the breeze and fuckin' wonder what the qurtab-club would think of that, of that girl lifting me up to the heights of a new Islamic character… the Romantic Muslim! Yusef Ali, have you ever heard of such a creature?"

"I might have."

"Only submitting to dumb-crush kitabs deep in his gut like a damned fool. Insha'Allah, I might get the mercy of old age and a chance to make up for these shirks…" With his hand on my head he pulled me toward him, knocking foreheads with our eyes too close for proper focus. "Because Yusef Ali, that girl's my qiblah."

He was drunk. And stupid. And in ten minutes he wouldn't remember saying any of that, but I loved him.

"Al-hamdulilah," I said, this time not as generic dialogue-filler but with real joy for the iman in Jehangir's drunken heart.

"I'll tell you another thing about the Masjid of Manassas," he said.

"Okay."

"Did you know that the first White House of the Confederacy was built by Zelda Fitzgerald's great-uncle?"

"No, I didn't know that."

"Montgomery, Alabama. I saw it. But anyway, back to the Masjid of Manassas. I had a Confederate ten dollar bill that I had bought over'n West Virginia, right? At an antique shop in Berkeley Springs. And I concocted myself a plan to smuggle my Confederate tenner into the Masjid of Manassas just to leave it somewhere safe so it'd be in the masjid forever but secret where nobody'd ever find it.

"So I was telling this girl about my plan, right? How I had to find a safe place in the masjid where no one would ever look. And you know what my girl says?

"She says, 'tape it to the ceiling.'"

I went to bed at maybe two-thirty. The party still went strong downstairs but I was tired enough to block it out. I fell asleep thinking about Pakistan; not the geographical location, nation-state or cultural tag but the word itself. *Pakistan.* I had noted the word coming up several times that night. Some people said it like my parents: *Pock-ies-taun.* Others said it the way kafrs say it: *Pack-iss-tan.* My own pronunciation fell somewhere in between.

I woke up to a blast of sunlight from my windows, feeling as though I had slept a long time but it turned out to be just a little after nine. Knowing the time had long passed, I heaved myself out of bed regardless and took out my prayer rug. Walked over to the bathroom, lifted the seat up and urinated without fear of anyone being awake to come in on me. Went back to my room and stood at the back of the rug, heels on the little tassels.

And I prayed unwashed.

Did not really feel like going downstairs, as I was sure some left-overs from the last night's goings-on were still on our couches feel-ing the damage. Well, not really *feeling* it. But they were still there. I submitted to my bed and slept 'til noon.

When I finally came downstairs I found only two Muslims in the living room, too wide awake and pleasant to have been vestiges from the party. At first glance I only knew that the girl was Mus-lim, as she wore a spotless white hejab outlining her face in a long oval. The guy could have been anything until I heard him justify the killing of apostates.

"It's like treason," he said boldly.

"How?" she replied gently. "How can someone's relationship with their Creator constitute—"

"You have a hard time understanding it because you were brought up in this Secular Western way of thinking."

"Oh really?" Her hands were covered in elaborate henna designs. Neither of them noticed me standing at the edge of the living room.

"You see," he answered, certain there was no successful argu-ment to what he'd say, "every society has its own concept of trea-son. In England, if you sexually violate a female from the Royal

Family, it is considered high treason. So with this in mind, you have to look at—"

"But that makes no sense. Polluting the royal bloodline makes raping a princess more criminal than raping just some common girl? That's completely ridiculous. You're backing up ignorant, irrational behavior with more of the same."

"No, it's just to say that each society has its own understanding of what it means to belong to a community, and what it means to be loyal or disloyal to that community. Now, with Rushdie; he owed a certain respect to his community and he did not live up to that obligation. To the contrary, he took the religion in which he was raised and subjected it to complete and utter desecration. Now the difference between Rushdie and a kafr is that we must expect more of Rushdie. He knows his religion and how to push the buttons to get a response. He writes this horrible book insulting the character of Rasullullah Sallaho alayhe wa salaam, and tearing down Islam itself which is the center of everything in our life." The guy pronounced Islam as *Islaam*.

"I disagree," she answered with a slow shake of her head. "I'm an English major, so I'm looking it at it from a literary perspective. If you look at W.K. Wimsatt's Intentional Fallacy, okay, basically you can't judge an author's message because the author himself—or *her*self—doesn't even know what the real idea is behind their work. We all have so many subconscious elements to our behavior, a big chunk of what an artist puts on the page, canvas or whatever is accidental. So to look at Rushdie's art, his fiction, and say you have therein a justification for his murder is completely ignorant of what it means to be an artist."

"Just as I said," he replied with polite bravado. "You're conditioned by Western secularism. We're discussing a religious issue and you bring up kafr theories! Can you find support for Wimsatt's Intentional Fallacy in the sunna?" He turned his head and saw me. "As-salaamu alaikum," he said with the same debating tone.

"Wa alaikum as-salaam," I replied. I then turned to the sister. "As-salaamu alaikum."

"Wa alaikum as-salaam." I abruptly turned and walked to the kitchen.

"Who's out there?" I asked Rabeya, sitting at the table with her morning paper.

"Bush is gonna kill us all," she said.

"Yeah, but who's out there in the living room talking about Salman Rushdie?"

"Oh, they're from the MSA."

"What are they doing here?"

"They're waiting for Umar. Don't know what's up with that."

"Oh."

"They're still arguing?"

"Yeah, about whether or not Muslims can kill apostates."

"Ah… earlier they were debating whether or not women can be heads of state in Muslim countries."

"Really?"

"I had to go out there momentarily, just to stifle him."

"I'd expect nothing less."

"I was like 'asshole, Ayesha led troops in battle.' He said that was only Allah's way of testing the believers. Some people you just can't argue with."

"Damn."

"Yusef, they weren't in here five minutes before he pissed me off. He looked around at the beer bottles and shit and was like, 'the MSA should be doing more to reach out to borderline Muslims like this.' Borderline Muslims? What the FUCK is a 'borderline Muslim?' I think the girl was almost embarrassed to be with him."

"I could see why."

"When I was younger and someone would question the status of women in Islam, I'd always point to Benazir Bhutto. There: a female leading a Muslim country, while America still hasn't had a woman president. It usually shut people up."

"That's cool."

"I was naïve on several counts."

"This might be a dumb question," I disclaimed, "but is it hard reading the paper with… the uh, burqa?"

"A little. You know what really pissed me off about that guy out there?"

"What?"

"He was like, 'women can't hold positions of authority because menstrual cycles have too much influence on their emotional state.' Can you believe that shit? God damn, Yusef. You think the testicles don't affect a man's mood at all? How about a guy who's getting lousy head, or a guy whose girlfriend will only give it up like once a month, or a guy who's stuck with an ugly wife and looks at all the hot young things hoppin' around and just wants to kill himself, or a guy who's so fucked in the head that he's repressing all his desires and backing up the pipes just to end up mean like Umar… or fuckin' Catholic priests who try so hard to stay asexual that their sperm spreads throughout their whole bodies like cancer poisoning them to the point that they touch little boys? Then there's the guy who secretly wants dick but can't admit it to himself, let alone society and so he turns into the biggest asshole hatemonger-homophobe, violent even. Eminem's a fag, I'd bet you a million dollars. And how about a guy who's so whacked that he forces women into nonconsensual sex because it makes him feel powerful? You think being a man doesn't fuck with your head at all? Jesus Christ, c'mon."

"Wow, I never even thought of that before."

"We should be happy that Clinton cheated. God forbid that

Bush ever gets blue balls, he'll be launching nukes left and right."

I then heard a loud cry muffled by walls and floors.

"Is that Fasiq?" I asked.

"He's outside giving the adhan, I think."

We went upstairs and to the bathroom, watching from the window as with his back to us in trademark Operation Ivy hoodie Fasiq did the whole thing—even the turning left and right for *hayyal as-salah* and *falah*. "What are you doing?" asked Rabeya after the final *la ilaha illah Allah*.

"It's Zuhr time, isn't it?"

"No, not yet."

"Oh. I thought it was Zuhr time."

"Pretty soon, though."

"Cool."

We prayed in less than an hour. It was only Rabeya, Fasiq and myself. I led. Umar had left with his new MSA friends. Jehangir was still sleeping upstairs. At least he had made it to bed.

He came downstairs wearing a black ski cap.

"Booze and girls," he said mournfully flopping down next to me on the couch. "Booze and girls, y'akhi, booze and girls, booze and girls, the biggest threat to my deen we'd all ever seen..."

"You missed Zuhr," I said smiling.

"Sleep," he added to his list. "Booze, girls and sleep."

"I've prayed twice today," I said.

"You just lost credit for it, bragging like that."

"Staghfir'Allah." He rummaged between two cushions, found the remote and turned on the TV. Flipped through the channels real fast until stopping on Spike Lee's *Malcolm X* at the spot where a Malcolm-led Harlem FOI storms the police station. I wondered how the movie looked through Rabeya's eye-grid.

"I could dig on Malcolm the Tenth," said Jehangir. "There's a truth to that."

"A truth to what?" I asked.

"Knowing you're right. Knowing you're a man. Being a soldier for it. Standing firm, standing tall, telling people off. Walking around all tough with index finger on your temple, thumb on your jaw." He mimicked the trademark Malcolm pose. "Look at us, we don't know who the shit we are. Look at *me*: drunk off my ass, chasing pussy, doing juvenile skateboard stunts, stupid haircut rebelling against everything because it makes me feel cool. Then you got these guys, you know they know their shit. At least they believe they know their shit, they believe it with all they got. Malcolm, man, sitting in a jail cell eating up books for sixteen hours of the day, copying out the whole dictionary by hand, all to be gunned down at his podium by dudes with sawed-offs. I'm just a little jerk-off punk, not a *man* like this guy. Tons of truth, y'akhi. More Umar's truth than mine, but it's legit."

"With all respect to Malik Shabazz and everything he did," said Rabeya, "he was a misogynist cock when he wanted to be."

The next day Jehangir and I were riding with his friend Hannibal, Jehangir leaned back in shotgun and me stretched out in back, Method Man's "PLO Style" on the CD player: *PLO style, Buddha monks with the owls... PLO style, Buddha monks with the owls... here comes the ruckus, the motherfuckin' ruckus...*

Jehangir sifted through Hannibal's CDs, occasionally offering comment when he saw one of interest.

"Professor Griff!" he exclaimed. "Never thought I'd see that again."

"Shit's mad old, son."

"Hell yeah it is." Jehangir's smooth transition to such a non-punk element had stunned me.

"When I was a kid," said Hannibal, "my dad hated rap—still does, actually—but if I convinced him that a CD had redeeming political content, he'd never say no. You'll see a lot of it in there, all the older stuff: Public Enemy, KRS-One, Intelligent Hoodlum—he calls himself Tragedy Khadafi now, though…"

"Oh shit! Brand Nubian, wow, this is fuckin' vintage."

"Yeah kid, like 1992."

"Can we put this in?"

Hannibal took it, index finger and thumb on the outer edge, hitting a button with his pinkie to release *Tical.* Jehangir removed it for Hannibal to slide in the Nubian.

"Allah U Akbar" began with the opening of an adhan looped over and over: *Allaaaaaahu Akbaru'Allaaaaah*, until the beat slowly surfaced. For those beginning seconds Jehangir seemed almost illuminated. The muezzin resurfaced a few times in the song.

We elected for a late lunch at the Greek diner on Elmwood Avenue, favorite of college kids because it was near Buffalo State's campus and you could get a relatively cheap breakfast any hour of day or night. Hannibal ordered their "2-2-2": two eggs, two pancakes, and your choice of two bacon, two sausage or two ham. Hannibal forewent the third 2 and just had eggs and pancakes. Jehangir got an omelet of some sort and I went for a grilled cheese sandwich.

Hannibal was a kafr but his dad was Muslim, formerly in the Nation and before that a Black Panther.

"So my dad was saying how Farrakhan's a Sunni now," he told us, his tone at the end almost making it a question.

"I heard something about that," said Jehangir. "He's just after money from the Arab states."

"Back a while ago he said he boarded a spaceship with Elijah Muhammad and W.D. Fard."

"Was it the Motherplane?" Jehangir asked. Hannibal laughed.

"I don't know about that," he replied. "But Farrakhan did some good in his time and place, even if he is a nut. And him going Sunni will at least get some of his followers off that white-devil stuff."

"Still won't help the yahoodas."

"No, definitely not."

"Did you hear about that old jail in the Carolinas?" asked Jehangir.

"Which jail?"

"There's an old jail in the Carolinas where they used to bring slaves right off the ships. I can't remember if it was North or South. It's still there, it's like a tourist spot now. But anyway, there's ayats from the Qur'an on the wall, like two hundred years old, still right there."

"For real?"

"Yeah, must've been some Muslims brought over here."

"My dad would be real interested in hearing that—if he doesn't know about it already."

Pulling out of the diner's parking lot, Hannibal popped out the Brand Nubian and asked, "want to pray?"

"Pray?" repeated Jehangir. "Is it time?"

"Should be time for Asr."

"Cool."

"Wait," I said, "I thought you were *kuf*—I mean, I thought you weren't Muslim."

"I'm not, but I can pray."

We went back to the house and Hannibal ran upstairs to make wudhu. Waiting for my turn I watched him, trying to make sense of the situation. He *wasn't* Muslim, right? Just his dad. Why was Hannibal making wudhu? Why was he praying with us? Why didn't he have bacon, sausage or ham in his 2-2-2? Why did he and not Jehangir or even I notice that it was Asr time?

Jehangir put one rug in front for the imam, with two behind it.

"Allahu Akbar, Allahu Akbar!" he said from one of the rear rugs, immediately removing himself from consideration for imam. "Allahu Akbar, Allahu Akbar, la ilaha illa Allah…" Hannibal motioned for me to lead. I shook my head and stood by Jehangir, just then realizing what it meant.

"Allaaaaaahu Akbar," said Hannibal facing qiblah, and the prayer was on. I did the same and folded my hands over my navel. When I should have been silently reciting *al-Fatiha,* I contemplated all our previous transgressions of fiqh. When we did manage to pray, we prayed with men and women standing side by side, even with feet and shoulders touching! We prayed behind female imams and even menstruating female imams. We prayed behind a Shi'a when Amazing Ayyub led, and often behind a stoned hashishiyya higher than the Ghurafs. This, however, went off the chart. I was praying behind an imam who wasn't even Muslim at all. As he went through each position something ugly swelled inside me. With hands on my knees, I stared at the floor feeling the ugly thing bubble up and get mean in my gut. Rising up—*sami Allahu-liman hamidah*—I looked at Hannibal's back and felt the ugly thing rise too, right up to my lungs. Then I put my forehead to the floor, *Subhana Rabiyal'Ala, Subhana Rabiyal'Ala, Subhana Rabiyal'Ala* and before we had even finished the first rakat I hated him. I felt the brushing of Jehangir Tabari's body against my left side and I hated him too because I knew it didn't bother him to pray behind a kafr. I wanted to storm out of the house and run down the street until coming across a Muslim who prayed right, ate right, dressed right and said things that made you feel good about Islam—*real* Islam, not this punked-out Jehangirism for which I sold out my parents and culture. I had removed myself so far from everything that mattered that I had a naked girl in my bed with big breasts and nasty dreadlocks trying to get me to stick it in her but *al-hamdulilah* I refused. From what people told me, I had received "contact highs" from sitting in smoke-filled rooms with Jehangir, Fasiq Abasa and Rude Dawud the Sudani who one day had just decided that he would completely flip his life over to the point that girls think he's Jamaican—which he probably doesn't even discourage because the Caribbean is sexier than the Sudan, right? Even his accent was changing from hanging out with Rastafarians all day. And I associated with every undesirable element at Jehangir's parties which I allowed to occur in a house that was just as much *my* home as his. *Booze and girls*, as he would say. People throwing up on each other and fornicating. Girls with no idea of what it means to have dignity. Men with no concept of self-control. Jehangir Tabari, whose *romanticism* just equaled a spiritual, cultural and ideological laziness: in all things the path of least resistance. Allah wills, right?

As a mumin I was ruined. How long had it been since I had attended a real jumaa? In a masjid, with men and women separate and khutbahs from qualified imams? Had I journeyed into apostasy? What did that even mean? We lived in a non-Muslim state where I had no fear of shari'a's penalty, but there's more than one way to chop off a head. What would it do to my parents to find out how this house really functioned?

"It'd be better for you than living in the dorms," Abu told me. "There are very bad things there."

"You live with Muslims," said Ummi, "and stay focused."

And there I was in my living room, praying behind a kafr, next to a stupid punk-rocker, before us a green Saudi flag with its shahadah marred by a spray-painted anarchy-symbol. And qiblah distinguished by a hole in the wall smashed with a baseball bat.

I was not an apostate, I reasoned, because I still had faith. *La ilaha illa Allah, Muhammadu rasullullah.* There. I had gotten close, however, listening to Jehangir Tabari whose version of Islam was only a sell-out to the seductions of Americanism. It appealed to me, sadly, because no matter how hard Abu and Ummi tried to raise me right, we were still stuck in the abode of kafr, surrounded by it at all times even in our own house when the television was on. Each of us had, in our own ways, allowed a little shaytan in our lives. A little leads to more; then more still, until how much shaytan you allow is no longer your decision but Shaytan's himself. I felt like a furnace burned inside me.

I then realized I was sitting on my legs. Hannibal, also sitting on his legs, turned his head to the right and said "as-salaamu alaikum wa rahmatullahi wa barakatuh," then did the same while turning left. I had gone through the motions, without even noticing, for three whole rakats. Immediately after salaams I stood up and went out on the porch.

Leaned back in the recliner, shoving away any empty brown bottles within my reach. Women really do need to be restrained, I thought. They don't know what's good for them. Look at Lynn. She went up to my room wanting to have sex with me. She let me see her breasts and tried to put my hand in her pants. I wasn't her husband. It wasn't mine. And what of Rabeya who kicked some guy's ass—rightly so—but she wouldn't have had to if she really practiced purdah, which is more than just a way to dress. Or Fatima, who would have let Jehangir stick his finger in her if he pursued it enough. Imagine, dirty Jehangir with his dirty fingers. How many girls had he done that to? She would have been tight, and it would have hurt. And Jehangir with all his charm would tell her it was alright and then try to hurt her more. Jehangir, the drunk. Jehangir, who I had seen passed out and Jehangir who I had watched throwing up with his face in a toilet. Jehangir who thought American Islam would be the best in history; Jehangir, nothing more than a cultural nationalist. And me, me conditioned in the same Western secular thought almost bought it. I had been raised in this society where one individual carries the same value as an entire community, and all that matters is whether or not you feel good—screw everything else, screw your values and families. I was studying to be an engineer—you know what? If it were up to me, I would have been a painter. I used to enjoy art class back in elementary school. Now, the typical American response: if you like to paint, if that's what makes you happy, then go ahead and do it. Someday my children would be starving and I'd have no security but what does that matter? I'd be doing what I like. And for suggesting I do something else with my life, all of a sudden my parents were these horrible insensitive people. Who's to say that back at eighteen I knew what was right for me? I hadn't lived at all or experienced anything. Just out of high school, was I qualified to know about careers or finding the right girl? What's wrong with a little help from your parents? I didn't know anyone who had a great time dating; according to all my kafr friends, it offered little more than anguish and inconvenience mitigated by occasional feelings of goofy weightlessness. To hell with that.

Was Umar really so awful? All he had done was practice his religion, make no bones about it and refuse to allow anything else to filter in. Islam says, don't drink. So he didn't drink. Islam says, don't fornicate. So he didn't fornicate. And this house made him out to be the bad guy, that's how perverse everything had become.

Western civilization was rapidly killing itself; not hard to see. Drug and alcohol addiction, teen pregnancy, AIDS, skyrocketing divorce rates. What happens when people don't live by any set of rules? Couldn't anyone see where we were headed? Why wouldn't we look back at those nations that came before us? Great empires like Babylon and Rome, wiped out for their decadence with barely a trace of having ever existed at all. Search the land; where'd they go? *Aoudhu billah.*

Then a car pulled up to the curb and let Umar out. I recognized the guy driving and girl in the back seat from earlier. I wish I had gone out with MSA kids instead of Jehangir and his kafr boy.

"As-salaamu alaikum," I called out.

"Wa alaikum as-salaam," replied Umar.

"How was it?"

"Did you hear what happened?" he asked.

"No."

"You didn't hear what happened in Saudi?" He looked ready to cry.

"No, brother. What happened?"

"A school caught fire, and the mutaweens wouldn't let girls out if they didn't have their *abayas.* Two died." His voice trembled, so he repeated it. "Two died."

"Oh God."

"A burning *fucking* building, y'akhi. Kids running, screaming, trying to get out, trapped inside by the motherfucking police."

"The mutaweens, you said?"

"Yep. Commission for Promotion of Virtue and Prevention of Vice."

"If that's virtue."

"I wonder if Rabeya's heard yet." With that he opened the screen door and went inside.

I sat on the floor of Jehangir's room shuffling through pictures from his trip to Pakistan, Crass' "Fuck All Government" briefly aggravating me in the background. Jehangir sat on his bed reading the back of an album cover.

He stood smiling before some landmark in almost every photo, hair covered and at least a few years younger than the Jehangir I knew. Jehangir standing barefoot in blue jeans at magnificent red-and-white Badshahi, Lahore's Mughal glory; Jehangir ankle-deep in a stony creek in the lush valley of Swat; Jehangir haggling over the price of a goat head in a Rawalpindi bazaar; Jehangir at Buddhist ruins in Taxila; Jehangir stepping off a psychedelic Ken Kesey bus; Jehangir on the Khyber Pass looping around green mountains; Jehangir in front of Faisal—a gift from Saudi Arabia—largest masjid in the world, it looked like a sci-fi spaceship with four long rockets. Jehangir put on Roger Miret and the Disasters, starting at "New York Belongs to Me."

"I'm really going to do it," he said out of left field.

"Do what?"

"Put on a show."

"A show?"

"A punk show. A Muslim punk show. Call up the taqwacore bands out West, find a date when they can all come out here. Make a big thing of it. I think it can work. We have a lot of Muslims coming to the house Friday afternoons, and a lot of kafr punks here Friday nights; if we got 'em all in one spot at the same time, that's a lot of heads."

"I can't even *imagine* those worlds colliding, Jehangir."

"That's because you haven't been to California."

"I don't know…"

"There's a whole scene of it out there. *Khalif*ornia, Jesus." He laughed and whipped the album cover at me like a square frisbee. The front featured a portrait of Ayatullah Khumayni with eyes and mouth blocked out by ransom-note lettering like the famous Sex Pistols defacing of Queen Elizabeth. On his eyes: *Salaams up the Ass.* Over his mouth: *the Ghilmans.* "Good band," he explained. "The Ghilmans have been around a long time. From what I understand they have a punked-out Sufi thing going on. Like they're spiritual but it's a 'fuck you religious assholes' spirituality, and they're not exactly *big* on the whole sociopolitical Islamic-thing."

"I see." I flipped it over and read some song titles on the back. "Shaykh Omar Bakri Can Suck My Cock." "Protocols of the Elders of Zion." "Houri Gash." "Fuck the Umma." "Our Holy Prophet Fingered His Six-Year-Old Bride In Her Dirty Asshole." "Where Mullahs Fear To Tread." "Allah's Name Was Found In A Honeycomb." "I Twirled The Ka'ba On The Tip Of My Dick."

"A lot of taqwacore is just to throw shit out there and really piss people off," he explained, noting the reaction on my face. "People are so uptight and emotional about religion and take it so seriously, sometimes you need a punk to say 'fuck you, fuck you, fuck you, fuck everything you stand for, you're full of shit and there's sperm in your hair.' Nobody needs to be on a high horse about themselves."

"How are these guys Muslims, though? Totally disrespecting the Prophet and everything—"

"I don't know but they are. You can say *Muhammadu rasullullah* and then still own up to the fact that he was a pedophile, right? The guy was human and capable of evil and sickness as much as anyone. Nothing special. His shit smelled just as bad as yours. In fact, Muhammad being a sicko is totally punk rawk. Tears down any chance of him being a Christ or sacred cow. You don't need to condone his hanker for that itty-bitty-titty. And forget about Qurayza. Don't come off like a mealy-mouthed fundamentalist weirdo for trying to defend that shit. Just accept that Muhammad had his darkness. He had demons, temptations, compromises; look at the shaping of Islam as he rose to power.

"Anyway, the Ghilmans… they're as generous with what they have as the fuckin' Tabligh Jamaat. They have the talent to be big but instead they commit commercial suicide by playing taqwacore. What a fuckin' demographic: gay Muslim punks. Not just gay, not just Muslim, not just punk. Gay Muslim Punks. Not exactly a gold mine but it's what they want to do, so at least they're devoted."

"You think they would play your show?"

"Insha'Allah, I'd love to have those guys out here. The Ghilmans, are you kidding me?" I tossed the album sleeve back and resumed looking at his photos.

Then I saw the Minar-e-Pakistan, marking the spot at which the Muslim League passed its resolution calling for an independent Islamic republic. And right there in the foreground: the same skinny American teenager, hands in denim pockets.

I went down to the kitchen and heard Propagandhi's "Fuck Religion" blaring from Rabeya's adjacent room.

"Salaam alaikum," I called out, proceeding to prepare myself a glass of orange juice.

"Wa alaikum as-salaam," from behind the curtained doorway. "Hey Yusef,—"

"Yeah?"

"Come in here a sec." I left my glass on the counter, walked over to the curtain and gently pushed it aside. For some reason I was nearly startled to see Rabeya's room behind it. Though of course I knew she had always been there, my rare delves past the curtain boundary had left me with little in the way of a retained image. Her walls were covered with photocollages and fliers from protests, the far wall bearing a souvenir from the 2001 Presidential Inauguration: black marker on white posterboard reading "HEY LAURA—MY BUSH IS BETTER." She had posters of red-haired Tori Amos in white t-shirt reading "Junkies Baddy Powder" and the famous WWII image of a woman in work-shirt and red bandana flexing her bicep above the words, "WE CAN DO IT!"

She motioned for me to have a seat on one of her four-columned monoliths of books. I chose a pile only to notice that one of the books on top was Pickthall's translation of the Holy Qur'an. I picked it up and resituated the others to fill its space. For all the degradation accorded organized religion in that house, at least Allah's Book would be spared the indignity of lying beneath my ass. Moving only my eyes I looked around the room. Another thing on the walls: poetry written in tiers of light-tan masking tape with black Sharpie sloppy punk-rock font. They crammed in wherever posters, protest placards and photos left space: she even had some on the ceiling. The ones near enough to read I instantly recognized from Rabeya's coffeehouse recitals and zine. There was "Redemption Center," in which Prophet Muhammad (PBUH) waits at Kauthar with a big sack of severed body parts to be returned to those believers who had lost for the Law: be it a hand, foot, head, clitoris or whatever. And there was the classic "72 Cocks," in which Rabeya described her Jenna as being something like the notorious porn film "The Houston 500." *Big black dicks that never go soft, even after blowing their milk-honey Kauthar... line 'em up and spread me—oh wait, sorry—that's not in my nature. I meant, 'cut off my labes and give me 72 sons so I can cook them macaroni with halal cheese.'*

"I like your room," I said, opening the Qur'an and flipping pages.

"It's a ceiling and some walls," she replied. I then found in her Qur'an a large block of black marker-strokes censoring an entire ayat, both the original Arabic and Pickthall's English interpretation.

"What's this?" I asked, holding it up.

"What?"

"This—you crossed out an ayat?"

"Which one is that?"

"It's—wait, let me see... 4:34."

"Oh, right. Okay then."

"So you just felt like you didn't need a whole ayat?"

"Well, that ayat advises men to beat their wives. What did I need it for?"

"But there's a wide variety of interpretations as to what that verse actually means," I argued. "You know, most translators say it means 'beat lightly' and there's a great deal of legal rulings on the subject. And there's the story of Job, how he only used a blade of grass to—"

"Yeah Yusef, I know. I went through that ayat up and down. I looked at what all the scholars said, even progressives like Asma Barlas; did you know that in that context, the word *daraba* might not even mean 'to beat?' It could also mean 'to prevent.' Sure, I did all the gymnastic tap dancing around that verse a desperate Muslima could do. Finally I said, fuck it. If I believe it's wrong for a man to beat his wife, and the Qur'an disagrees with me, then fuck that verse. I don't need to stretch and squeeze it for a weak alternative reading, I don't need to excuse it with historical context, and I sure as hell don't need to just accept it and go sign up for a good ol' fashioned bitch-slapping. So I crossed it out. Now I feel a whole lot better about that Qur'an."

"Wow. I see, I guess."

"Problem solved—and you won't find anything in there about a woman's testimony equaling half a man's." She switched CDs on her multi-disc player. I did not recognize the band or its female singer, but they were covering the classic "I Heard It Through The Grapevine."

"Who's this?" I asked.

"The Slits."

"Oh."

"But Yusef Ali… I have something for you."

"For me?"

"Yep. I was thinking about it when you asked if it was difficult reading through the burqa, so…"

She whipped out her surprise and presented it to me with the pride of an Olympic gold medalist, saying "here": a vaguely complicated armful of solid black clothing. Upon closer examination, I discovered the eye-grid.

"A burqa?"

"That's right."

"What am I supposed to do with this?"

"I don't know… *wear* it?"

"You want me to wear a burqa?"

"Just for a day. See what it's like in there."

"I don't think so."

"Well, promise me you'll hold onto it. Just in case you change your mind."

"Does it at least have any cool band patches on it like that one?"

"No, it's plain."

"I'll keep it. But don't expect to see me sporting this thing around town."

"That's fair. Just so you have it."

"Well, thanks then, kind of." I glanced at each of her walls. "That's funny…"

"What?"

"You're the only one in this house who doesn't have a flag in their room."

"Is that right?"

"Yeah. Some even have two. I just have a little one, but still—"

"Yusef, what flag am I going to hold up?"

"I don't know." I then remembered that I had no idea of her ethnic heritage.

"There's no flag for me," she said. I examined the black fabric in my hands and thought of black flags waved by aspiring mujahideens in the hazy cheap desert-mountain footage you saw on CNN from time to time that always looked like it was shot in the 1970s: sinister-looking mystery men hop-stepping tires like a high school football squad, except that they carried Kalashnikovs.

I then noticed that she had a mirror on her wall, right by the closet. It struck me as kind of humorous; why would Rabeya need a mirror when she never had to do her hair or makeup and she just threw the same old hood on herself before leaving the room. By the mirror hung a poster of a hejabi carcass lying in a pool of its own blood, only the feet exposed. On the body was written, "Muslim Woman." Eleven daggers hovered above as though claiming credit for the murder. Next to each blade was a word in Arabic, with English translation offered at the bottom of the poster.

According to the translation, each dagger constituted a "Danger Threatening Muslim Women." They were:

1. telephone
2. song
3. riding car with non-mahram driver alone
4. traveling to the foreign country
5. having no covering
6. amusement and co-public park
7. co-marketing
8. porno magazine
9. porno film
10. harmful TV programs
11. disagree to be married or late marriage

"Where did you get that?" I asked, my eyes still on it.

"Came with some books I ordered."

"Oh."

"I like how 'porno magazine' and 'porno film' were two separate threats," she remarked with a laugh. "I guess porn is an especially grave danger."

"Looks that way."

"Maybe just as dangerous as the telephone!"

"Wow," I said. I had nothing else to offer. I then found words among the masking-tape strips that were not hers, covering five rips of tape and a sixth for the author's name.

at heart, i am a muslim,

at heart, i am an american,

at heart, i am a muslim,

at heart, i am an american artist,

and i have no guilt.

—patti smith

"You ever hear the hadith about the prostitute lost in the desert?"

"No," I replied.

"Well, there was this prostitute lost in the desert—starving, dying of thirst and heat, et cetera, the whole deal—and when she finally comes to a well, she notices this dog lying there in the sand and dust and sun totally about to die. So what does the prostitute do?"

"I think I heard this one before," I said.

"You probably have."

"She takes her hejab off, lowers it into the water and then puts it in the dog's mouth. And for giving the dog water before quenching her own thirst, Rasullullah said all her sins were forgiven."

"It's a good one to remember," she said pointing to the *Dan-*

gers Threatening Muslim Women poster, "when you find yourself thinking that this is our religion."

"Makes sense."

"There *is* a Cool Islam out there, Yusef. You just have to find it. You have to sift through all the other stuff, but it's there."

CHAPTER VI

With the end of August came a new school year. Jehangir led Fasiq Abasa, Rude Dawud and I on a mission to the campus of Buffalo State College.

"Find the new characters," he said, drunk before we even got there. We ended up at Porter Hall, where packs of eager freshmen still clustered out in front. Jehangir put his mohawk under a black ski hat and looked more like a worker on construction sites or loading docks than a punk. Fasiq spiked his up and donned the Op Ivy hoodie. Rude Dawud wore his trademark pork-pie hat. My clothes were kind of generic. I don't know what to say about them; they were just clothes. I bought them at the mall. Didn't really say anything about me, I thought.

Standing in front of Porter Hall, I relaxed my eyes as with those 3-D hidden pictures and glazed over on the thirty-two slabs of fluorescent light in eight floors of lounge windows; and at the same time, relaxing my ears to blend all the conversations around me into one light rumble with no actual words. College life, an assembly line of fresh faces that dropped off and disappeared just as they became worn-out and tired. Campuses never lost their vitality and youth, but this truth came across as almost depressing. We were surrounded by kids just out of high school. I found it sad that I viewed them as *kids.*

Somebody was walking inside and Jehangir yelled for him to hold the door. Jehangir's drunkenness was still at the stage that it only made him more charming. Just like that, we were in. Ran up the stairs to the second floor. Whatever songs the music industry was shoving down kids' throats at the time were blaring from open doors decorated with stupid college decorations: corny name tags made by the RAs, clipped headlines and sexy photos from magazines. At the end of the hallway was another stairwell and we hit the third floor. Same thing.

On the fourth floor we chilled in the lounge on ratty dorm furniture. A white kid in thick black-rimmed glasses and a Less than Jake shirt came up and tapped me on the shoulder.

"It's 4:20," he said.

"What?" I had no idea what he meant.

"It's 4:20, you got a minute?"

"What do you mean?" Then Fasiq observed and called the kid over. The kid said he wanted "trees." Fasiq and Rude Dawud got up and followed him to his room, leaving just me and Jehangir in the fourth-floor lounge.

"You gotta love the first week of school," said Jehangir, arms spread out on the fire-resistant couch. "Shit like that only happens in the first week."

"What do you mean?"

"All these new kids, they desperately want to be cool but they don't know anyone. That's why all these doors are open and people are just starting conversations with perfect strangers. There's no cliques yet. It's a level playing field. Give it just a week, all this dies and people are resigned to their own circles. Kind of sad." I looked at Jehangir and wondered how he knew so much about college society.

"S'up guys," said a scruffy young man coming down the hall. Young but not too young, not young enough to make me feel old. He had a cynical old jerk's wisdom that made it obvious he had been there awhile. He shook both our hands and plopped down on the lounge couch that once hosted Fasiq and Dawud. "Yo, I just sucked on a fresh pair of eighteen-year-old tits." I knew then that he was older. Jehangir had once worked in a gas station and explained to me that the porn magazines with titles like *Just 18* and *Barely Legal* aren't bought up by eighteen-year-old guys.

"That's hot," Jehangir replied. He had the gift, especially when drunk, of reaching anyone on their level; even a wretch like this guy. "What she look like?"

"She was cute, man. Had some nice ol' titties."

"Awesome."

"Her room's fuckin'... shit, what was her room... fuckin' 610, man."

"Nice."

"You should go check her out."

"Might do that," said Jehangir.

"Just like they treat snakebites with snake venom," said the guy, "I need those eighteen-year old tits. They're my disease and the cure. I suck on 'em like they lactate self-respect."

"What's your name, man?"

"Billy Plunger."

"I'm Jehangir."

"Wha—"

"It's just like John-geer."

"Oh. Cool. And you?" He looked at me.

"Yusef."

"Yusef?"

"Yeah."

"Oh. What's up man." Jehangir pulled out his flask and took a swig. "That is the shit," said Billy Plunger. "I fuckin' love college."

"Hell yeah," said Jehangir, who as far as I knew had never seen a classroom after high school.

"You got a girlfriend?" Billy asked.

"Nah. You?"

"Shit no."

"Cool."

"Once you settle down," Billy explained, "you can never go back to being young and stupid."

"Exactly," said Jehangir, raising his flask.

"Girl was fuckin' eighteen," he repeated. "I'm fuckin' twenty-three, bro."

"That's not too old," replied Jehangir.

"It's old enough. Old enough for me to be a piece of shit. You think it's old enough?"

"Who's to say."

"Yeah, I hear that. Fuck it, man, I don't give a fuck. Right?"

"Right."

"I was five whole years old before she even appeared on the planet, man! Think about it like that. I had a fully developed personality before she was even conceived. But she was hot. Even through her jeans she had a fuckin' sopping damp crotch. I wrote a poem about her, you want to read it?"

"Sure." Billy Plunger straightened his body to reach deep in a pocket, pulling out a folded yellow paper. He handed it to Jehangir, who nodded his head as he read it.

"That's good shit," said Jehangir.

"Thanks man. Show it to your boy." Jehangir handed it to me.

"That's cool," I said with a smile.

Billy's piece went like this:

poem composed
while getting blown
in room 610,
porter hall,
buffalo state college

with blue ballpoint pen
on a yellow legal-sized notepad
resting on top of her head

shit
i can't write
with you bobbing
so much

ah
fuck it

"There's a lot of fuckin' sluts at this school," said Billy.

"Yeah," I replied. Jehangir took another swig.

"Fuckin'... cunts, everywhere. At the end of last semester we drove around as parents were all helping load their kids' shit into the family vans, you know, and we'd fuckin' yell 'thank you for your daughters!' Fuckin' crazy, man."

"Wow," I said.

"Imagine being some old guy and your daughter goes here and some asshole yells that at you. It'd fuckin' eat you up inside."

"I couldn't even imagine." I wondered how I turned out to be the one doing our talking. Jehangir just stared off into space and drank.

"You gotta own up to that shit, man. Someday you're going to have a daughter who's going to have all the rotten things done to her, in her and on her that you did to somebody else's little girl. You know what I'm saying?"

"That's true," I replied.

"What goes around comes around."

"Yep."

"Look at this shit," he exclaimed, retrieving a pen from his pocket, presumably the pen with which he had written his poem. "It's a fuckin' Catholic pen."

"A Catholic pen?" I repeated.

"A Catholic pen. Check it out." He held it with both index-fingertips and thumbs and read the inscription. "Newman Centers at UB. Catholic Campus Ministry."

"Hmm," I replied, not meaning anything by it.

"It fuckin' says on the cap, 'if you see someone without a smile, give them one of yours.' Isn't that some shit?"

"Yeah."

"Got it from a girl I work with. She always leaves her fuckin' Catholic pens at work. That's how she saves the world, I guess. I know it's her because she always wears Catholic t-shirts. I think about her the whole drive home, like every fuckin' day."

"She's hot?" I asked.

"Not so much hot as pretty. You know what I mean? She's cute, real cute and when all is said and done that's what's so hot about her. She's petite, maybe a hundred pounds at best. Ties her hair back in a ponytail. Pointy little tits. Nice ass. Small waist. I'd fuck her."

"Cool," I replied. Jehangir looked at the ceiling and sighed loudly.

"Part of it is she's Catholic and I could just see her all dirty gomping down a dick and choking on it. Do her from behind, smack the white ass pink and yank that little ponytail. I'd fuck 'er real good. She's an uptight girl, but it's like the cause of the uptightness is something buried deep up her cunt by that no-good Catholic Church and only Billy Plunger can dig it out."

"Wow," I said. I faked a laugh.

"With my cock, naturally."

"Later guys," said Jehangir as he stood up. I watched him walk down the hall, flask in hand. All of a sudden it was just Billy Plunger and Yusef Ali. Looking back on that night, I think Billy Plunger had struck Jehangir with a twisted reflection of himself that he found very hard to deal with. The difference, however, vindicating Jehangir in my eyes was that while Jehangir loved sex, he also loved women. Billy Plunger loved sex and hated women.

"I know what I'm talking about when it comes to that girl," Billy Plunger continued. "I grew up fuckin' Catholic."

"Yeah," I replied. "I grew up Muslim. We're fucked up too."

"I wonder if that girl'd take it up the ass."

"You think she would?"

"It's hard to say. At first you'd be like no, no, not that girl, not ever. But you never really know. Sometimes they surprise you. Sometimes man it's the nice girls that are so dirty, you know what I mean? They're the ones that, if you unleash it, man they know what to do with a dick. They know what they want, they know how they want it and they will fuckin' work for that shit, right? My one buddy, he was with this girl who was like the typical high-school sweetheart. The really nice smile, silky soft hair, great smell, never did anything wrong—but she took it in the pooper. The whole time they dated, it was just dirty butt-sex. She was super-paranoid about getting pregnant, so that was the only way she'd do it. Her parents were real strict, you know, they probably would have thrown her out of the house if they even knew she had sex. Isn't that ironic, man? This girl, to not look like a dirty whore to her parents, she only takes it up the ass. Isn't that amazing? It really makes you think."

"Yeah it does."

"You know who F. Scott Fitzgerald was?"

"Yeah."

"*The Great Gatsby*."

"Right."

"Did you know he grew up in Buffalo?"

"No, I didn't know that."

"29 Irving Place, his fuckin' childhood home."

"Really."

"Yep." Billy took a second to think about it. "Me and my ex, we used to go to fuckin' historical sites all the time. Just New York state history, I don't know why. It was just our dumb couple thing. You know, some couples do puzzles together. We were into state history. We went to old graves and battlefields an' shit. We used to go to plenty of old houses too. Kinderhook: Benedict Arnold's house on Broad Street. Auburn: Harriet Tubman's house. I would have taken her to F. Scott Fitzgerald's childhood home too, but we broke up."

"That sucks."

"He was no Hemingway, though. Fuck 'im."

"Was your girlfriend dirty?" I asked, thinking that was the place our conversation would inevitably head. Billy looked at me as though I had just shot him.

"Man, that shit's not cool."

"I'm sorry."

"She was my girlfriend."

"I know, man. I didn't mean anything by it."

"You know," he mused, "there is such a thing as gloomy masturbation."

"What?"

"I got it down to an art form."

"Really," I said.

"Dude, sometimes I go into the bathroom at Butler Library, you know, and I look in the mirror, stare deep in my own eyes and I just punch my own fuckin' face. I clench up a fist, tighten my face and I wail on myself."

"Why?"

"I fuckin' hate myself, kid."

"But why?" I asked again.

"I'm fuckin' wounded. Look at me. I'm a hurtin' sack of shit."

I then wondered where Jehangir had gone off to and what became of Fasiq and Dawud, and what I could do to ease myself away from Billy Plunger.

My limited social skills could not provide me with a reasonable exit from the conversation. When Billy finally had enough and decided to call it a night, I began searching for the crew I had arrived with. Fasiq and Dawud were burned-out behind some door, but I had no idea where. Jehangir could have wandered to Seychelles for all I knew. Starting at the fourth, I hit every floor to the ninth—where I found Jehangir, on a lounge couch sitting absurdly close to a beautiful freshman girl (people just don't sit like that with each other unless they want to hook up). Both of them were too drunk to notice me.

"Your name has religious significance," he told her.

"Really?"

"Sure. Khadija was Prophet Muhammad's wife."

"Oh wow. I didn't know that."

"Sure." Jehangir explained, "Khadija was his first wife. He loved her, like the real true-blue love. He didn't marry anyone else while she was alive. His later marriages were mostly political, to build ties with other tribes. His wives after Khadija used to complain that he'd still talk about her too much. But he just really, really loved her. When he first began his holy mission and thought he was going nuts, she was the one who reassured him."

"That's really cool," she exclaimed. "Now what about my middle name?"

"What's your middle name?" Jehangir asked.

"Ayesha."

"Ayesha? I don't know anything about Ayesha." The topic changed and Jehangir continued his booze-slurred segue into her pants. I stood there wondering if they'd ever see me. She took his hat off and played with his hair.

"Are you in a band?" she asked.

"No."

"We can be in a band together."

"Yeah?"

"A secret band, so underground we're the coolest band because nobody knows about us."

"So underground we've never played a show or put out a record."

"A band so underground, the band's two members don't even know each other's names."

"I know your name. Your first name is Khadija, and your middle name is Ayesha."

"You don't know my last name. I don't know any of your names."

"My name's Jehangir." His head became too heavy to support and he just let it gently descend to her shoulder. His forehead then pushed off her for leverage; struggling to hoist his skull back up, they clumsily kissed with awful alcohol-breath, and with that I headed for the elevator.

Outside Porter had died down, most of the freshmen having ventured to the dorm rooms of new friends or the staples of student life on the Elmwood strip: the gas station, the pizza place, the diners, the bars. Slumped on a picnic table were Rude Dawud and Fasiq Abasa.

"Jehangir's on the ninth floor with a girl," I explained.

"Shit," said Fasiq.

"I think we missed Isha time," said Rude Dawud.

"What are you talking about?" Fasiq snapped. I then realized that they were both wasted. "You can't miss Isha time."

"Sure you can."

"No you can't."

"If it were past Isha," Rude Dawud replied.

"Does it look like the sun's coming up anytime soon? You can make Isha whenever."

"Let's make it then. Allahu Akbar, Allaaaaaahu Akbar..." And the two of them stood in a hashishiyya jamaat right there in front of Porter Hall. I watched and struggled hard not to laugh. They kept forgetting what to do or say next and what rakat they were in. The prayer never formally ended but just drifted off while they were in sitting position. "I'm moving to Costa Rica in a month," said Rude Dawud.

"Really?" asked Fasiq.

"Yeah. I met some guys who are going down there and I'm going with them."

"That's cool."

I sat on the picnic table. Fasiq and Dawud stayed on the grass right next to each other as though still praying. We waited a long time for our boy to come out.

"Keeping a pilgrim's mind is harder than actual pilgrimage," declared Jehangir as he stumbled out the door. "It doesn't matter how close you are to a grave or relic, or how far and long you've traveled to get there if your mind isn't a million miles away from the nearest vagina."

"D'you fuck her?" asked Fasiq.

"Y'akhi, insha'Allah, you wouldn't believe her eyes," replied Jehangir as we began the long walk to his car. "She had these lovely sad eyes that just cried 'Jehangir don't fail me, don't lose that pilgrim's mind' and I couldn't let her down. That was my jihad, the struggle between me and Jehangir Tabari—the greatest jihad, right? Five floors below me was Billy Plunger, a muezzin to all the heterosexual men of the world, calling us to throw ourselves down in sujdah at the feet of our women and not be him. Shaytan lives in the testicles, if he lives anywhere. Yusef, the keys." He pulled them from his pocket and handed them to me. I was, after all, the only sober one in the group.

On the way home, Fasiq riding shotgun put in a mix tape he had made that had the Rolling Scabs on it, their accidental classic "We're the Scabs."

"These kids were like twelve years old," Fasiq remarked. "They were all on heroin an' shit. The lead singer went down an elevator shaft when he was fourteen."

"Kullu ardh'n Karbala," said Jehangir.

"This song," said Fasiq, "if you listen to it… it's like Sufism."

We all laughed. "No, really. First it's like 'I just want to be your sexy scab,' like '*Your* sexy scab,' you know? And second, when they're all 'we have no producer, we have no lyrics' that's like Sufism, like 'we have no scholars, we have no scripture.' Like fucked up, take-it-as-it-comes Islam. Like Islam stripped down to its bare core."

"Jesus Christ," said Jehangir. "Hey Yusef—"

"Yeah man?"

"Yusef, Yusef Ali, you know that Rumi wrote 'when the Prophet said put females behind, he meant your soul.' That's somethin' right there."

"Yeah." I nodded my head and kept my eyes to the road.

"Bro, I have a big dick that burns out eyes… but Ya'Allah, grant these balls no victim but me… that's my du'a, Yusef Ali. Ya'Allah, grant these balls no victim but me."

"That's a cool du'a."

"These vesicles are seminal, bro."

"So tell me about your new Porter Hall girl," I said.

"Her name was Khadija, I think—we were talking and you know what got to me, bro? There's a lot of Americans who don't know that they have holy names. Khadija. Ayesha. Raheem. Malik. Umar. Ali. I once knew a Christian guy named Hasan. Isn't that some shit?"

"Yeah," I replied.

"And I was talking with Khadija about music, and mentioned taqwacore and she didn't know what it was. So I'm like, 'ever see that movie, *The Naked Gun*?' And she says yes, she's seen it. So I ask her, 'remember the part where Ayatullah Khumayni's black turban comes off and he's got a big orange mohawk underneath?' And she remembers it. So I tell her that's taqwacore."

Fasiq Abasa and Rude Dawud stayed silent, presumably passed out or at least fallen asleep. By the time we got home, they were all out. I left the three unholies in Jehangir's car and went to bed.

Two weeks later Fasiq Abasa came into some money and bought a video game console for the house. He hooked it up in the living room, which technically was his bedroom, the same living room where mumins piled in on Friday afternoons and drunks passed out on Friday nights. Jehangir Tabari bought a game for it, a baseball game where you could create characters, giving them all the necessary details, the right face, build, skin tone, even gender, put names on their backs and have them fill entire rosters. The first team Jehangir made was the All-Time Oakland A's, with Mark McGwire at first base, Nap Lajoie at second, Carney Lansford at shortstop and "Home Run" Baker over at third. At left field he put stolen-base king Rickey Henderson, at center "Mr. October" Reggie Jackson.

"I know he belongs at right," Jehangir explained, eyes locked on the television as he clicked away on his paddle, "but it was between him and Canseco. I thought Reggie a better fielder so I gave him center." Catching, Terry Steinbach. The starting pitchers: Lefty Grove and Catfish Hunter. Reliefs: Rollie Fingers with the big handlebar moustache like an Old West villain tying beautiful girls to railroad tracks, and Dennis Eckersley.

"Who would you put as manager?" I asked, though I had no frame of reference for his response to hold meaning.

"I was torn," Jehangir replied, "between an undeniable legend and my childhood. Connie Mack from the old Philly A's is still the heart and soul, blood and guts and patron saint of the team. But Tony LaRussa skippered during the late 80s Bash-Brothers Earthquake-Series dynasty, my all-time peak of baseball enthusiasm. Look at all the guys I got from those days: McGwire, Lansford, Henderson, Canseco, Steinbach, Eckersley. You can't beat that."

"Yeah," I replied, with no idea about any of it.

"I think if I could, I'd have Tony run the show and just keep Connie around as a diamond sage telling stories."

"That'd be cool."

The second team he made was *us.* Rude Dawud the first baseman, Lynn with dirty-blonde dreadlocks at second, Fasiq Abasa at short, Fatima on third. The outfield: Jehangir at left, me at center and Umar out in right with all his tattoos. Amazing Ayyub for catcher. Starting pitchers: Rabeya and a mystery guy named "Bloody." Reliefs: Sayyed and the newest addition, Fatima's friend

Muzammil who we had only met a few days before.

"Your guy is pretty good," said Jehangir.

"Really?"

"He's a solid hitter. My guy steals a lot. Umar's a slugger. You should see him swing those big inked-up arms, it's nuts. Like he's putting another mihrab in the wall." I laughed.

"Who's Bloody?" I asked.

"He's a kid I knew out in Pasadena, craziest fuckin' kid you'd ever meet. Big, tall goofy bitch with a frizzy mohawk half-brown and half-black, at least when I knew him. Safety-pin in his nose, the whole nine. He was originally from New Jersey but faked an English accent—that's a punk thing, what can I say. He could pull it off, though. But he pronounced 'Hackettstown' as 'Haketstan' or 'Hackistan.' Kind of a nut but I love that kid to death."

"Wow."

"I don't even remember half the stories I could tell about him. Going into diners drunk off our asses, getting food all over ourselves, shouting curses to anyone who came in, spitting in people's faces, running mankind from our little third-world dictatorship booth in the smoking section."

"Oh my God."

"That's Punk Rawk," he said proudly. "Not this harmless mall bullshit. Punks all clean-cut and cute with skateboards and wallet chains, baggy khakis and Airwalks."

"Hey Jehangir—when you were making us on the game, how did you know what kind of face to give Rabeya?"

"I've seen it, bro."

"What? When?"

"An Indian sweat lodge in Michigan," he said, still playing the baseball game.

"Indian sweat lodge?"

"Okay, Native American. She knew someone who was going

and we both tagged along. It's like a domed tent covered with layers and layers of blankets and you cram inside, men on one side and women on the other, all around these stones that have just been pulled from a fire outside. And the elder, he pours water on the hot stones creating this insane sauna-like effect. It gets so hot in there, bro, with the steam and packed in there with so many bodies, you think you're gonna die. You just sweat all the badness out of you."

"That sounds cool."

"Needless to say, you don't want a lot of clothing. Before entering, the men all stripped down to their boxers and the women were down to shorts and t-shirts. I only saw her for a second and I wasn't going to gawk at her—it was pretty awkward for both of us—but I did see it, bro."

"What did she look like?" I asked.

"I don't know," he replied without looking away from the television. "Not what you'd expect, but at the same time you don't really expect anything so, whatever. I guess she looks like a person."

"What was the sweat lodge like?"

"The most physical discomfort I've ever felt in my life, but also some pure fuckin' joy. First you're outside standing around the fire that's heating the stones. The stones represent your ancestors, I think. You take some tobacco and throw it on the fire, and it makes a *pop!* kinda sound—" He turned off the game and we went into the kitchen. "It was mostly women," he explained, pouring himself some coffee. "Or at least it felt like that because the women were much more comfortable than the men with being cramped together in a little hut and sweating on each other and singing in the dark. Besides me and two guys James and John, the men were all in their mid-thirties. On the females' side were old women who had been doing it for twenty years, little girls and everyone in between. There we were—a bunch of sweaty hot bodies in the dark—blessing our mothers and grandmothers and great-grandmothers. And in them… in *Rabeya*… I saw something I had never seen before.

"In Islam, Yusef—if you're a man—female spirituality is like a distant land you can only read about. Women pray far away, up in balconies or behind dividers and you never hear a woman's voice in jumaa. This is justified by the idea that men could never be around women without thinking of them indecently."

"Do you think it's true?" I asked. "Can men really be innocent around women?"

"Maybe, maybe not, who knows. But if you believe that you can't, and you live like you can't, it messes you up inside."

"What do you mean?"

"The more you accept man's intrinsic weakness, the easier it is to hate girls. Suddenly all your bad thoughts are their fault since they should have known how weak you are and not take advantage of it. When you're enslaved to your nuts you can hate all sorts of girls. Girls who laugh loudly, girls who show their knees. Girls who go to bars and dance. Suddenly you can't handle anything."

"I see."

"Shit, Yusef. If the problem is *men's* wicked thoughts, why aren't we the ones behind dividers?"

The new guy—Muzammil Sadiq—made his debut when Fatima brought him along to Friday jumaa. Knowing that she had discovered the kid out in San Francisco, Jehangir immediately took to Muzammil like a long-lost brother, pulling him into a world that only the two of them knew: street names and interstates, restaurants and clubs, good neighborhoods and bad, dialectic quirks and geographic interests. Muzammil even knew about taqwacore, which helped make that scene seem a little more real for the rest of us who had only heard of it through Jehangir's legends. Muzammil came with tales of his own of a growing genre, the blending of taqwacore (Muslim Punk) with homocore (Gay Punk) into something entirely new: liwaticore, subculture within subcultures of a subculture.

"It's only a few bands right now," he explained. "But it's a start."

"So who are the big ones out there?" Jehangir asked.

"The Ghilmans, mainly—"

"Those guys are awesome—I'm trying to get them out to my show this winter."

"That'd be hot," Muzammil replied. "And there's the Wilden Mukhalloduns, and Istimna, they're both pretty good bands. The Guantanamo Bay Packers have some good songs. Gross National's good, high political content. Their singer's a Pathan bi-girl. There'll be more, I'm sure as the gay Muslim population grows into its own coherent community."

"Insha'Allah," said Jehangir smiling, a brown glass bottle in hand even at jumaa.

"There was even going to be a gay masjid in Toronto, from what I heard."

"No shit?"

"Yeah, but they didn't do it for fear of violence or something. I would have loved to see that."

"I'm sure it's on its way, somewhere. With al-Fatiha and Queer Jihad and all these groups and conferences popping up, all the new Sulayman X's out there… it'll definitely happen."

"Insha'Allah."

"Islam used to be a lot more enlightened about that shit," said Jehangir with a swig off his bottle. "Back in the day, you know, with Bin Quzman and Abu Nuwas of Baghdad, and Sarmad who studied with the religious scholars and then dropped all of it to walk naked through Delhi singing his love for a gorgeous Hindu boy—"

"They killed Sarmad," Muzammil replied.

"Huh?"

"They killed Sarmad. Aurangzeb had him executed."

"Oh, shit. I forgot about that."

"He still has followers in India, though. They see him as a Sufi saint."

"That's cool," said Jehangir.

"He was yahooda," interrupted Umar, who had been lurking on the conversation's periphery unnoticed. "His parents were Iranian Jews."

"And," said Muzammil, "your point is..."

"He was a yahooda rabbi, he even said it himself. Another outside force coming to Islam just to destroy it from the inside. Refusing to cover his private parts, rejecting all the laws of Islam, glorifying his sodomy. What would happen if instead of killing Sarmad, we lifted up and exalted him?"

"I don't know," Muzammil sighed. With sarcastic woe he resigned, "I guess he'd convert everyone to Zionist Faggotism. In fact, that was our plan all along."

"What do you mean?" asked Umar.

"You see," Muzammil whispered so as to keep it top secret, his eyes wide open like he was going nuts, "Sarmad lived when—the sixteenth, seventeenth century? That was when it all started: our global conspiracy between Jews and homosexuals to cripple the Muslim Umma! The wheels have been rolling ever since. We've overtaken every major government. From behind the curtain, we manipulate world events to our liking. See how the Muslims have been weakened? We're responsible for everything, Umar: Mughal

India's fall to the British, the collapse of the Khilafah, Kemal Ataturk, East Pakistan breaking away to become Bangladesh, the creation of modern Israel, the rise of television, birth control, the phony Moon landing, subliminal brain-washing radio waves, *riba* banking, AIDS, abortion, Benazir Bhutto, the Gulf War, Bosnia, Chechnya, Somalia, the Bush-Taliban oil connection, child porn, Ebola virus and the disintegration of Michael Jackson's face… we caused all of it, Umar. Even though they got Sarmad, they couldn't stop all of us. When we put our wicked heads together, there's just no stopping yahoodas and queers."

Twenty minutes later I overheard Umar continuing his argument to an entirely new audience of passive listeners.

"It's like Yazid and Husain. Yazid flouted Islam, he was a drunkard and corrupt. What if Husain gave Yazid his pledge of allegiance? Just imagine Muhammad's beloved grandson endorsing that behavior; what would that have done to Islam? But no—Husain fought Yazid, fought him with every step and every breath until his last, even when he knew that victory was completely beyond his reach. And in so doing, by opposing the unlawful, he saved Islam."

"Mash'Allah," said one of the brothers.

"Rasullullah sallallaho alayhe wa salaam," added Umar, "said he would rather fall from the heavens to the earth than lay eyes on another man's *awrah*. You know, back when Mustafa lived here, the *ahlul-Lut* would never have come through that door."

I had no idea where Muzammil and Jehangir had gone until I went to use the upstairs bathroom and found them out on the roof with Fasiq, Fatima and Rabeya.

"Come on out!" Rabeya called. I climbed through the window.

"We only have two months of this left," added Jehangir, "if we're lucky."

"Hey Yusef," said Fasiq with a puff off his kief, "did you know that William S. Burroughs called weed the official drug of Islam?"

"Where'd you hear that?" I asked.

"Muzammil was just saying," he replied.

"He had fled the United States on obscenity charges," Muzammil explained. "And he went to Tangiers, got caught up in the whole scene there. Jack Kerouac went too to help him work on *Naked Lunch.* But anyway Burroughs said that culturally hashish was Islam's drug, whereas alcohol was Christianity's."

"That's interesting," I noted. "It kind of makes sense, in a way."

"Burroughs got big on Hassan bin Sabbah, mystic leader of the Mushashins back in medieval times. Hassan bin Sabbah's famous line was, 'nothing is true; everything is permitted.'"

"They didn't teach me *that* in Muslim summer camp," said Fatima.

"And Imam Burroughs," said Fasiq—"what else did he say?"

"He said that Muhammad was an invention of the Mecca Chamber of Commerce."

"Hey Muzammil," said Jehangir, "are you looking for a place to stay? Rude Dawud's movin' out of here next month, so we'll have a room open."

"Oh, no thanks. My parents said I should stay in the dorms this semester, to stay focused on my schoolwork; I don't think they really know what dorms are like."

"That's cool," said Jehangir.

"My parents wanted me *out* of the dorms," I interjected, "to save my deen."

"Parents are kind of funny," said Muzammil.

"And uncles too," added Fatima. "Except when they'd kill you."

"Your uncles would kill you?" asked Jehangir with a quick swivel of his head. "For what?" She looked at him as though he more than anyone should have known the answer. "Oh," he said. "So they'd really kill you?"

"They're the real deal," she answered. "And I'm a disgrace."

"That's crazy," said Jehangir.

"Yep," Fatima calmly replied. "If I ever have kids, I don't think I'll teach them about religion."

"Really?" I exclaimed. "But it's your culture, who you are—"

"There's more to my heritage than thinking it imitates the devil to eat with your left hand. That's not where I get my cultural identity."

"But aren't you Muslim?" I asked.

"Sure I am. But my kids don't need to be."

"I'd just give my kid a Qur'an," said Fasiq, "and then send him on his way. Go find your own truth, you know?"

"I don't need my kids saying 'Allahu Akbar' when they pray," said Rabeya. "That works for me, and I would teach it to them so they know me and who I am and where they're coming from. But if they found something else, cool."

"I want my kids to be smart," said Muzammil. I admit that it took me a second to remember that homosexuals do raise families. "If I was ever a father I'd take my kid to every kind of temple, real early on. By the time he or she was eight years old they'd have been to a masjid, a church, a synagogue, a Buddhist temple, a Sikh gurudwara, whatever we could find. I want a worldly child. By second or third grade my son-slash-daughter will have more appreciation for diversity and the beliefs of others than most adults."

"I believe in teaching my children Islam," I offered. "Just as Pakistan is part of their heritage, so is our religion. You can't separate it. I don't know how strict I'll be; maybe we'll just go to the masjid for Eids and that's it. I doubt we'd pray five times a day, though we wouldn't admit that outside the house. I don't know how I'd be if I had a daughter who wanted to go to the prom, and things like that... or if my son came home drunk one night. But my own values are constantly changing, so it's hard to say. I honestly have no idea but I have a nice little image in my head of what Islam can be for them."

During the brief silence that followed, I realized that Jehangir had said nothing on the topic. I looked at him. He was looking at his hands. It were as though he knew the question would never apply to him.

Though Umar was not up on the roof, I imagined what he would have said. He had once told me the story of a man who raised his son to have no knowledge of Islam. Nearing his thirtieth birthday, the son was involved in a horrible car accident. The man rushed to the hospital, only to hear that his son would not survive. At his son's deathbed the man cried that he would pray for him.

"You should not pray for me," the dying son replied, "but for yourself. Because you did not teach me Islam when I was a child, the punishments for all my missed prayers and fasts will fall upon *you.* The punishments for my drinking alcohol and mixing with girls will fall upon *you.* The rewards I missed for not saying 'la ilaha illa Allah' will be extracted from *your* baraqa."

The next day Jehangir, Muzammil, Fasiq and I met up with Amazing Ayyub at a gas station. With Muzammil, Fasiq and Ayyub crammed tight in the back seat we headed to the mall. Ayyub still had on his Confederate flag t-shirt.

Punks in a mall—when they're not snotty mall-punks, of course—can be a fun time. Fasiq and Ayyub did their old stunt where Ayyub pretended to be a mental patient and Fasiq his good-hearted care staff. Ayyub ran into stores slapping his head, hollering, careening into merchandise displays and Fasiq would just take him by the arm, and coddle him with a gentle voice while store clerks stood frozen not knowing what the hell they could do. Jehangir had gotten a little vial of stinking prank-perfume and would bring it into the uppity stores—Kaufman's, Bon-Ton and the like—all prim to the customer-service people—"yes, um, I was wondering if you had this scent… I can't find it anywhere, but I just love it so much—" and watch their reactions when he twisted the cap and had them smell. Neither Fasiq or Jehangir, of course, had dressed their parts. I doubt anyone took us seriously, but at any rate our crew made a great deal of people uncomfortable so it was at least fun for that. Amazing Ayyub whipped out his Mexican wrestling mask, put it on, ran into an AAA office, stuffed three brochures into his mouth, made a weird animal noise, hopped around and ran out while we all stood twenty feet from the place laughing our asses off. Though I never did anything to entertain the group, just being with them made me feel like one of *the cool guys.*

"No good can come out of this," said Jehangir as Amazing Ayyub made a beeline for Victoria's Secret and we followed. The attractive young lady out in front holding a bottle of perfume for passersby to sample looked the other way. "I guess we don't look the type to have girlfriends," Jehangir observed.

"Maybe she was afraid you'd share *your* perfume with her," I replied.

"MY COCK WEIGHS TEN POUNDS RIGHT NOW!" bellowed Amazing Ayyub at us from the opposite side of the store, gripping a flowered red slip on its hanger. I heard a crash and laughter and turned around to see the tail-end of Jehangir shoulder-tackling Fasiq. With that we all ran out of the store.

"Where's Muzammil?" Fasiq asked.

"I think he's still in there," said Jehangir. We waited. Muzammil came out with a pink-and-white-striped plastic bag.

"I bought a catalog," he said. Figuring either Muzammil dragged or was having sex with a guy who did, we let the topic die fast.

We walked around some more, bought pizza (to go) at the food court, pushed Ayyub into a fountain and left for fear that it was only a matter of time before someone called security. Soaking-wet Ayyub took the front passenger seat. As we pulled out of the parking lot, he rolled down the window and whipped his pizza at a stationary station-wagon. The slice plopped and stayed, cheese-side down, on the victim's windshield.

"Get out of here quick!" I shrieked to Jehangir, immediately embarrassed that there was no avoiding my role as the group's relentless nerd. Jehangir blended into traffic and our escape was complete, Blanks 77's "I Wanna be a Punk" providing the perfectly anthemic but aggressive soundtrack.

"Put on Sham 69," said Amazing Ayyub.

"Don't," I replied, knowing he only wanted to sing me his rich-boy song.

"Is it Asr time?" asked Fasiq.

"Probably," said Jehangir.

"Do you want to pray?"

"Sure."

We dropped off Amazing Ayyub at the City Mission, or Camp Fun as he called it, and headed home. Umar and Rabeya were there and said they'd join the jamaat; but when Jehangir invited Muzammil to lead, Umar suddenly remembered that he had already made Asr.

After the prayer, Jehangir cupped his hands du'a-style and said, "my Beloved shits Truth, but intellect is a can of Lysol by the toilet."

"What the hell is that?" asked Fasiq.

"I think Rumi said it," Jehangir replied. "Shit, shit, I know a guy who doesn't even defecate anymore and he's prayed with the same wudhu for ten years. I guess he doesn't sleep either. Me, I sleep. And I fart. I eat Taco Bell which wrecks me and I fart out zikrs. Thirty-three al-hamdulilahs, thirty-three subhana'Allahs, thirty-four Allahu Akbars. Phbbbbbbbbt! Phbbbbbbbbbbbt! You know what I said just there? La ilaha illa Huwal'Hayyul Qayyum!" I went upstairs and flopped out on my bed. Within twenty minutes Muzammil appeared in my doorway.

"Here you go," he said, underhand-tossing me the pink-and-white Victoria's Secret bag. I took out the catalog.

"What's this for?" I asked.

"It's for you."

"For me?" I asked with raised eyebrows.

"Rabeya said you could use it."

"For what?"

"I'm sure you'll figure it out. Baby steps, brother. They're not naked, so at least you won't be confronted with a gaping snatch yet… but at the same time, their faces haven't been airbrushed out."

"So wait; I'm supposed to… self-abuse with this?"

"I wouldn't call it 'abuse,' Yusef. Have fun." He closed the door and I heard his footsteps heading toward the stairs.

There I was. In my closet a woman's burqa, which its owner expected me to wear in public. In my hands what would become my first masturbatory material, purchased for me by a gay man. Both the burqa's owner and the gay man were Muslims. I think.

Aoudhu billahi mina shaytani rajeem.

I wondered what was happening downstairs. Maybe Jehangir was still talking about the holiness of his farts. Maybe Fasiq was on his way upstairs to smoke pot on the roof and would walk by my room with my door closed. Rude Dawud would soon move to Costa Rica, a few weeks or so. I wondered how that would all play out and what he would do down there. He hadn't been around much lately, always with his adopted reggae/ska scene. I wondered if anyone downstairs besides Muzammil and Rabeya knew that I was alone with the Victoria's Secret catalog. Maybe everyone was outside my door with cups to their ears. I wasn't really going to jerk off, was I? I went to the door and stood silently behind it. Then I swung it open. Nothing. My penis was hard and sticking out.

At first I did it clumsily, moving my whole body. I soon discovered it was easier just to move my hand. Then it got good but I stopped once to make sure I had locked the door. I took my shirt off; I don't know why but it just seemed proper. I listened for sounds in the hallway. They had some beautiful girls in that catalog. I focused on one who reappeared page after page in different poses and pouts and bras. She had big breasts and a face that could pull off all the desired moods. On one page she cast her face down and rolled her eyes up, as though looking at me from below. On the next she wore cute pajamas and gave a sweet smile. As I flipped through the book I kept looking for her. She posed topless lying on her stomach, showing off the panties; or on her knees giving you the bird's-eye view of her bra. As my passion accelerated I snatched quick glances of details around my room as a whitewater rafter might notice a rock or tree in that split-second the rapids whisk him by. I saw my alarm clock with robotic red digital numbers but didn't even notice what the time was. I saw the color of my walls. I saw my desk and computer. My Pakistani flag. Mustafa's old Bukharis. The thought occurred to me that Mustafa may never have ejaculated in this room, for all the time he had it. Before I could really consider it the thought was gone, left behind with everything else. I felt a tremor in my body I had never known before, surprised that it wasn't centralized in my penis but seemed to just jolt through my torso. I went faster. My eyes locked on the girl's eyes and we just stared at each other. Then my eyes wandered to her shoulder and a single green bra strap. Round breasts. Shadow of cleavage. Her stomach. Little waist. Panties. Breasts again. Bra. Lips. Her eyes like she was looking at me. Like she knew. Like she wanted it. We were together. I wanted to fuck her. I *did* fuck her. She was my hand with a face. A sweet face, smiling like this was cute and not at all dirty. I fucked my hand and fucked it faster like I was raping myself. Tits. Cunt. Fuck. Lynn. Lynn's tits in my hands. Her blue bra that was still in my room somewhere. The load surging inside me, building to launch. I squeezed tighter and jacked and jacked and fucked myself until it came out and then it *really* came out, the second blast like a shotgun arcing high and landing on my chest. I kept going, feeling the hot first shot gliding down my furious pumping hand. More came. An endless barrage of little shots, castaway drops scattering here and there. My fist slowed down. Inside I felt dizzy but clear and warm but numb, charged but relaxed with perfect precision: a buzzing calm if that makes any sense. I felt like all that semen had once been inside my skull, coating my brain with a thick skin of baby batter slowing down the synapses and now I had gotten it all out. I was free and clean and too at peace to care about the sticky mess all over me, the clean-up only becoming more of a future nuisance as I lay there allowing my sperm to gel and dry and turn into crust in my pubic hair. I looked at it intently. Liquid, but not quite a liquid. Off-white puddles with texture. It seemed to freeze my hand in its perverted claw-hold pose. It was gross. I had known it before but only in my sleep. With my clear and empty head I thought strange things. Strange that if the woman was a real woman and not just a sheet of paper with ink on it, we could have turned those drops and gobs into a whole new human being. Strange that she might have swallowed it. People swallow potential people. Isn't that weird? But I think I would have liked her to do that. Is that weird too? Then it occurred to me that when a man masturbates, he plays the role of the vagina. Because he's not moving his body, having sex with the hand as I had initially done; he's moving his hand, having sex with the penis. So the active role a man plays is that of the woman. The woman—the hand—is dominant. At the very least he is both, because it is still *his* penis. My heart slowly returning to its normal rate, and all the facts of the world crawling back into my brain, I felt stupid and got up, grabbed a towel, scrubbed my body hard to get it off and left marks where the semen had been. I got dressed, grabbed another towel and headed to the bathroom for a shower.

CHAPTER VII

Umar told us that Sayyed had keys to the masjid in Rochester and we could borrow them for *i'tikaf*.

"No women, though."

"Umar," replied Rabeya, "I'm from Rochester—I used to go to that masjid all the time."

"Rules of the mosque. No women."

"Oh right, there's that hadith—how's it go? 'The woman, the dog and the ass all interrupt prayer.' That's a good one."

"And I don't want the *liwatiyyah* coming either."

"The wha—"

"Muzammil Sadiq," said Umar. "Muzammil from the *ahlul-Lut*. Nothing personal against him, if he says *la ilaha illa Allah* he's my brother but I don't want him there."

"Why not, if he's your brother?" asked Fasiq.

"Because what if I fall asleep?"

"I think he'll manage to control himself," moaned Rabeya. "I mean, it'll be tough because you're so fucking hot, Umar. Maybe if you tie him up before you fall asleep, then you'll be safe." Umar rolled his eyes.

"I think Muzammil would feel unsafe if your hating ass were there," said Jehangir. "How do you like that?"

"That's fine with me."

"Well nobody's fitting in your fuckin' pickup," Jehangir countered. "So if we're taking my car, Muzammil and Rabeya are in the jamaat."

"Mash'Allah," replied Umar.

"No," said Rabeya. "I'll respect the rules of the masjid. It's bullshit but you don't know who else'll be there."

"Okay," said Jehangir. "But Muzammil's in."

"Fine," said Umar. "Maybe it'll help him."

"Help him with *what?*" snapped Rabeya, but Umar ignored her as he walked away.

"No beer," said Umar as we loaded our bags in the trunk, glaring straight at Jehangir. He looked at Fasiq. "And no weed." He looked at Muzammil. "And no… uh… no gay material."

"Damn!" said Muzammil with obvious sarcasm. "I was just about to ask if we could swing by the campus an' pick up all my big stacks of fag porn—because, you know, that's what I usually do in mosques."

"Hilarious," Umar replied.

"Sometimes I bring my Zionist cohorts and some pigs—"

"That's enough."

"What time is it?" asked Fasiq.

"Almost eleven," said Umar. "We'll be there around midnight, insha'Allah wa Ta'Ala."

"Not bitch," called Fasiq as he climbed in the back.

"Not bitch," called Muzammil, leaving me stuck in the cramped middle.

Jehangir drove. Umar sat shotgun with Sayyed's directions in hand. We took the I-90 East, going by the sci-fi lights of an airport runway, green and red and white. Then it was a lot of nothing.

"Did I ever tell you about the masjid I saw out in Montana?" Jehangir asked.

"I don't think so," I replied, squeezed in tight with my hands on my knees.

"It was right on this road, the 90... I pass by a barn with a giant rusty crescent on top of the silo. On the roof a giant 'Allah' in Arabic, and in English it says 'MASJID AL-TAQWA.' So I pull over, hop the fence and run through a cornfield. Kind of had to. The imam was real cool. He was from Yemen, I think. He had a beard, kufi, flannel shirt and blue jeans dirty from the knees down with dirty work-boots at the door because I think he was still a real-deal farmer."

"What was the inside like?"

"Weird. Kind of a barn and kind of a masjid. Had a mihrab and even a minbar. Nice carpets. But you could tell it used to be a barn. I don't know." Jehangir put in a tape. The Jim Carroll Band's "People Who Died" came on. With nobody talking and nothing to look at, my only mental stimulation was the darkness and the song—the darkness dramatized by road lights and car lights, the song energetic in sadness, vibrantly mournful—and I couldn't help but imagine that this car ride to Rochester, to a masjid, five young men seeking Allah in what looked like a movie... and maybe that was why Allah made us, just so He could curl up on the Couch with a bowl of Popcorn to watch little ants find Him... and I was being stupid. Jehangir got off at exit 46, the suburb Henrietta which he informed us was named after the daughter of Sir William Pulteney. Then we got on 390 North. Took the third exit, ended up on 252 East and within a mile or so we were on the right street. And there it was. As Umar turned the key I couldn't help but feel like we were doing something wrong. We had among us a mohawked drunk fornicator, a mohawked pothead, a homosexual and me, whatever I was. Umar was the only *real* Muslim, the only one who could have hung in the old days of Hijras and Badrs; and even he was covered with stupid tattoos any scholar would call *haram* regardless of what they said.

I made sure to enter with my right foot first. Immediately to our left was a wall of cubbies to house our shoes. To our right was the locked office. Umar took a pair of courtesy slippers and went into the bathroom. The rest of us walked straight ahead to the glass doors and unlit prayer room, careful there too to go in with the right foot.

Then the place was ours. It was wide, a decent walk from one wall to the other. Looked even bigger due to the super-high ceiling. I looked at the crazy haircuts and Jehangir's spiked jacket. Invasion of the taqwacores. I pictured us in the Ka'ba fourteen centuries past, an army of maniacs and hooligans running around with baseball bats smithereening stone al-Lat and al-Uzzas with double-handed, out-the-park swings.

"Look how clean this place is," remarked Jehangir, looking at the walls. At first he seemed unnaturally loud, but I realized that it was just the acoustics of the room and it didn't matter because nobody else was there. "That's why I love masjids. You go into a church, they bombard you with images of Christ and Mary and whatnot. Or a Buddhist temple, they got a gold Buddha as big as the whole room and there's no escaping him. But you step into a masjid, bro, with these walls bare except for curvy calligraphy so complicated you can't even read what it says, and it doesn't matter who you are. There's nothing in your way, nothing imposed on you."

"The only thing that ever made me uncomfortable in a masjid," said Muzammil, "was *people.* With the place empty, this isn't half bad." Fasiq went to the bookshelf, sorted through paras until finding the Juz Amma, took it and sat propping himself against a wall to read—in the dark, until Umar came in and turned on the lights. At first he put them all on, then switched off a few.

"We should make two nafl rakats," he declared. "Out of respect for the masjid." We each took a corner of the wide open room. Umar prayed in the center of the room, directly in the lights. Jehangir stood towards the left wall. I walked up to what would have been the front row in a jumaa. Fasiq and Muzammil had dark corners. I later heard Umar say loud enough to be heard everywhere in the room, "now make your sunna for Isha." So we did that. I think we all did. I felt like I had to, thanks to my brother Umar enjoining the right. Then Jehangir got up, went to the mihrab and flicked a switch on the wall to turn on the microphone.

He crooned it like a hammered Sinatra with matching face and posture.

"Allaaaaaaaaaaaaaaaaaaahu Akbarullaaaaaaaaaaaaaaaaaaaaaahu Akbar; Allaaaaaaaaaaaaaaaaaaaaaaaahu Akbarullaaaaaaaaaaaaaaaaa-aaaaahu Akbar!" Umar was probably ready to kill him but he didn't say anything, just silently mouthing the words.

We made a beautiful Isha. Jehangir led. I prayed between Umar and Muzammil and never felt anything negative flowing from one to the other. It was a good prayer. We were brothers with bare feet.

"Look up there," said Fasiq. The women's balcony. "Let's check that shit out." We headed for the door. "Staghfir'Allah," he added, realizing that he had said 'shit' in the masjid. We left with our lefts first and went up the stairs, finding a large open space with long tables leaned against the wall with their legs folded in and a mess of folded chairs. Chalkboards and a podium. "This is where they have their Sunday school and banquets," said Fasiq. Then we stepped through another glass door and found the balcony. "We could spit on Umar from here... staghfir'Allah."

"Salaam alaikum," I called to our brothers below.

"Wa alaikum as-salaam, sisters," joked Jehangir.

The upstairs also had a kitchen but all we could find in the refrigerator was a bag of chipatis and, covered in aluminum foil, a bowl of leftover *something* that Fasiq identified as "spicy-ass shit."

"You're not down with South Asian cuisine?" I asked, smiling.

"Man, I don't know how you do it."

Went back downstairs to find Jehangir sitting in the mihrab, forearms resting on his knees. Muzammil leaned against a wall in contemplation, of what I don't know. Umar seemed lost in zikrs or du'as. I looked at Jehangir again. High orange mohawk, spikes, red plaid pants. Looked at the tiled mihrab around him and the prayer rug beneath.

"Come here bro," he said, nodding to the bookshelves as he got up and walked over. He reached into his leather jacket and pulled out a flimsy booklet, the cover yellow with white creases and rounded corners.

"What's this?" I asked.

"My gift to the masjid," he whispered in reply.

Jehangir held it so I could see the cover and catch its musty attic smell. *The Punk.* "It's a novel," he explained. "The first punk novel. This kid Gideon Sams, he was like fourteen when he wrote it. He fuckin' worked at his dad's pizza place and dreamed of becoming a brain surgeon. Did his homework in a pool hall. Wanted to design a skateboard that he could pogo on. Look at that on the cover: *'Romeo and Juliet' with Safety Pins.* Haha. Shit. This book, man, it's like reading a book by one of the old Sahabas." Jehangir slid the thin volume among the paras that Fasiq had been sorting through before. "Who knows who'll find it."

"Yeah," I said.

"Hopefully someone cool."

"Did that kid write anything else?"

"Shaykh Sams? I don't think so. He died when he was twenty-six. I don't even think *The Punk* was meant to be anything big, it just kind of happened. Alayhe salaam."

I watched him walk away and find a spot to lie down.

"Brother," said Umar, gentle but firm. "It is good to lay with your head facing qiblah."

"Right," Jehangir replied, turning around with no tinge of hostility. It was a good night like that.

Among all the Qur'ans and paras and hadith collections I noticed a magazine, the official publication of some prominent American Muslim group. Picked it up and flipped through the pages past big colorful ads for Qur'ans on CD-ROM and Islamic children's videos, something about Chechnya, something about Bush and Iraq, something about Allah's Name found in a watermelon, something about matrimonials. Islamic matrimonials. Brothers Seeking Sisters. Sisters Seeking Brothers. Parents inviting correspondence for Salafi daughter (Arabic origin), searching for a very pious Salafi with beard, and strong Iman and arabic origin... parents seeking correspondence for daughter in final year of university, studying software engineering; 5'5" with fair skin, wears hejab... Gujarati Parents invite correspondence for final year MD resident daughter, 28, 5'4", slim, fair, beautiful. US born, raised with east/west values, preferred US born, never married and professional, in medical field... Egyptian parents seeking correspondence for their daughter, 30, 5'1", caring, attractive, with master's degree. Looking for USA born/raised professional between 29-36 years... Hyderabadi parents inviting correspondence for their doctor son raised and educated in USA. Specializing in Neuro-Radiology, age 34, 5'9". Father, brother and sister all doctors. Girl should be educated, slim, fair, from a very cultured, well-to-do religious family... and so it went, column to column. *Preferred already in a strong engineering, medical or related occupation... son in computer programming... preferred Hyderabadi professional... graduated Radiologic Technology, pursuing MRI certification... prefers someone in medical field... employed in computer field... seeking a US born/raised medical doctor/lawyer/engineer/CPA (24-30) for their US born/raised daughter... send resume and picture.*

I looked at the pack of raving weirdoes with whom I shared the masjid that night, imagined us replying to these ads or better yet, showing up at the families' doorsteps.

Hi, I'm Jehangir. I'm here to marry your daughter.

Hi, I'm Fasiq. No degree but I'm in pharmaceuticals.

Hi, I'm Muzammil. I hear your son's a doctor.

As-salaamu alaikum, I'm Umar. These ads are haram!

Hi, I'm Yusef. Sunni, Pakistani origin, engineering student, good family.

Lying on the carpeted hard floor, the five of us shared those corny late night, male-bonding philosophy sessions and pulled it off surprisingly well. Umar was still Umar, but he didn't seem as nuts as usual. Maybe in the masjid he toned down his act. Maybe in the masjid he just made more sense to the rest of us. We were spread out all over the room so you had to speak loud to be heard by someone on the other side. Eventually it just became too much effort and we either spoke only to the nearest brother or drifted off to sleep.

"Umar," I said just before falling asleep, "is masturbation halal?"

"No."

"Really?"

"Rasullullah said it was better to fast... but you know what, brother? Allahu Alim."

We were awoken by Umar's eloquent Fajr adhan hitting us from every corner of the place at once.

"Was the microphone really necessary?" whined Fasiq. We pulled ourselves up and plodded to the bathroom, peed away the morning erections and washed our feet for prayer. Nobody wanted to lead so Umar got in front and Muzammil gave the iqama.

"Make your line straight," Umar commanded. "Shoulder to shoulder, feet to feet." We could barely keep our eyes open.

After Fajr Umar went to the shelves and grabbed Qur'ans for each of us, failing to notice Maulana Gideon Sams. "Okay, we are turning to Suratul-Nur, the thirty-fifth ayat… aoudhu billahi mina shaytani rajeem, subhana kallahumma wa bihamdika wa tabara gasmuka wa ta'Ala jedduka wa la ilaha gayruk… bismillahir rahmanir raheem. Allahu nuru al-samawati wal-ardi mathalu nurihi kamishkatin feeha misbahun almisbahu fee zujajateen alzujajatu kanaha kawkabun durriyyun yuqadu min shajaratin mubarakatin zaytunatin la sharqiyyatin wala gharbiyyatin yakadu zaytuha yudeeu walaw lam tamsas'hu narun nurun ala nurin yahdee Allahu linurihi man yashau wayadribu Allahu al-amthala lilnasi wa'Allahu bikulli shay'in aleemun… sadaq'Allahul azeem. Now brothers, this is called the Ayat of Nur, or Light. Scholars throughout the centuries have tried to find the correct interpretation, but the true meaning is known to Allah subhanahu wa ta'Ala and nobody else except as He wills. Brother Yusef, would you like to read the English interpretation?"

"Aoudhu billahi mina shaytani rajeem," I said quickly under my breath, "bismillahi rahmanir raheem.

"Allah is the Light of the heavens and the earth. The parable of his Light is as if there were a niche and in it a lamp, the lamp enclosed in glass. The glass as it were a brilliant star lit from a blessed tree; an olive, neither of East nor West, whose oil would almost glow forth though no fire had touched it. Light upon light!

Allah guides to His Light whom He wills. And Allah sets forth parables for man, and Allah knows all things."

"Jazakullah khair," said Umar. "Now brothers, first we need to note that Allah subhanahu wa ta'Ala tells us that this is a parable, so that is how we need to look at it. Allah subhanahu wa ta'Ala is the Light of the heavens and the earth. Light is warmth, warmth is life. In the pre-Islamic days, people used to think the sun was Allah subhanahu wa ta'Ala because when the sun seemed to make them warm and cause their crops to grow. But in reality, Allah subhanahu wa ta'Ala is the real Light because without Allah subhanahu wa ta'Ala there is no sun. And though we think the sun is this great big thing, so many millions of times larger than our own earth, it is smaller than other stars and its light and warmth extends to only a tiny corner of a tiny corner of even this galaxy. But you see, Allah subhanahu wa ta'Ala's Light is everywhere, throughout the universe.

"Now Allah subhanahu wa ta'Ala's Light is like a lamp inside a niche. Brothers, in the olden days people would build a niche in their wall and place the light in that niche, and they would build the niche high so the light could shine throughout the room. The niche is made especially for this Light; and the glass, you know, it reflects the Light, the Light shines through it; so if Allah is the Light, all these devices through which He shines are the creation, the created universe. Just as you can look to the stars and feel incredible rushes of iman come over you, or look at the ocean and tremble with appreciation of Allah subhanahu wa ta'Ala's Will, or look at the animals or even at your own bodies—your internal processes, your fingerprints, your eyes, your brain, your skin, our reproductive systems, the development of a fetus in the womb—these are all Allah's Light shining through His created things.

"And the glass, it says, is like a brilliant star lit from a blessed tree neither East nor West. If something is only in the East, it is cold and dark when the sun is shining upon the West. And vice versa. But this tree is neither East nor West, it is never cold and dark. It receives Allah's Light all the time.

"Like I said there are many volumes written about this ayat. Imam Ghazali devoted a great deal of time to the study of its meaning and he wrote a great book, the *Mishkat al Anwar*, that I wish we had with us right now. But not even Imam Ghazali could find the complete meaning, insha'Allah wa Ta'Ala." Umar closed his Qur'an, cupped his hands and led us in a lengthy Arabic du'a. Then we rubbed our hands down our faces and got up.

"One time I read that verse with Amazing Ayyub," said Fasiq as he gently placed his Qur'an back on the shelf. "Out on the roof and we were both pretty gone, you know. But he said the niche was Fatima, and the lamp symbolized Hasan and Husain."

We made sure to step out left-foot first.

"Shotgun," I called. The sky was an interesting color most of us rarely got to see. Umar double-checked the masjid door before climbing in back. Jehangir pulled out of the empty parking lot to the Dead Kennedys' "Kill the Poor" but turned it down a little because it was still so early.

In roughly an hour we had made it back to our home planet. Most of us slept the rest of the day.

Rude Dawud's going-away party filled the house with his Caribbean scene that we barely knew existed in Buffalo. Jehangir had made it a rule that for the night it'd only be classic ska, starting with Prince Buster's "Judge Dread." Lynn showed up with that Marcos kid who found himself privy to a drunken Jehangir Tabari briefing on the Moors.

"Gibraltar's named after a Muslim," Jehangir reminded him, haphazardly waving his green Heineken. "It's actually Jibral-Tariq:

'Mountain of Tariq,' named for the general who took Spain."

"That's awesome," said Marcos.

"And you got fuckin' cathedrals that started out as masjids and nobody knows it. All these Catholics going in on Sunday to eat their wafers and there's fuckin' Qur'an all over the walls."

"Wow."

"And you know, brother, Muslim Spain had such an incredible freedom of thought... that's why the Inquisition happened. When the Catholics retook Spain, there were all these Christian heresies that had flourished because the Muslims didn't give a shit... and all these Jews—like fuckin' Maimonides their greatest medieval thinker, right there in Muslim Spain. And of course, lots of mumins. So when the Church got it back they had to clean up, wipe out all that free thought."

"Damn," said Marcos.

"Yeah," said Jehangir. "We used to be the good guys, and *they* were the assholes."

"What happened?"

"Allahu Alim."

I watched Rude Dawud hugging everyone and getting lots of attention from girls.

"You think we'll ever see him again?" I asked Jehangir. By then it was a point in the night, and Jehangir's drinking pattern, when I knew he'd give a hyper-sentimental response that may be low on rationale.

"If not in this world," he said, "the next. You never know, y'akhi. It's all the al-Zariyats."

"The what?"

"The al-Zariyats. The fuckin'... Winds that Scatter. It's a

sura… fifty-one, I think. 'Wal-zariyati zarwaa—'"

"And?"

"Yusef, Allah is the Wind, the fuckin' Winds that Scatter." Jehangir put his arm around me. He smelled bad and his eyes were red. "You see all these people, Yusef Ali? They're like fuckin' leaves on the ground. One leaf, two leaves, three leaves. A fuckin' mess of leaves. Okay, now look at that guy over there with the spiked hair. See him? Here he is tonight, with all of us. Here he is at Dawud's Costa Rica party. Here he is in Buffalo with circles of friends and who knows what else. Maybe he goes to school here, and-or works. He's got a life here filled with people of varying values. And then Allah the Winds that Scatter just picks him up and takes him to fuckin' Michigan or something. Bam! New people. Like a fuckin' leaf caught in the breeze flying here and there, in this pile, in that pile. Look at me, Yusef, and all the scenes I've seen. The Winds pick me up and toss me around. It's beautiful."

"Right."

"Now Allah is taking Rude Dawud to Costa Rica. We have no idea how long that'll last. Maybe in a month he's back up here, he misses the fuckin' snow or something. Maybe the plane crashes and everyone dies. Insha'Allah, you know? Or maybe he goes down there, loves it, and then ten years from now you and your wife go on a second honeymoon? Where? Costa Rica. And without even thinking twice that you have a friend in Costa Rica, you go down there and bump into him on the beach. Holy shit, takbir!"

"Allahu Akbar," I replied.

"And if not, then there's Kauthar."

"Insha'Allah."

"But you know what, bro? I've had enough of all… this." He waved at all the punks and Jamaicans drinking together. "Time for me to go upstairs and make my salatul-Isha, right? That's where I'll be if I make it up the stairs." He patted my shoulder and walked off. A few minutes later I decided to join him. Increases the reward of prayer twenty-seven times, after all.

I went up to his room and found him passed out in sujdah, his anus pointing to heaven.

Standing in front of China Buffet, I felt a *moment.* It disappeared as soon as I noticed it, but it was real. It was the moment when Buffalo weather begins to get nasty; the first time an autumn breeze hurts your face. Weeks can go by from that moment to the hard Buffalo winters and massive thigh-high snow. But that moment tells you it's coming.

"I bought this for Jehangir," said Amazing Ayyub in his Confederate t-shirt which was dirtier every time I saw him. He handed me a red tulip.

"Okay."

"I'm not a fag."

"I know."

"That's on the Iranian flag, you know."

"The tulip?"

"Yeah man. If you look at the flag, the fuckin' red crescents and sword, you know, they spell out 'Allah' but it's all shaped like a tulip, if you look at it."

"I never saw it like that before."

"It's for Jehangir. I'm not a homo. It's for fuckin' martyrs an' shit."

"I know, Ayyub. So how are you doing, man?"

"I'm hurting, bro."

"Really?"

"I walk all day. My left foot's green and swollen. I limp all the fuckin' time. They got a curfew at Camp Fun so sometimes I sleep between pillars at the Albright-Knox."

"How's that going, Ayyub—with Camp Fun, I mean."

"Besides the Bible stuff and having to take a shit in front of everybody, and having to be in by seven at night, it's okay. I met a girl there."

"What's her name?"

"Devon. She's a cool girl." He nodded in agreement with himself. "She's nineteen."

"She sounds cool," I said.

"She jerked me off and then licked her hand."

"That's fantastic," I replied. Amazing Ayyub smiled.

"Tell Jehangir about that."

"I will."

"I can get girls, even if it's at a homeless shelter."

"You want to go in and eat?" I asked.

"Sure."

We entered the China Buffet but Ayyub never ordered anything, electing instead to swipe things off my plate when the manager wasn't looking. "Get some more sesame chicken," he suggested each time I stood up. Ayyub ate like a creature on the Discovery Channel; urgent, paranoid, snatching up a handful and stuffing it into his mouth with eyes darting back and forth for his enemies. I was sure someone noticed, but nobody said anything.

Somebody pounded on our door. Jehangir, Umar and Rabeya were slouched on the living room couch, none of them appearing too eager to move.

"I'll get it," I volunteered.

"I'm here about the room," said the guy on our porch.

"Ayyub, man, I don't know. I think Umar's still pissed at you."

"That was months ago, brother. I've seen the fliers all over, I know you got a room."

"Okay, but—"

"I missed this place," he said walking right past me and into the living room. "As-salaamu alaikum guys." Jehangir was no less than stunned. There was no gauging Rabeya's reaction behind the burqa. Umar did not move. "Umar, man, um, I guess… brother, I'm sorry about doing shit in your bed."

"Mash'Allah, y'akhi."

"If you can forgive me, I don't know, I was kind of wondering if I can rent Rude Dawud's old room."

"Do you have a job?" asked Rabeya.

"Yeah, I work at Wal-Mart now. Maintenance on the overnights. Mopping floors, cleaning toilets. That kinda shit." I imagined what his matrimonial ad would be in those Muslim magazines. *Graveyard shift janitor, tattoos and poor hygiene, seeks hand-jobs for self. Preferred: attractive Shi'a in medical or related field.*

"If you're good for the rent, I don't care," said Rabeya.

"He's fine by me," said Jehangir. "Hey man, thanks for the tulip."

"No problem, bro," Ayyub replied. "Did you hear about that girl at Camp Fun?"

"Which one?"

"The licker?" He pretended to lick his hand.

"Oh—oh yeah, yeah I heard about her. Good job."

"Thanks. Umar, what do you say?" We all looked at him.

"Okay," Umar replied. "Okay, insha'Allah." Ayyub's face lit up and he tackled me in a joyous mock dry-humping.

The heat had been in Rude Dawud's name. I volunteered to switch it over to mine. I parked a healthy walk from the gas place because much of Main Street isn't even accessible by car. The old buildings wore masks of plywood which themselves were dressed in spray-painted apparel. I noted one reading, HELP! UNREGULATED SPRAWL IS ROBBING BUFFALO'S DIGNITY. Dead businesses, boarded-up stores and a glass door leading nowhere with blue and gold lettering telling me it had once been an office of the UNITED STEELWORKERS OF AMERICA, AFL • CIO • CLC—LOUIS J. THOMAS, DIRECTOR. Above it now hung a sign reading WHOLESALE JEWELERS. Stood up close to the glass door and looked past the lettering and I saw no jewelry or steel, just chipping walls and a paint roller long abandoned.

Then I veered into Theater Place quick to defecate. I really had to go. Suddenly, like sneaking to a Warp Zone in the old NES Super Mario I was ported into a different, distant Buffalo. First thing I saw was a long line of middle-class people waiting to buy tickets at the Shea box office. To my left was Melanie's Sweets, the walls covered with portraits of Elvis, everything well-lit with faint jazz in the background. I walked up the winding banistered stairwell in search of a restroom, finding the second floor all offices. I came across a men's room that turned out to be locked. I took the elevator down this time, wishing I could just take a dump there and leave it.

Stepping out of Theater Place, Buffalo hit me differently. This time I noticed all the placards advertising art and theater events. Don't know why I had missed them before.

I crossed the metro tracks and walked past the M & T building where outside loitered a pack of attractive, professionally-dressed young women smoking cigarettes. They were lovely but looked spent. You could have seen on the stiff faces that their romantic vehicles had sputtered out. Then I passed the bronze soldier with tilted hat and gun resting slack on his right arm, dedicated to veterans of the Spanish War and Philippine Insurrection. I could have seen Amazing Ayyub looking up at him like hey bro, what if a hundred years from now there's a statue of *me* on this street? And how could you reply but "that'd be fucked up, Ayyub."

Down the street further I saw one of heroic Pulaski with sword and cape like a lion's mane flowing behind him. Just the word is funny to me. *Pulaski.* There's a town named after him up north of Syracuse on the I-81.

I walked past a wig store and the Christian Science reading room, then noted a tag on one of the boarded-up storefronts reading BULLET 716 accompanied by a bullet with motion lines behind it. I still had to defecate bad. HUD office. I also had to urinate. LaFayette Court. From there it wasn't far at all before National Fuel, 455 Main.

I went in, signed my name and sat in the expanse of open chairs. Posters hung in various spots so all could clearly read the two vital messages: 1) if you leave and your name is called you must sign in again, and 2) no public restrooms. I wondered how long it would take.

In maybe fifteen minutes they called my name. I sat down in the guy's cubicle, signed whatever he gave me.

I walked out of there refreshed and bursting power, despite the physical discomfort of all my waste still inside me. Now responsible for something, my name would go on bills. My legacy in the history of that house had been sealed.

That week I sat by Amazing Ayyub as Jehangir gave khutbah.

"It feels good to be back," Ayyub whispered.

"Don't talk during khutbah," I replied in his ear.

"Oh. Okay. Sorry bro."

"Islam is fuckin' surrender," said Jehangir to the jamaat. "That's it. Being aware that you don't run the show, staying mindful of it in everything you do. Is surrender getting up off the toilet halfway through a poop to go look in your Bukhari and see how Rasullullah wiped his ass? Maybe, brothers and sisters. Insha'Allah. But to me, surrender can be laying outside at night to see shooting stars—you know what that means, right? That's another eavesdropping jinn knocked out of heaven. So lie on your back, watch and get scared, real-real scared but not of Jehennam or anything like that; get scared because this universe is being controlled by Somebody besides you. Know that, realize that, dwell on it. And then you're not scared anymore because that Somebody loves you in a way you can't even begin to comprehend.

"When Somebody's administering this creation and it's not you, what can you do? Surrender your shit. Take your hands off the wheel a second, see how it feels. What can you worry about? Insha'Allah, Mash'Allah, Subhana Allah, la ilaha illa Allahu Hayyul Qayyum. Fuck it. Allah's arranging things beyond all our grasps. The earth isn't spinning because you told it to. Your intestines aren't digesting by your command. You're made up of a trillion cells that don't ask your permission before offering their rakats. And we think submission's about applying a strict discipline to our worship? We think surrender's about not eating a pig? It's not that small to me. I can't fit my deen in a little box because to me, everything comes from Allah. Birds sing Allah's Name. To say Allah's in this book and not that one, or He likes this and not that... do you know Who you're talking about? The Allah that made you from a clot and clothed it with flesh, you know it, you've heard it. The Ayat ul-Nur and this business with the lamp, niche and olive neither East nor West? It's about people. I do zikrs counting your names on my knuckles: Yusef, Amazing Ayyub, Umar, Rabeya, all of you. *We're* the Nur, and Ghazali can eat a dick.

"Allah's too big and open for my deen to be small and closed. Does that make me a kafr? I say Allahu Akbar. If that's not good enough then fuck Islam, you can have it. Imam Husain said, 'he who has no religion, let him at least be free in his present life.' So there you go. Now let's pray."

Then he turned his back and led us.

"We're putting on a show," he told me from the front porch's recliner. I sat on the steps. It was the last day of October and he was dressed like Hulk Hogan, the post-1996 Hollywood with black penciled three-day beard and heavy blonde mustache, dumb sunglasses, black bandana, black feather boas and a toy championship belt that he'd strum like a guitar when someone put on Jimi Hendrix's "Voodoo Chile" mouthing along *Well I stand up next to a mountain/and I chop it down with the back of my hand...* " I've been calling my boys out West, y'akhi, and they're comin' like a big fuckin' caravan of taqwacore punks. These guys are nuts but they're sincere. Al-hamdulilah, because if they weren't such spiritual-types I'd never afford this shit."

"When's the show?" I asked.

"December twenty-first."

"Where?"

"The Intercontinental. You know, that place downtown."

"How many bands?"

"A shitload."

The next day it snowed. Buffalo had the ingredients to be a good writer's town: the whole dying-industry, working-class grit. Jehangir Tabari said it reminded him of Pittsburgh and Detroit. Said he knew a guy they called Pittsburgh, who actually hailed from Karachi and had never seen the yellow Allegheny bridges.

I told a girl in one of my classes that I'd drive her to the airport. Jehangir went for the ride and sat shotgun. The girl came with a friend who insisted on seeing her off. They were both freshmen; this was their first college snow.

"Remember that hippie guy in front of Pano's?" one asked the other.

"Oh my god! That guy was insane! Remember that guy in the Princeton hoodie?"

"Oh my god! That guy was nuts!" They laughed out their words. I had no shot with either of them. I was the good guy that would give rides to the airport in a pinch. That was my role. They thought Jehangir's hair was cool.

First time I ever flew, it was December so now all airports give me a nice Christmas-ish feeling.

"Cute girls," said Jehangir, sounding almost mournful. "They're at the height of their power, too."

"What do you mean?"

"Youth, y'akhi." I looked over, having never imagined that Jehangir Tabari could feel old. But right then he *looked* old, like something had worn him down without any of us noticing. "Yusef, you ever hear of Marie Laveau?"

"Nope."

"Marie Laveau, the Voo-Doo Queen of New Orleans. People go to her tomb leaving coins and food or whatever. You mark an X on it in red brick and tuck a tulip in your hair, it's supposed to do something."

"Like what?"

"Win you true love, I don't know." I could sense him going through the motions, effortlessly trudging along with no spark in his voice at all. "Ever read Buzz Sawyer?"

"Who's Buzz Sawyer?"

"He was a redneck truck-driver who got all into Sufism. A real tobaccy-chewer, you know? And an American Sufi saint. He drove big rigs all over the country in his faded blue jeans and big belt buckle and John Deere cap with a flannel shirt and plastic vest, all alone for thousands of miles at a time doing Sufi mental exercises in his cab, like reciting Holy Names all the way from New York to Colorado."

"He sounds interesting."

"Those poets like Rumi, they wrote love poetry that appeared to be about human passion but really expressed their longing for Allah. Buzz Sawyer, he wrote these really lusty poems about truck-stop whores who would CB truckers and fuck them at prearranged meeting points. It gets quite dirty actually but that's his expression of the same idea. He's really searching for his Beloved."

"That's awesome."

"He's out there right now."

"Wow."

"He was a Sufi of the Uwayysi Mashrab. You know what that is?"

"No."

"The Way of Uwayys. You know who he was?"

"No."

"Uwayys-i-Gharan, a shepherd in the time of Rasullullah. He never met Muhammad personally, but received guidance from him through telepathy or something. So it became like a whole big thing: following not a physical teacher, but the spirit of Muhammad himself."

"Oh."

"Uwayysi Sufism. No school, no shaykh, no tariqa. It's just you out there on the road by yourself."

"Makes a lot of sense."

When we got back Jehangir dug around in his room and found a Buzz Sawyer poem that he had photocopied right out of the book he had borrowed. The piece was untitled.

right now
here in the bayt ul-waffle
staring down
three long strips
of bacon,
i make du'a.

i love allah,
and muhammad
is a dead bird on the sidewalk
but i mean that
in a beautiful way,
in the tawhid way.
so knowing that,
i love muhammad too.

sallallaho alayhe wa salaam.

to avoid
greasing up
my pen,
i eat
with the left.

"Buzz Sawyer had mixed feelings about being a Muslim poet,"

said Jehangir.

"Why?"

"Because Prophet Muhammad said, 'it's better for your belly to be filled with pus than poetry.'"

"Oh."

While watching Conan O'Brien it occurred to me that we were in Ramadan. It's easy to forget when you keep odd hours. We all fasted but when you wake up at noon and go to bed at four in the morning, I'm not sure if it counts. At any rate, when the sun was up we didn't eat. Umar did it hardcore, getting himself up before the sun rose every day. At least it was winter and the days were short.

"There's a gate in Jenna that opens only for those who fast," he explained.

I miss when things were easy. Before I moved into that house, my concept of Islam was quite simply defined. I knew what it was and what it wasn't, even if my actual lifestyle lurked somewhere in between. At least I was aware of it.

"Dude, dude bro!" yelped Amazing Ayyub with panic and a hand on the dashboard as Jehangir rolled to the first in a long line of stop signs. Jehangir wore a brown wool pakul, earning him looks from passerby who had only seen the hat on CNN Talibans. "Dude man, on campus you gotta make complete stops. The campus cops are everywhere, they'll get you."

"Okay." Jehangir got up to the next sign slow and methodical, pressed his foot on the brake a full Mississippi, looked both ways and moved on. It was barely a hundred feet before the one after that.

"It's 4:20," said Fasiq from the back seat.

"Gotta wait til the sun goes down," Jehangir replied.

"Oh yeah."

"Nothing can pass the lips," said Ayyub. "That means Muzammil can't give blowjobs, haha."

"Ayyub, man," said Jehangir. "That shit's not cool."

"I'm sorry."

"Subhana Allah," said Fasiq. "Once the sun's down I'm getting SHIT FACED." In fact, that was the purpose of our drive. We were on our way to the liquor store on Grant with the big white horse out front.

"Bro," said Ayyub, "if you're gonna screw around don't do it on campus, it's like a different government here man. It's a fuckin' police state." We arrived at the liquor store and Jehangir parked in the bank's parking lot across the street. Ayyub made a comment about how *ghetto* Buffalo was, then darted in front of a grimy bus, hopped on the store's wooden white horse, and acted like he was humping it.

The entrance of the store looked like a classroom with school-style plastic desks occupied by sketchy old characters with eyes on the electronic gambling screen hanging from the ceiling. Alcohol is a foreign culture to me. Was then, is now, always will be. Fasiq grabbed his Beefeater like an old pro. Ayyub bought a vinegar sausage stick, the kind with the fiery packaging. He made a joke about the fire symbolizing Jehennam, the place Allah would send you for eating sausage.

Back outside on Grant, Ayyub gave a repeat performance of simulated bestiality, yelling in his special crazy voices. "Buffalo's dead!" he hollered. "Once I buy my truck, I'm taking us all out West." I thought about all the bums playing lotto sitting empty and hopeless in their grade-school desks inside the store. Made me feel good to be a clean-livered Muslim. I'll admit that religion can be dumb sometimes, but there's really no positive argument you can make on behalf of liquor. "It's so fucking COLD," shrieked Ayyub. "What the shit are we doing in Buffalo? Our ancestors are from warm places, bro. I'm not meant for this shit."

"If I ever see you drink," Jehangir said with a handful of my jacket, "if I ever hear of you having so much as a spoonful of beer, so help me I'll kick your fucking ass."

"That's fair," I replied, unable to hold in my smile. I loved it when Jehangir got into his whole big-brother complex.

"It's got me by the balls," he continued. "But you're still good because you don't know what it's like to be drunk."

"Okay."

"While you're at it, stay off the pussy too. It's like those fuckin' potato chips, y'akhi. You can't eat just one."

"I'll remember that."

In Muzammil Sadiq's dorm room, he and Jehangir considered possible bands for the taqwacore show as Propagandhi's "Fuck Religion" played in the background. With nothing to contribute I eventually zoned out of the conversation altogether. My eyes stuck at the flag on his wall: rainbow stripes, red orange yellow green blue purple, with a shiny bronze star-and-crescent in the middle.

Dialogue floated through my head without any of it registering.

"Vote Hezbollah," said one of them—I wasn't involved enough to know which. "We gotta have those guys."

"And Eight from the Ukil." A pause as their name was written down.

"The Mutaweens."

"Hell yeah, and the fuckin' Imran Khan Experience."

"Cool."

"Probably the Zaqqums and Bin Qarmats, they're both pretty good bands."

"The Zaqqums are straightedge, right?"

"I think so. But they don't really sound it."

"Burning Books for Cat Stevens."

"Yeah."

"We got the Ghilmans down."

"Get the Wilden Mukhalloduns too."

"Right."

"The Infibulateds."

"Who?"

"The Infibulateds."

"What's their deal?"

"They're this riot grrrl band dealing with sex and gender issues. Most of their songs are along those lines. Like how a female can't express her sexuality to any extent and still maintain Islamic dignity, a girl who enjoys sex and would freely talk about it must automatically be suffering from low self-esteem, shit like that, they just fuckin' tear all that apart."

"Nice."

"How about Osama bin Laden's Tunnel Diggers?"

"Yeah, definitely. Have you ever seen those guys? They fuckin' rock."

For some reason that pulled me back to the conversation.

I knew the band's name didn't mean anything. Punk bands gave themselves dumb names all the time, whether to be funny or for shock value. There were bands called the Child Molesters, the Nipple Erectors, the White SS, the Sniveling Shits, Raped. But still it made me think of the man.

His image popped easy enough in my head. The long beard made his face almost seem narrower. Eyes quietly magnetic. Extended index finger in limp holy point. White turban, camouflaged field jacket over white jalab. He had the right look to be a Che in other hemispheres, portraits unassuming but baronial, with t-shirts and posters and his own action figure.

"How about Bilal's Boulder?" mused Jehangir.

"Shit no," said Muzammil. "Those guys are assholes."

"Yeah, they kind of are. They're a pretty good band, though."

"Bilal's Boulder? They don't even allow girls at their shows!"

"Yeah, but they're taqwacore."

"I don't know, bro. That might cause some problems."

"Well we're telling them it's an all-gender show right off the bat, and if they don't like it then they don't have to come."

"Some of the other bands are going to piss them off."

"That's too bad," said Jehangir. "I don't want to exclude anybody."

"These guys are total cocks."

"I know, y'akhi. But the whole point of taqwacore is that Islam can take any shape you want it to. If we deny a band their spot because we don't like their attitudes or their interpretation, then we're no better then all the Conformist Chickenshit imams out there."

"Okay," said Muzammil. "Bilal's Boulder, cool."

The three of us drove around Buffalo in Jehangir's car, hitting the broken-down decayed parts of town. Jehangir had his Rancid tape in, starting at "The War's End." Went down Tonawanda Street and the giant porn shop with big yellow billboard-style placards all over it. *Adult Videos. Over 75,000 titles.* The wind pushing gusts of snow off closed-down factory roofs. Whole streets of shameful redbrick cubes with plywood windows. Everything seemed to wear a layered-on film of grime and grease that would take dump trucks of lye to remove. Jehangir's brown wool pakul gave the drive a third-world hardness look. Third-World Buffalo. Drove by a lot with weeds poking up out of the snow and could still see the concrete outline of where something used to be. Four steps that might have once led to a door. Half-buried shopping carts. Tires. Palettes. Orange cones. Plenty of useful things stacked up in ignored pyramid-piles. Bricks, concrete cylinders, metal pipes. A skeletal car with all four doors open, everything torched so you couldn't even know what color it used to be, the seats gone and a mass of red wires under what used to be the dashboard. In the surrounding background, more buildings with windows boarded or even bricked.

"Wish Amazing Ayyub was here," said Jehangir, "to tell us how dead Buffalo is."

"Yeah," said Muzammil.

"Remember that dog Fasiq found?" Jehangir asked me.

"Ilm?"

"Yeah, Ilm. Ilm the Dog."

"Yeah."

"You think he's still alive?"

"No, probably not."

"Insha'Allah. Lake Erie winter, y'akhi. All these California bands don't know what they're getting into. Just the other day Rabeya was complaining that Muslim clothes are so paper-thin… they don't make shalwar kameezes for Buffalo."

From there we went to the Galleria Mall, where smiling Jehangir had his picture taken on Santa's lap. Pulled out of the parking lot to the sounds of Uncool's "Finale," Jehangir holding his Polaroid on the edges.

Back at the house I considered another romp with my right hand when Jehangir popped in my room.

"Got something for you," he said, tossing a book my way. I caught it and examined the cover with cheesy old illustration of some Flash Gordon type villain sneering sinister with his laser gun and the title in big bold obsolete font. *Twenty-Four Septendecillion*, by Abu Afak.

"What's this?"

"The great Islamic pulp novel," Jehangir replied. "It's from the 1940s—the heyday of *Amazing Stories* and all that shit, the shit that guys like Ray Bradbury grew up on. Abu Afak, he was like a fuckin' philosopher disguising his ideas in cornball outer-space stories. He was like Islam's Robert Heinlein."

"So what's this one about?"

"Muslims landing on Pluto."

"Ohhhhh-kay…"

"It's cool, check it out. It's like, in the future where Pakistan's the world superpower. The main character grows up in this fictional city called Jinnahabad where his dad's the muezzin of the largest masjid in the world, and then he ends up being an astronaut on the first-ever expedition to Pluto and after taking the first human steps on its surface he gives the adhan."

"Interesting."

"Give it a chance."

He left and I sat on the bed with Abu Afak. The pages were brownish-yellow and smelled musty.

CHAPTER VIII

The crew looked outside at the ice dunes that reflected their ship's blinking lights. With every pounding heartbeat as the landscape was illuminated for a brief flash they saw their captain's silhouette in the glow. He did not look back. His eyes were wet and the hairs on the back of his neck stood on end as he raised his hands to his bubble-helmet. Allahu Akbar, Allahu Akbar! His voice cracked. Allahu Akbar, Allahu Akbar! He did not expect to become the holiest man of his time but he did, largely by default.

As his cry on the solar system's outer rim blared home to a broken, hunched-over umma he remembered his father's adhan blaring from the minarets of Masjid 'Alamin. Now he, too, was a muezzin.

Allahu Akbar. Allahu Akbar. La ilaha illa Allah.

Then all was still on cold Pluto, while in considerably sunnier Pakistan believers made their wudhu.

—Abu Afak, *Twenty-Four Septendecillion*

Buffalo winter.

Snow came so constant it never had a chance to get dirty. Came down light and harmless but added up on the ground. Covered the roads and made your car's rear tires swing a different direction than the front.

Road salt stained everything. Cars, parking lots, the bottoms of your pantlegs. The sky looked like that too.

President McKinley was assassinated in this town, by an anarchist named Leon Czolgosz.

Jehangir and Fasiq hid their more or less bald skulls in various headwear. Fasiq's kifaya scarf made from a necktie and old NOFX shirt covered his ears and wrapped around his neck. Jinnah caps and black ski hats, standard. With brown wool pakul and jacket spikes Jehangir resembled a post-apocalyptic mujahideen like the Taliban met *Mad Max*.

He kept on pushing toward his show, making phone calls and arrangements and pulling it all together between a date, a venue and however many bands. What really amazed me was that all of Jehangir's force and ambition could blossom in a town like this: home to industrial decay and four Super Bowl chokes, rotten weather and smells of crack cocaine cooking outside. I had never known the smell before living on that street. It's like sweet dog food.

Back to Buffalo winter. The bathroom window stayed closed. Skateboards were shelved. Spending all our time inside, each of us had interludes of being sick of everyone else.

I took to chronic masturbation. The routine repeated itself at least twice a day. Obligatory pre-game urination, handful of toilet paper for the wipe-up, locking of the door, unveiling of *Victoria's Secret*, focus on the same pictures almost every time.

Sometimes I felt bad—usually in the split-second following ejaculation. Right after you spill it, you forget why you had ever needed to in the first place. Once I swore off self-abuse but made it barely twenty-four hours before striking a deal with myself: jerking was fine, but without the aid of supermodels in lingerie. I threw out the catalog and touched myself to its memory. Within a week I hit the mall and bought another.

I once walked in on the girls when they were talking about it. The clitoris serves no other purpose, Rabeya preached to Fatima. It's your body. How can you be open to someone else touching you but then can't touch yourself?

I turned around to dip quick out of the kitchen.

"Wait, Yusef," Rabeya called. "Sit with us a sec."

"Ok."

"I want to ask you something."

"Sure."

"Do you jerk off?" Fatima looked down at the table.

"Whoa," I replied. "I don't know if—"

"C'mon, we're big kids. You like girls, right?"

"Of course."

"But you're not doing anyone."

"No."

"So you're taking care of your shit, right? You're not all backed-up I hope. That just leads to nasty attitudes."

"No. I mean, sure. Yeah, I do."

"You masturbate."

"Yeah."

"I think masturbation's different for guys than for girls," Fatima interjected.

"Maybe," said Rabeya. "But what does that have to do with you being afraid to touch your own freakin' anatomy?"

"Has anyone made Asr?" I asked. "I think it's time, I'm not sure though."

"No," they both answered at once.

"I don't really feel like it," said Rabeya. She knew what I was thinking. "And no, it's not my period."

One of the diners off Elmwood Avenue had a promotion offering free ice cream whenever it snowed. Jehangir, Fasiq, Ayyub and I went when the snow was still manageable.

"It's not snowing," argued the manager.

"What are you talking about?" scoffed Jehangir. "Look outside!"

"That's freezing rain."

"Bullshit MAN!" freaked Ayyub.

We walked out and the manager saved himself four free ice creams. Amazing Ayyub ran around the parking lot throwing his arms up and shrieking like a nut. "THAT'S FUCKING BULLSHIT!" he yelled at a passing car. "DON'T EAT HERE THEY'RE FUCKIN' CHEAP ASSHOLES." Fasiq went to a small hill of snow that had been shoved into a corner by the plow, grabbing himself a dirty handful. He then went back in the diner, only to emerge with the same snow now in a cup with cherry-flavored syrup on it.

"Look, Ayyub," said Fasiq, getting him to stop his crazy-man dance. "They gave me a free sno-cone."

"No shit! I'm getting one too."

"Don't worry about it, man. Take mine."

"Are you sure?"

"Yeah. Rock it out, bro."

"Thanks Fasiq." Ayyub took the cup and spoon and went to town.

"How is it?" asked Jehangir, lips posed unnaturally to hold in the laugh.

"It's good man. Fuckin' cherry with chocolate bits."

The three of us simultaneously howled. "What's so funny, guys?"

Then we went to Target so Jehangir could buy Christmas lights for his room.

I spent Thanksgiving break in Syracuse. The two-hour drive from Jehangir to my parents was essentially a straight line down I-90 East. It was cold at home and we had *some* snow but no Lake Erie effect.

That Friday I went to our regular masjid less than a mile from the Carrier Dome. It had lost all its religiousness, but not in a bad way. I felt towards the place the way you might look at your old elementary school: a museum of my more innocent years, a comfortable naiveté that you could wrap all around yourself and hide in for an hour or two. Back when that mosque was my world, it was a nicer world. Abi sat by me for jumaa. Ummi was off somewhere, wherever they put the women.

At first glance nothing had changed. The carpeting, walls, mihrab, calligraphy, place for your shoes, fliers on the bulletin board for protests and Islamic clothing. It threw me off a little to see unfamiliar faces. Couldn't help but feel that a new generation was creeping in on my turf. Just by their newness they were improper and inappropriate.

At least we had the same imam. I have heard very few khutbahs in my life that were delivered with any sort of enthusiasm. That day's was not one of them. Came out dry and flat but even this fueled my warm spot for the place.

Then the imam addressed the room's large number of college students. There are many dangers facing us, he said. Alcohol, drugs, mixing of men and women. If you cared about your deen, he explained, you would have no kafr friends. The word came to me like a slur. **Kafr**. It's an ugly word. I think it's meant to sound ugly. Maybe it's just ugly because we use it in ugly ways. There are varying pronunciations, but they're all ugly. **Kafr. Kafeer. Kafirun.** It's our us-and-them word to push *them* away. Don't listen to that, that's *kafr* thinking. President so-and-so has sold us out to the *kafrs*. It's so difficult raising your children Muslim in *KAFR* society. The *kafrs* and their alcohol. The *kafrs* and their teen pregnancy. That's a *kafr* problem. Good thing we're Muslims.

I thought about Rabeya not praying because she didn't feel like it, and Jehangir the womanizing boozehound, and Muzammil the liwatiyyun, Fasiq Abasa the hashishiyyun calling himself with a bad name like Fasiq Abasa, Fatima fearing for her hymen with Jehangir's hand at the threshold, Amazing Ayyub spitting at football players; what would the imam call them? Did they count as kafr friends? I knew I was Muslim, though still not a good one. But these guys, they took it to a whole new level. Lynn was a kafr, I knew that. Reading Sufi poets doesn't make you Muslim. Rumi wasn't the Prophet, as Umar would say.

Now Umar, he was Muslim. But he didn't look it.

Apart from the masjid and a brief excursion to the mall, I spent the whole Thanksgiving break in my parents' house living out of my duffle bag, watching television, studying occasionally and enjoying free food. I found one of Fasiq's hoodies smuggled among my clothes. The front said "Wesley Willis" and the back featured Wesley's giant laughing face and the words, "Good News is Rock n' Roll." I did not know who Wesley Willis was.

"He's the Qutb," replied Fasiq when I asked.

"Besides that," said Jehangir, "he's a rock star from Chicago. Put out over sixty albums and wrote two thousand songs."

"Wesley's awesome," said Rabeya.

"He whups the camel's ass with a belt!" boomed Fasiq in what I imagined was an imitation of him.

"He can really rock it out," said Jehangir in the same voice. "He is a rock star in God's joy world."

"He can rock it to Russia," Fasiq added.

I wore the Wesley hoodie to what would become, after upcoming construction, the largest mall in North America. It was in the history section at Borders Books that I received my first comment.

"Yo," said a girl behind me. "That hoodie is HOT." I turned around. She was a short South Asian with shoulder-length black hair. Her jacket and the strap of her big purse were decorated with band buttons. I could not tell how old she was, but knew she was younger than me.

"You like Wesley Willis?" I asked.

"I LOVE Wesley Willis!" I noticed that when people say they *love* Wesley Willis, they intonate it like he's an actual guy down the street. "Rock n' Roll McDonalds, Chicken Cow, he's the Shit."

"Yeah he is."

"Your mullet is the reason people hate you," she bellowed in the same voice Jehangir and Fasiq did. "Take your ass to the barbershop. Tell the barber that you're sick of looking like an ASSHOLE!" I laughed to feign knowledge of what any of that had meant. One of her buttons said *sXe.*

"You're straightedge?" I asked, proud that at least I was cool enough to get *that.*

"Yep-pers."

"Me too."

"Yayyy!" I could not tell if she were being sarcastic or just cute.

"My name's Yusef, by the way."

"I'm Fareeha."

"Nice to meet you."

"Likewise."

"So... have you always been straightedge?"

"I had a cigarette in seventh grade, but other than that yeah."

"I had a cigar in spring 1998," I replied. "But that's it." I read her buttons. The Lindsey Diaries. After School Knife Fight. Black Paper Diary. Poison the Well. A Life Once Lost. Beloved. Between the Buried and Me. A mess more bands and one reading NEVER APOLOGIZE FOR YOUR ART.

"Nice. Well, I guess I'll catch you later." She then walked away. I spent the rest of the day wondering if I should have asked for her number.

The next day I shaved my testicles. I don't know why. I also shaved around the base of my penis, which Jehangir had once told me would make it seem larger. Umar had often said it was *fard* to remove your pubic hair.

My bald scrotum had the texture of those red stress-relief things you'd buy at Spencer's Gifts. You know, where it has protuberances almost resembling a face and you can squeeze or pull on it and it slowly returns to the original shape. I think it was due to my balls retracting from the cold of shaving cream and water. Usually they just drooped.

Al-hamdulilah, the I-90 was okay for my drive back. When I returned to the punk house I found a mid-20's Arab on our porch.

He stood tall and confident in a spiked leather jacket like Jehangir's but green, blue jeans, Doc Martens, white cotton kufi. His white t-shirt bore the cover design for Rancid's *...And Out Come the Wolves* album with the spray-painted red stencil lettering and the mohawk-punk with tattooed arms sitting on the steps with his face buried in his lap.

Most interesting about the man: his beard was half off. On one side it went full mufti-length. On the other he had completely shaved it.

"As-salaamu alaikum," I said going up the steps.

"Wa alaikum as-salaam, brother. I'm Harun."

"I'm Yusef."

"Yes, mash'Allah."

"You met Harun?" asked Jehangir as the screen door swung open.

"Just now," I replied.

"You know who this guy is? He's a fuckin' cult hero in California. Legendary zine writer, right? He travels the country hoppin' trains and hitchhiking or bummin' rides off friends and lives off dumpsters, sleeps in masjids, stays in youth hostels, befriends hoboes, rides with truckers and Tablighs and his whole life is just a big sociological experiment."

"Wow," I said.

"This guy and his fuckin' zines are nuts. His shit's going to be the canon for taqwacore ten years from now, it'll be like the fuckin' Muwatta or some shit."

"Staghfir'Allah," said Harun.

"Harun," said Jehangir, "tell him why you shave half the beard."

"Oh, right," said Harun. "You see, during the time of the Crusades, when Muslim soldiers were captured, the Christians would shave off half their beards and then send them back to their homelands like that. It was intended as a complete disgrace. These troops would have to return to their wives and families looking like emasculated half-men."

"Damn," I said.

"So the reason I shave half my beard," he continued, "is to highlight the current condition of our umma today. For a variety of reasons, some from external forces and some killing us from within, the Muslims are stripped of their power and respect."

"Harun's crashing on Ayyub's old couch until the show," Jehangir explained. "Then he's putting it all down in his zine. This shit's gonna be immortal, bro."

Harun and Jehangir got drunk that night and regaled us all with stories of their separate travels and shared experiences in California.

"Remember Bloody?" Harun asked.

"Hell yeah!" Jehangir yelled with eyes half open. "Bloody's still around, from what I hear."

"Where did you guys ever find him?"

"He'd been around awhile."

"Crazy shit, that guy," said Harun. "But one thing I'll give 'im: he's fuckin' fearless, fuckin' crazier than a shithouse rat. I've seen Bloody do things at shows—shit, not even shows; he'll pull the same shit in a diner or fuckin' kindergarten for all he cares but man, you wouldn't believe."

"We've seen him test Allah's patience many a time," said Jehangir.

"But you know, a guy like Bloody is proof that Islam has lost its creative drive."

"What do you mean?" asked Rabeya.

"Because they can't handle someone who startles and scares. If

Bloody were to step into a regular old masjid," Harun replied, "you know it'd just be a matter of time before somebody said to him, 'you know brother, it's not sunna for you to carry a bad name like Bloody, you should pick a nice name like… oh, Muhammad.' And they'd take his jacket, you know they'd take his jacket. And do something with his hair. And give him leather socks. But shit, Bloody'd just punch 'em all in the brains, every last one of 'em."

"So there's going to be how many bands staying here?" Umar asked Jehangir.

"I don't quite know yet. A shitload, I think."

"Where are they all going to sleep?"

"In the living room, in the dining room. In the halls. Under the kitchen table."

"Some of these taqwacores are girls?"

"Yeah."

"And you have liwaticore bands coming?"

"A couple, yeah."

"And they're all sleeping out here together? Guys, girls and liwats?"

"Yep."

"You see, brother," said Jehangir with a hand on Umar's shoulder, "I was worried about the men and women together, and that's why I invited the liwats. The liwats are going to corrupt all the men and turn *them* liwat, and the women will be safe, insha'Allah." Sarcasm had become the only way anyone could deal with Umar.

The next week all four members of One Trip Abroad showed up in their sticker-covered van. Jehangir ran out, flew over the porch steps and hugged them like old friends. He threw his arm around a spike-haired Syrian who I later learned was the lead singer, Dee Dee Ali. He sported a navy blue pea coat over baggy pants with Union Jacks all over them. Red suspenders hung at his hips. Safety-pin in his nose like two-dimensional stereotype Hollywood punks. Behind him three likewise, one carrying a big bulky guitar case.

Dee Dee Ali's knee-high leather boots curled at the toe like a genie.

"You got the Iron Sheik boots!" shrieked Jehangir. "Holeeee shit! That's hot, brother, wow—"

"Got them from the guy who makes 'em for wrestlers," replied Dee Dee Ali.

"Amazing," said Jehangir. "We used to talk about that shit *all* the time." I could observe from the giddy schoolboy smile that Dee Dee Ali was for Jehangir what Jehangir provided me: the mantled big-brother invincible with Persian fire-halo and football-star heroics. He was also, from what I gathered, how Jehangir Tabari might have liked to view himself.

"Look at this nonsense," said Dee Dee Ali with a gesture to the white streets. "What the shit is with this?"

"Welcome to Buffalo," replied Jehangir.

"We're the coldest Muslims on the fuckin' planet."

Inside Dee Dee Ali saw Harun and Harun saw Dee Dee Ali and they raced to each other like long-lost brothers. Between the three Khalifornians something special had just happened that made me at once warm and jealous to see it. Dee Dee Ali and the rest of his band sat in the living room, the guy with the guitar case opening it up to unveil the acoustic. As he strummed and Jehangir stood beaming, Dee Dee Ali belted out a taqwacore anthem. *I see*

Muhammad down at the corner store/rockin' on Galaga, getting the high score/when he delivers sermons the kids think he's a bore/but when he smashes idols, everyone cheers for more—

Muhammad was a punk rocker/he tore everything down/Muhammad was a punk rocker/and he rocked that town…

Sitting on the sidewalk in front of the liquor store on Grant, the one with the white horse—Ayyub, me and One Trip Abroad's bass player, a feral head of curly black hair with wildman's beard speckled by tufts of gray. Six foot eight, three hundred pounds but wiry and agile like he could just up and dropkick your face off with big furry boots. Beyond our little sheltered patch of dry pavement everything was covered in snow or wet with melting snow and slush. I looked across the street at a pair of dirty, poverty-costumed, late-middle-aged Hispanic men standing in discussion by the bank and then heard a physically uncomfortable sound that just got louder and louder as though some horrible machine was on its way—like shaking rocks in a tin can in front of eleven microphones—and I honestly got scared as it came near. Then past the bank and old Puerto Ricans rode a black boy on a bike with no tires.

The three of us watched him ride on tirelessly down Grant, his ass hovering above the seat.

"Buffalo's dying," said Ayyub. "Time to get outta here." However, he was soon distracted. "Look at that dog over there. That's a big dog. You'd have to shoot a gun eight or nine times to kill that dog."

"Alcohol," said the bass player without provocation, "is the curse on American sex."

"What?" I asked. Something about him—maybe the holy beard—made him look like his opinion actually weighed something.

"America's so fucked about sex," the bassist explained, "that the guys need alcohol for confidence and girls need alcohol to drop all their ingrained hang-ups. So by the time people get to banging, their brains are so dulled by beer that there's no personality or spirit to anything they do and they're just like two humping animals."

"Wow," I said.

"In Europe they're much healthier about everything," said the bassist. "Sex, drugs, drink—Europeans are cool, they're just chill about it. Americans can't get over this whole rebelling-against-the-parents complex. It's pretty childish." I saw a trace of Jehangir-ness in his urge for spontaneous philosophizing and wondered if all taqwacores carried the same mournful rugged romanticism.

"What's that shit on your forehead?" asked Ayyub, causing me to study the bassist myself. Above his eyes crinkled a virtual road map of ancient scars.

"Qumma-zani," he replied.

I felt self-conscious about masturbating with our new guests in the house but went ahead and shook my pipick knowing it'd only get worse once all the other bands showed up. I got over the post-ejaculatory guilt and would come downstairs relaxed and somehow more confident. Perhaps it was that any sexually interesting females I might encounter had temporarily lost their hold on me.

The vans came streaming down the interstates, knowing whatever big cities they rumbled through only by the big flat green signs reading in the same font everywhere. It all looked the same. Road and more road. Rest stop parking lots for sleep. When one van broke down its cargo and passengers were distributed evenly among the rest. They came strong and steady like a caravan, like Bedouins across the Hejaz.

They wore kifayas and knit ski caps, turbans and Aqua Net mohawks. They were dirty and rugged, their bodies wearing the grime of roads: sweat, oil, stale salty odors; their insides wrecked with Mobile station cuisine: vinegar sausage sticks, potato chips, thirty-five cent cinnamon buns, Pepsi; their brains worn down by bad sleep and lack of stimulation from the Eisenhower System landscapes; their bodies growing hard and mean as they went from a warm place to a cold place.

The vans lined up along our street. It was Thursday, December nineteenth.

Every room downstairs was crowded with taqwacores. There were maybe forty new characters, all of them presumably sleeping over for the next two nights. Jehangir had no idea where they'd all go, but they weren't the type to complain about sleeping on a crowded floor.

I viewed each face only in terms of what band he or she came with. It was like the United Nations. "The bass player for the Mutaweens now has the floor…"

One guy stood out: a big barnhouse African in GBH t-shirt, DogPile pants and Doc Martens. He could have been three hundred pounds but it was solid and strong. I felt like a child shaking his hand. He hit a room hard with the kind of awesome imposition that Umar wished he could pull off. I could have pictured him as a third-world dictator with gold epaulets on each shoulder and a wide red sash across his chest. His name was Mahdi and he played the drums for Osama bin Laden's Tunnel Diggers. He came from Chad, which I think left an impression on me because you rarely hear about Chad. All I knew about the place was that Qadhafi had once invaded it.

As I walked through my house feeling more like an anthropologist than actual member of this strange society, I could not help but note one detail setting these taqwacores apart from your average punk—one article figuring prominently in almost every costume—one symbol jumping out at me from t-shirt iron-ons, necklaces, patches and even tattooed forearms, calling my attention away from eyes and faces and names so all I saw was *it*—usually in blue and white—with all its years of meaning: good meaning, bad meaning, burning-flag protest meaning, evil occupiers shooting AK-47s at boys with rocks meaning, the meaning my imams gave it, the meaning my parents gave it, the meaning it carried every time I ever saw it in an Islamic magazine.

The symbol was this:

"I don't understand," I said to Jehangir, pointing to a huge one on the back of some guy's leather jacket.

"Pretty punk rawk, huh?"

"The Star of David?"

"Bro, it's like back in '77. The old-school punks like Iggy Pop and Sid Vicious, they used to wear the swastika and all this Nazi bullshit. Doesn't mean they were racists or anything like that—they were just trying to piss people off, make passersby on the street uncomfortable. So if this is Muslim Punk, and our community and audience is all fuckin' Muslim, what symbol's more unsettling than the Star of fuckin' David? Doesn't mean any of these guys are Zionists or anti-Palestinian fuckin' whatever, it's just to get a reaction."

"But what's the point?" I challenged. "With Sid wearing the swastika or these guys wearing the Star—beyond offending people, what's it all for?"

"What do you mean?" he replied as though amazed I had not yet grasped the concept.

"Why the need to rile everyone up?"

"Because it's fun."

Punk rock means deliberately bad music, deliberately bad clothing, deliberately bad language and deliberately bad behavior. Means shooting yourself in the foot when it comes to every expectation society will ever have for you but still standing tall about it, loving who you are and somehow forging a shared community with all the other fuck-ups.

Taqwacore is the application of this virtue to Islam. I was surrounded by deliberately bad Muslims but they loved Allah with a gonzo kind of passion that escaped sleepy brainless ritualism and the dumb fantasy-camp Islams claiming that our deen had some inherent moral superiority making the world rightfully ours.

I think it's a good thing.

There's no room in taqwacore for half-assed Muslims playing off as though they never miss a prayer. The ones who live pseudo-cool and then come to the masjid wearing masks. They're weak and have no real personality and taqwacores would eat them alive. If you don't pray, don't pretend. Don't build a complex thinking you're beneath all the Super Mumins of the world because you went to the prom and think you have to hide it from everyone. Be Muslim on your own terms. Tell the world to eat a dick.

Look at me, saying this. I stand for almost everything that taqwacore is not. But I fake it reasonably well.

Riding in the back seat of Fatima's car—Fasiq took shotgun—to the liquor store on Grant Street, Fasiq reading Sufi-ness into Fatima's Saves the Day ("In 'At Your Funeral' he says *the food that celebrates your end* is a fuckin' pig, you know? It's like Muhammad's dying, it's the end of Shari'a") and Islam's plight in Moxy Fruvous ("D'you hear that? *I'm telling you I was the King of Spain... now I eat humble pie...* "). I was beginning to accept that Allah spoke to Fasiq through weed and song lyrics. Why not?

Returned home with armfuls of liquor for the guests.

"You're about to see how it really is," warned Jehangir as he passed out clear-bottled Coronas to waiting Muslim hands. The taqwacores were all loud. I didn't hear a damn thing anybody said. Someone turned on the music, beginning with the Germs' "Fuck You" but it just drowned into everything else. There were a mess of girls. Some covered up completely like Rabeya. Others wore regular hejabs but decorated them with band patches. On one I saw a Bettie Page button.

A skinny, wiry punk with a war-torn forty-year-old face, barbell in his septum and high black mohawk with the rest of his hair growing into a crew-cut turned to me, grabbed me by the neck and I watched his mouth move though I couldn't hear anything he said. I looked at him with puzzled eyes. He pulled me closer and yelled.

"As-salaamu alaikum!"

"Wa alaikum as-salaam," I yelled back.

"I'm the fuckin' proof of everything this whole fuckin' shit says."

"What do you mean?"

"Everything Islam tells you to do," he screamed into my ear

with beer breath, "let me tell you something: you *do* it, or else you end up like me. The Qur'an forbids alcohol, right? Look at me, bro. I've crashed cars, got my nose busted a fuckload of times and once I threw up right on a bitch as I was going knuckle-deep in her dirty little twat. That's right, I got my fuckin' puke in her hair and all on her shirt. But Islam tells you to keep your thing dry until you're married, right? Bro—you know how many haram cunts I've had? And now I have green shit coming out of my dick at all hours of the fuckin' day and I got cauliflowers growin' on my asshole. And do I have fuckin' kids out there somewhere? Shit if I know, fuckin' sad-sack bastards. So there you have it, man. Read your fuckin' Qur'an."

"Okay."

"I'm telling you that because I love you."

"Thank you, brother."

"You ever read?"

"Read what?"

"I dunno… books?"

"Yeah, sometimes."

"Here." He reached into the back pocket of his tight jeans and pulled out a beaten-up old flimsy paperback. "You ever read this guy?"

The author's name was Abu Afak. The book was titled *The Rose Gardens of Mars.*

"Yeah," I replied. "I've never seen this one, though."

"He's a fucked-up dude," said the punk. "He was like a fuckin' science-fiction guy, you know what I'm saying? He wrote about the fuckin' future."

"So what's this book about?"

"It's fuckin'… Christ, it's about the future and in the future Saudi is the fuckin', fuckin' where America is now… you know what I mean? Saudi rules the world. So Saudi leads the colonization of Mars. And when they're colonizing Mars they find all these fuckin' Martians, right? And the Saudis, the first thing that comes to their minds is whether or not these fuckin' Martians have the free will to choose between Islam and kafr... because if they do, then it's the Saudis' responsibility to give the Martians daw'ah and bring them to Islam, insha'Allah."

"That sounds interesting."

"So yeah, fuckin'... they have this big conference of scholars and shit in Riyadh, and they debate whether or not the Martians have souls, and this that and the other thing, all that fuckin' mullah bullshit—"

I saw the door open and four more taqwacores come in. Everything stopped. Each of them wore a headwrap. Full beard, shaved mustache. Heavy winter coats leaving their jalabs visible from the waist down. They didn't look anything like a punk band except for their mean eyes.

"As-salaaaaaaamu alaikum," yelled Jehangir, running to them with open arms and a Corona in his left hand, "wa rahmatullahi wa barakatuh!" He wrapped himself around one of them in a big brotherly hug that left the guy unsure of what to do.

"Wa alaikum as-salaam wa rahmatullahi wa barakatuh," he replied coolly.

"Hey everybody," proclaimed Jehangir with his left arm around the poor Muslim, peering from the corners of his eyes at Jehangir's Corona. "It's fuckin' Bilal's Boulder!" The room gave salaams of varying confidence.

"Brother," said the one by Jehangir. "We just came to say hello. We're sleeping in our van."

"Are you fuckin' nuts?" shrieked Jehangir. "We have plenty of room here—well, not *plenty* of room but we got a big-ass house, what's four more guys—"

"Brother, al-hamdulilah. Thank you so much but we are sleeping in the van, insha'Allah."

"Yo y'akhi it's fuckin' freezing out there. You guys don't really know how it gets here in Buffalo, so why don't you just stay in and—"

"We are okay, brother." And with that they turned around to go right back out the door.

"What's with that?" asked somebody.

"I've never seen such scary dudes speakin' so gently," said Rabeya.

"They're a different bunch," replied Jehangir, his eyes stuck on the closed door.

"They're a buncha cocks," said Muzammil.

"They're decent guys," said Jehangir. "They'll give you anything. If all they have to give you is a fuckin' Bic pen, they'll fork it over. But they're a little rough to deal with sometimes—"

"Hatemongers, Jehangir. Fuckin' bigots. If they had their way I'd be tossed from a minaret." Jehangir paused for a moment.

"Yeah," he said softly. "Yeah, Muzammil. They hate you. And they hate me too. They hate all of us for something. Me for the beer in my hand, you for the cock in your mouth, Rabeya for having her clitoris intact. We're all doing something haram. Look at us. We're the ones that have always been fuckin' excluded, ostracized, afraid to be ourselves around our fuckin' brothers. They don't build masjids for us. We have to get our own. A fuckin' fag mosque in Toronto, you know I'm all for it. Female imams, God bless 'em. Whatever. You know I don't give a shit. But let's not play that bullshit game where once we get our own scene we can push people to the sidelines, to the fuckin' fringe like they did us. Do you only want a community so you can make someone *else* feel like the Outsider?" His voice gradually raised. "Fuck that," he said sharply. "Fuck being as small as they are. I say be big. Be bigger. Kill 'em with kindness. How the fuck are they going to hate you when you love them?"

Then somebody pushed his way through the people. "Brother, man—" was all Jehangir said before Umar opened the door and stepped out.

Suggested soundtrack: "California Babylon" by the Transplants.

When you have dozens of people in a house and none of them are going anywhere, how does the party end? How does anyone ever sleep? I began wondering that when things were still up and going at four a.m. There was no room to move downstairs. Even the upstairs hallway had turned into an obstacle course with drinkers and small-talkers and sleazy hook-ups of every persuasion. Liwats, sihaqs, Ayyub with a girl whose belly spilled out of her shirt. Umar spent the night in a van with Bilal's Boulder. I imagined what sermons they gave each other about how rotten all of this was. In the house there were no sermons but thousands of stories, legends and lore about crazy things that happened on the other coast, unforgettable monsters, unbelievable shows, tales that made the tellers more worldly for having been there and the audiences feeling like they had just stumbled into the genuine wealth of their shared culture.

At Fajr time at least half of us were still conscious. Dee Dee Ali made the adhan. Everyone put their bottles down and took their boots off. I looked around. There were a lot more bottles than people. Fasiq turned off the music. My eyes were heavy. Big Mahdi from Osama bin Laden's Tunnel Diggers led the prayer with a tuba voice that matched his frame. Dee Dee up in front gave the iqama. I have no idea who stood by me on either side. I never even learned half these guys' names.

Halfway through the short prayer I realized that none of us

had made Isha. Whatever. After Fajr the taqwacores laid down anywhere there was room. Everyone gave up their floor space. Dee Dee Ali and a bunch of others went into Jehangir's room. Rabeya took three or four riot grrrls in hers. Taqwacores piled in Umar's room. Two liwats were already asleep in his bed and none of us cared what he'd say about it. I had all four members of Vote Hezbollah plus a few miscellaneous on my bedroom floor. I fell asleep thinking something holy had happened.

CHAPTER IX

How many prophets? The hadiths differed but Asif never heard a figure less than 120,000. Did that include prophets of other worlds? Probably not; then it'd be billions, even trillions. Unless, of course, we were the only ones with souls.

Asif knelt in the crimson dust and made tayammum. In the distance, two Martians out for an evening stroll noticed and watched him.

"What is it doing?" asked one as Asif made his first prostration.

"I have watched Earthmen before," the other replied. "It is praying to its gods."

"Heathen," said the first. "What kind of gods do they worship? What are their ideas about religion?"

"We don't know—but we'll have to learn if we're to teach the Earthmen Islam."

—Abu Afak, *The Rose Gardens of Mars*

Friday the twentieth of December, jumaa full of wooly Muslim punks. From the back row they looked like an outer-space carnival, each an epic in his own right with comic book haircuts and unknown band names everywhere in white on black—patches or painted on leather, dangling chains and spikes. At the door collected a mountain of army-surplus combat boots and Doc Martens like these bass players and drummers and singers went tromping through Chechen wastelands fighting on our behalf.

Fatima sat next to me.

"Where's Jehangir?" she asked.

"I haven't seen him but it's really packed in here." With the taqwacores added to our usuals there was barely room to breathe and my sujdahs would unavoidably fall upon someone else's heels. Muzammil Sadiq kept his khutbah quick for our physical comfort. Packed in real tight we witnessed a five-minute monologue all in English about how when African Muslims came to Mecca the Prophet allowed them their native drums and dancing and spots and it made them no less Muslim than the Arabs. Jehangir would have liked it. My eyes scanned the characters but couldn't spot his big orange mohawk. We stood up. Noting the Star of David more than once in the row in front of me, it hit me again how truly weird this whole scene was. Would have made as much sense to see the guy on my left just burst into flames and the one on my right grow a second head like Surrealist Dada Imam Dali Islam. Somebody gave a stiff iqama. Then Muzammil led us through the prayer—in English. At first it didn't sound right. *In the Name of Allah, Most Gracious, Most Merciful.* What the hell was that? But I can say it wasn't that big a deal, what with all the house's daily heresies. What really got me was the fact that before that Friday, I never knew what 'Sami Allahu liman hamidah" meant.

I waded my way through all the people to the front porch, stood out there shivering with my hands in my coat and my shoulders hunched cold, and I saw Jehangir coming down the sidewalk with quiet sad holy steps enveloped in white jalab, his drooping head haloed in white turban—the tail dangling down his back.

"I had to park around the corner," he said, warm exhalations escaping in gusts out his mouth.

"Where'd you go?"

"The masjid."

"Why'd you go there?"

"It's not so bad." As he went up the steps his eyes resigned to my feet. He spoke slow as though disoriented. "Nobody knows me there. I just did my thing and left. Felt good to just be a regular old Muslim."

"I could see that." Pause. "Isn't it cold in just a jalab?"

"It's ass-cold. But the masjid was warm."

"Right."

"You know they say Neil Armstrong's a Muslim?"

"Neil Armstrong?"

"First man on the moon." His words weighed more with the visibility of his breaths. "They say that when he was doing his *that's one small step for man* thing bouncing on the lunar surface, he heard the adhan."

"He did?"

"No. They made it up." He stood with stoic vigor though the air must have been like ten thousand cold knives in that thin white cotton. He said it again. "They made it up." I looked up at the sky thinking then would be as good a time as any for Elijah Muhammad's Motherplane—or the Mahdi, or Isa or whatever it is you're waiting for.

Umar's truck drove by blaring Qari Abdul-Basit. Maybe ten minutes later he came walking up the street.

"All these taqwacore vans," he said.

"Yeah there's nowhere to park," Jehangir concurred.

"Where did you go?" I asked Umar.

"I went to jumaa with Bilal's Boulder."

"Which one?" asked Jehangir.

"MSA over at school."

"How was it?"

"Al-hamdulilah."

"Where's the band?"

"They're sleeping at the masjid tonight."

"I went to the one in Amherst," said Jehangir.

"Really?" Umar replied with surprise.

"Yeah, it was pretty cool."

We went inside. Jehangir flew upstairs while I delicately pushed my way through the house, catching tidbits of everyone's mini-khutbahs as I passed. Fasiq ran his game to a white girl with jet-black hair and a Bouncing Souls t-shirt about how the Qur'an never specifically forbade hashish even though it was around at the time. Just by his posture and coolness and her enthusiastic replies I knew he'd get it, something at least. Then I overheard Amazing Ayyub's escalating objection as Rabeya ran down all the awful things Ayatullah Khumayni said in his *Tahrirolvasyleh*, how you can have sex with a baby but are financially liable for any internal damage you cause and you can bang a ewe if you kill it after squirting. I thought Ayyub would kick her in the teeth but I kept going and passed some liwaticores, Muzammil right there in the middle talking about alternative readings to the Qur'an and how maybe

Lut's people weren't punished exclusively for being gay but perhaps for robbery or something. Right behind them Umar reminded a skin that the Prophet cursed effeminate males and males who pretended to be females.

"And Rasullullah *sallallaho alayhe wa salaam* said that he would rather fall from the heavens to the earth than see another man's awrah." The skin just nodded. "You know what the *awrah* is, brother? It's the place between your navel and your knees."

With a violent yank the skin undid the button on his jeans, flung down the zipper, pulled out his junk and swiveled his hips so it flapped around, making crazy eyes with his mouth open the whole time and ugly tongue wagging. I instantly thought Umar would kill him but in fact he just stood there, eyes gaping and jaw dropped. The skin put his thing away and disappeared into people. Passing Umar, I looked the other way.

That night, I believe, we were ready to change the world. No matter how drunk and stupid everyone got, the pervading feeling was *hope.* Jehangir had succeeded in bringing his taqwacore from the West coast to the East and there they all were filling my house with empty bottles and urinating in buckets or off the front porch because both bathrooms were constantly occupied. Jehangir had shed his jalab for the usual gear, but remained somewhat aloof amidst all the carrying-on. I looked at him and missed the happy drunk Jehangir who hugged everyone, loved everyone, put his arm around everyone and sang buddy-songs no better than the beer would allow him. I missed it as though Jehangir had been ripped from me tragically, unfairly, stolen away in the night as a lesson of how mean life could be.

"Shit," he said standing on the stairwell—I sat on the same

step—with a look of sadness for the carousing taqwacores. "There's all these ayats and hadiths against making divisions in your religion, and there's going to be seventy-two sects of Islam at the end of the world but only one can be right… what if we're just another of the wrong sects? Who's to say we won't fuck things up, in our own way, as much as the Taliban?"

"We're not hurting anybody," I replied. "This whole scene is just obscene gestures and idol-smashing. It's not like we're denying people education or health care."

"It's like the fuckin' Imam of Manassas said," continued Jehangir, ignoring me. "He said not to form the *farga,* you know, the groups. That's why I wanted Bilal's Boulder here. Yeah they're cocks, y'akhi, but this isn't a sect. Please, please Allah, I know You have no reason to listen to me because, I mean, look at me—I'm shit—but please don't make this a sect."

"The night before the Tragedy," a wasted Ayyub explained, "Rasullullah appeared to his widow in a dream. He was all weeping and pale with grief n' shit. She asked Rasullullah what made him so sad and he fuckin' said, 'I have been digging the graves of Husain and his companions.'"

Saturday, December twenty-first. Kullu yawmin'Ashura.

Somebody rose before the sun, I don't remember who, but he climbed gingerly over bodies waking up whoever could wake up and we made wudhu in the kitchen sink and then moved the table to pray right there because it was the only part of the house with any space left on the floor.

There were only nine or ten of us to the jamaat. At least a few of them hadn't even gone to bed yet. Jehangir was there, and Dee Dee Ali, the others a mishmash from various bands. Jehangir and Dee Dee Ali politely bickered, each trying to get the other to lead before Jehangir finally announced a brilliant solution.

"How 'bout we *both* lead?"

"How the fuck would we do that?" asked Dee Dee Ali.

"We both stand up in front, an' we both do all the Allahu Akbars."

Dee Dee Ali looked at Jehangir Tabari with the look of *you old codger, I should have expected as much* time-blessed friendship that had adventured in years and years and survived numerous social circles and traveled the world. They had something, the two of them, and you couldn't touch it. Anything they did went beyond concerns of making sense. What's so great about making sense? Why not two imams? Rock it out, two best friends standing together to lead a gang of rejects through two rakats.

Dee Dee Ali shook his head, put his arm around Jehangir and together they walked to where the imam would stand. I proudly gave the iqama, but quiet enough so as not to bother the sleeping.

The two imams looked at each other unsure and gave a roughly synchronized Allahu Akbar. It was a clumsy prayer: Jehangir and Dee Dee stood feet-to-feet, the rest of us feet-to-feet behind them as they darted looks at each other to stay together. I'm not sure if it really worked but it happened and maybe it never happened before in the whole history of Islam. After the salaams Jehangir looked up and pointed out to Dee Dee Ali all the spots of water damage in our ceiling. Dee Dee Ali laughed the hearty kind of male laugh suggesting that maybe life could beat death.

"So how'd you do?" he whispered to Jehangir.

"What do you mean?"

"I saw you with the guitarist from the Infibulateds. Anything happen there?"

"Shit," said Jehangir. "We were talking and went into my room. She's looking through my records, we talk some more and then it's on. You know? It's fucking *on.* It gets to the point that I'm wondering where this is headed, so I'm like 'what are you up for?' And she says, 'I'm up for anything.' So I think about it and shit just snaps in my brain. I pull away from her and I tell that girl to go in the bathroom and make wudhu."

"Are you serious?"

"Shit yeah. I don't know what possessed me to do that, but that's what I fuckin' said. I told her to go make wudhu because neither of us had made Isha yet. So she just looks at me like I'm nuts but she's too drunk to really piece it out, so she gets up and goes to the bathroom while I just sit on my bed wondering what the shit is going on. Took her forever to make it, it had to be drunk-wudhu. When she came back I stood up and said I had to make wudhu. So she sat on my bed and I went to the bathroom. When I came back she was passed out."

"Holy shit."

"So I told Rabeya what happened and Rabeya had me go downstairs back to the party while she stood guard in front of my door the whole night, protecting that girl from whoever."

"Damn." They both sat there awhile in prayer posture. "Hey Jehangir, whatever happened to Hi My Name is Allah?" I raised my tired head. Jehangir turned to me, knowing he'd have to explain.

"Hi My Name is Allah was a band," he said. "It was *my* band. I played guitar and sang."

"Why'd you call it 'Hi My Name is Allah?'" I asked.

"It was the most blasphemous thing we could think of," he replied. "But then, if you think about it, instead of being a prick right off the bat… it really wasn't so bad. It was like al-Hallaj."

"Who?"

"Al-Hallaj. Abu al-Mughith al-Husayn ibn Mansur al-Hallaj the Sufi saint of Baghdad. He was one of the Sufi Drunks, you know, the ones who got so intoxicated with Allah's Presence that it fuckin' annihilated their sense of self. So al-Hallaj he fuckin' yelled out 'I am al-Haqq!' and all the assholes came out of the woodwork to get him. Put him in jail for fuckin' years, put him on trial, called him an apostate and a blasphemer. How can you say you are al-Haqq, right? *Al-Haqq* is one of Allah's Ninety-Nine Holy Names. Are you saying you're Allah?

"But al-Hallaj didn't give a *fuck*. Not even when they found him guilty and tortured him to death. He just took it all and asked Allah for their forgiveness." I looked at my hands, then the floor. I was almost too tired to take all of it in. "You know what they call al-Hallaj today? 'The Prophet of Love.' So anyway, we had a band, called it 'Hi My Name is Allah.' It was a spiritual, beautiful thing but at the same time had that whole punk ethic of alienating people."

"So what happened to the band?" I asked, repeating Dee Dee Ali's question.

"I can't sing."

"That's bullshit," snapped Dee Dee. "You can totally fuckin' sing."

"Yeah," I added, knowing that his drunken crooning left much to be desired in range and technique but carried the charm that really mattered. You couldn't *not* listen to Jehangir and you couldn't *not* love him.

"It's fuckin' punk rock," said somebody else. "Who needs to fuckin' sing?"

"Exactly," said Dee Dee. "So what the shit are you talking about?"

"Brothers," Jehangir replied, "we had some crazy songs. I

mean really, really fucked up songs. Even though we were totally sincere in our intentions—we were all fuckin' Sufis back then—it came off as really, really fuckin' disrespectful."

"That's what this whole scene's about," said Dee Dee.

"Yeah, and I love it. But I couldn't do it. I'm singing shit about Islam that, if I weren't coming from a Muslim background, you'd call an artistic Hate Crime. Seriously. I'm talking shit like the Feederz, you know, 'Jesus Entering from the Rear.' Shit like that but about Muhammad. When I sang, I used to get these awful fuckin' stomachaches like a mess of open scissors jumbled up inside me. My internal organs were still submitting to Allah, you know. My own body disagreed with what I was doing."

Neither Dee Dee Ali or I had anything to say after that.

When I finally got a turn at the bathroom I locked the door behind me, sat on the floor and beat off. I hadn't done it at all on Friday. With my piece in my hand I imagined a petite white girl from one of my classes the previous semester. As I imagined it, I snuck into her bedroom at night real quiet so as not to wake up her parents in the next room. I sat at the edge of her bed. She half-woke up and made room for me to lie down next to her. We kissed and I worked into her cute pajama top to palm her breasts—little but not pointy, they were nice and full and round and she said I could come on her if I wanted. We switched sides so I could use my right hand. My left arm under her neck, I reached around to hold a breast while I jerked. Caught just a slight glimpse down her top in the window's moonlight but then she pulled her top up, either to afford me the whole picture or just to avoid getting semen on it. We made out while I felt her with my left and jerked with my right, and for one more stimulus I asked that she ran the tip of her fingers along my balls. At first she complied passively but before I was done she seemed into it. When I was ready I got up and supported my weight with left hand on her headboard and I hovered above the girl, beating hard while she waited for it. First came a gob on her right breast, then a stronger one that shot too far. I aimed my penis down for lesser bombs and dozens of stray drops. A stream trickled from the arc of her ribcage down to her belly button where it formed a small pool. I said something funny. She said *don't make me laugh. If my body shakes it'll spill out.*

Lying perfectly still in precarious balance, she sent me quick to fetch a towel from her closet. She took it and rubbed her skin hard to get it all, starting with the pool in her navel. Though it was too dark to see I knew her skin was pink where she went rough with the towel. *You got it on my neck*, she said, exaggerating her annoyance as she wiped it off and checked her hair.

Sorry, I said.

Feel better?

Yeah, I definitely do.

Sleepy?

I think so. I thanked her and kissed her and snuck back out her window, beginning the long walk to wherever it was I came from lonely but refreshed and psychologically lifted.

As I imagined this sequence through the course of my self-abuse her outfits changed—sweatpants with pooh-bear on them, nightgowns, slips, sometimes just a camisole and panties, sometimes an oversized t-shirt. Scenes became disjointed. I ejaculated on her, then saw myself getting up to ejaculate. Then I ejaculated. Then I came in through the window. Then I was ejaculating on her. Then we were making out. Then I ejaculated. Then I began to masturbate. Then I woke her up. Then I had my hand in her pajama top. In some visions my semen hit her face.

When I approached real-life climax I found one image in my

mind and locked on it: the milky crescents of her breasts, pajama top pulled up to her collarbone. I got up and went to the toilet, propping myself up with a left hand on the wall, and I spunked. In the second of my last shot and the slow calm return to life that followed, I loved that girl. In real life I couldn't even think of her name but in fantasy life I knew she was the sweetest girl in the world. Ejaculating made me stupid. I almost got metaphysical on it and wondered if our fantasies were things that really happened in parallel universes or something and maybe somewhere else far away I really had gone into her room at night.

She was the sweetest girl in the world.

I flushed.

As I came downstairs Jehangir stopped me.

"See that guy over there?" he asked, pointing at a spike-haired lunatic. "He was telling me how there's a new wave of Taqwacore Ska starting out west. Can you believe that shit? Made me think of Rude Dawud and his old band Skallahu Akbar and how he would have loved to hear that but he's gone to Costa Rica and missing all this. Isn't that some sad shit, bro? The fuckin' world, Yusef Ali. Little deaths every day."

"D'you ever hear of Futrus?" Amazing Ayyub asked.

"No," I replied.

"It's some crazy shit."

"Okay."

"Listen to this. On the day of Imam Husain's birth, angel Jibril was sent by Allah to congratulate the Rasul. On his way, Jibril passed over the island where angel Futrus was spending his exile. He'd been punished by Allah for not performing a task or some shit… Allah took his wings away.

"Futrus saw Jibril and asked where he was going. Jibril replied that Rasullullah's grandson was born. Futrus asked Jibril to take him along so that he could plead his case to the Rasul. Jibril said okay and took Futrus. When they arrived Rasullullah was holding baby Husain in his arms. Jibril congratulated him and then told the story of Futrus. Rasul was like, 'touch my baby grandson' and Futrus did it and his wings fuckin' returned to him and he went back up to heaven."

"Wow," I said.

"And think about how that fuckin' baby turned out."

One of the taqwacore riot grrrls had a tattoo of angel wings on her shoulder blades. I noticed them when she led our Asr in a little top with her black bra straps showing. During the prayer I noted that we hadn't made Zuhr. I also realized that I prayed in a state of ritual impurity from my earlier ejaculation. Afterwards Jehangir and all his bands left for the Intercontinental to set up and get wasted before the show. The house was quiet again.

I stood surrounded by food wrappers, empty beer cases, empty beer bottles, dirty clothes and improvised ashtrays. Amazing Ayyub went up to the stereo and put on his old standby.

"HEYYYYYYY LITTLE RICH BOY," he bellowed along, "TAKE A GOOD LOOK AT ME! HEYYYYYYY LITTLE RICH BOY, TAKE A GOOD LOOK AT ME!" As Ayyub hopped around shaking his fists I suddenly felt really, really good. I had lived at that house for some time. I had made contributions to the history of the place. There was a chance that if I moved out someday, they might remember me. Maybe when that song came on at a party Ayyub would get teary-eyed and miss the time that I was in his world.

I gave him a good-natured shoulder-tackle onto the couch. "NO YUSEF, PLEASE!" he shrieked like a nutjob. "YOU DON'T KNOW WHO HUMPED ON THIS COUCH, ARGHHHH!"

Fatima swung by, found the place empty and said she had to go to the mall, inviting me to tag along. I think it was the only time that we hung out just the two of us. She played Dashboard Confessional on the ride there.

"You should be proud," she said with a smile. "You're the only one in that whole house I'd let know that I listen to such shitty music."

"What do you mean?" I asked.

"You think the taqwacores would accept me knowing that I had a Dashboard CD?"

"You *don't* think they would?"

"Yusef, please. I know you're not Mr. Punk Rock, but you've been around these guys too long to be that naïve." I attempted a coy laugh. The song, "Age Six Racer," was a duet with some unnamed female. I briefly dwelled on the idea that Islam's problem was its absence of a girl singing between the lines. Made sense in the moment.

At the mall it felt kind of cool to be seen with an attractive young woman. Other guys probably thought that we were dating. When we passed the Disney store, Fatima made a crucifix with her index fingers and hissed. If it was any of the rejects I lived with, they would have done it so loud everyone in the store could have heard it. Fatima hadn't yet reached that level of crass confidence.

"They're just the devil," she said.

"Why?" I asked.

"The whole sweatshop thing."

"Oh, right."

"Just like these jerks over here—look at that, it's disgusting. Gap, Gap Kids, Gap Body, Gap Baby, Jesus Christ—"

"And there's Foot Locker," I said, knowing she'd hate them too.

"Yeah, they're great. Nike's the worst."

"Totally."

"I don't even buy clothes at malls. Mall clothes are totally not cool."

"So why'd we come here?"

"I had to get some pictures developed." Up ahead was the Ritz. Fatima withdrew a disposable camera from her purse and did all the necessaries while I looked at frames. For some reason as I turned around, I felt a vague sexual tension with the girl behind the counter. Perhaps she too thought Fatima was my girlfriend and this somehow made me more attractive. Sexual psychology is fascinating.

We hung out in the food court waiting for her film to develop. I got Taco Bell, Fatima went to Sbarro's. We sat across from each other at our white plastic table in a sea of white plastic tables with attached white plastic chairs and annoying consumers all around. "I got a present for you," she said, reaching across the table. I looked down at my paper plate and saw a small circle of pepperoni.

"I can't."

"It's gooood."

"I thought you were vegetarian."

"I was," she replied. "I kind of am on and off. My parents give me a lot of crap for it when I'm at home."

"Really?"

"They say I can't make haram things out of halal things and I'm innovating in my religion."

"What does it have to do with religion?"

"I don't know."

"Well," I said with a look at the Kennedy half-dollar of pig meat on my plate, "this is haram, anyway." Fatima laughed.

"For all the medical reasons Muslim scholars give for not eating pork," she replied, "we shouldn't be eating any of this food court shit."

"What do you mean?"

"You ever read *Fast Food Nation*?"

"No."

"You should. The whole industry is disgusting."

"Really."

"Yeah. Totally." She went into it with me, how they treated the poor creatures that became our Big Macs. Made me consider going vegetarian myself, or at least buying my meat from a halal store where they kill animals by the sunna way. Islam has a whole system for slaughtering. You can't kill an animal in front of other animals, you give it water, you point its head toward the qiblah, you make sure its calm and at peace, and you cut its throat in such a place that it no longer feels pain. Just when I'm ready to abandon religion, something like that pops up. It's not *all* bad.

Fatima turned out to be an interesting girl. I reached the point of not even seeing her as a girl at all; she was just somebody to talk to. We went back to the Ritz a little before the hour but they had her prints done anyway. Then we left, talking about the show the whole ride back. I said something about Jehangir, I don't remember what; but for some reason I mentioned his name, completely *forgetting* the whatever that happened between them. It shouldn't even be an issue, I think. Maybe it should. I don't know. She handled it coolly but I knew there was something deep in the back of her head that was sad about Jehangir Tabari. I wondered what it was and what he did. He might not have done anything really wrong but she was so sweet and young *in that way* that he should have left her alone. Maybe they just messed around and she was such a rookie to the ways of the world that she thought it meant something to him. I knew that if I messed around with a girl like Fatima, it would have meant worlds to me. For a second I wanted to kill Jehangir.

"See you at the show," she said pulling up to the curb.

"Definitely," I replied, climbing out of her car. She drove away when I closed the door.

Rabeya, Fasiq and Ayyub went in my car. There was room for Umar but he insisted on taking his truck. Fasiq had a Kahane t-shirt that one of the taqwacores had given him. It was blue with a big white Star of David, inside it a blue power-fist. It was explained that the fist-in-star symbol was used by Jewish resistance fighters during World War II.

A line of Muslims and punks started at the Intercontinental's door and wrapped around the block. We walked past them all and got in early. The floor was empty. Jehangir stood on stage messing with the microphone stand. The bands were all backstage, including, I assumed, Bilal's Boulder. Wondered how that was going.

They opened the doors at seven and Jehangir's dream came true. The Muslims and punks paid their four dollars, poured in, circulated, socialized, ordered drinks and took their places.

As cold as it was outside, inside it was hot enough for Amazing Ayyub to tear off his Confederate shirt and flash the big green "KARBALA" on his chest.

"YEAAAAAAH!" he screamed as he tossed his shirt somewhere. I knew he'd forget about it and leave the Intercontinental that night returning to Buffalo winter with goosebumps and hard purple nipples. Ayyub was that kind of idiot, the idiot that made you love idiots.

First band covered the Ramones' "Rock and Roll High School" on the Intercontinental's crumbling stage. I think they were the Zaqqums. Young Sid-Vicious-snarl-looking kid with hair like Pampero Firpo but dyed brown-red on one side and jet black on the other. Gangly frame and tight pants, leather jacket with standard spikes and some unknown band's huge black-and-white patch safety-pinned on the back. He bounced around while a parade of homely, misshapen characters in the crowd put their arms around each other and danced in a line of lost and weary. Then a lone dude with long, straight black hair ran weaving between clusters and couples, his fist in the air and his knees kicking high. People still filtered in. Much of the floor remained visible, the shiny floor reflecting the green off a stage light. Watching the ugly punks play and born losers dance, I realized again how cool I was not.

"You've never seen us here before," spat the young Zaqqums singer into the microphone, "and you probably never will again. So if you didn't like us, fuck you and if you did, fuck you too." Damn right. Punk Rawk. The next band came up, a slightly different flavor with the singer wearing a necktie, calling themselves Eight from the Ukil. They only did a few songs. Then came the next band with a few songs, and another and so on. After each group played its set they would just hop off the stage and join the pit. More than anything these guys were *fans.* Backstage I imagined Jehangir coordinating everything and telling bands when to go on and such. The Infibulateds came out and its lead singer threw her shirt off, letting her breasts flop around. Everyone cheered. Maghrib time came and went and nobody noticed. It was strange to think that the Infibulateds' singer and a large portion of her audience was Muslim. You just get certain concepts in your head that are hard to shake. The Ghilmans singer grabbed his bassist's nuts right there on stage as nothing more than a Fuck You to Islamic homophobia. Those guys were Muslim too. Their drummer wore hejab. Reminded me of the burqa that Rabeya gave me. Burning Books for Cat Stevens covered "Wild World" punk-style while everyone shoved at each other in the pit. The bisexual Pathan girl singer from Gross National did her anti-WTO song and burned an American flag. The Imran Khan Experience burned an Israeli flag though its guitarist wore the Star of David. The Wilden Mukhallodun sang anti-war anthems that got everyone going. Then Vote Hezbollah did a pro-Bush song that pissed everyone off but that was the whole point and even when the crowd booed, they had a great time doing it because they got the joke. You have to stop trying to make sense of Punk—what it's for, what it's against. It's against everything. The singer from Vote Hezbollah pissed on a Qur'an. Everyone loved it. Then he picked up the kitab, shook some drips off, carefully turned the frail wet pages and recited Ya Sin with absolute sincerity. Somehow the whole thing made sense.

Then Bilal's Boulder came out. All the bands pretty much got the same reaction when they first appeared on stage because none of these Buffalo kids could tell one taqwacore group from the next. The Bilal's Boulder guys looked scary. Their jalabs and turbans were gone. Their heads were shaved. They went shirtless, their arms covered in tattooed Qur'anic ayats. They wore green suspenders and combat boots. I didn't know what was going to happen. Backstage, I was sure, Jehangir had to be nervous.

"As-salaamu alaikum," said the singer. "We are Bilal's Boulder, and al-hamdulilah we are happy for this opportunity to come to Buffalo, insha'Allah subhanahu wa ta'Ala and spread the deen of Islaam. It is time for salaatul-Ishaa, so insha'Allah we are going to pray." Their drummer went up to the microphone and made a piercing adhan. They then jumped off the stage. The singer seemed to make calculations in his head. "This is the proper qiblah, insha'Allah," he said, walking to the far wall. Everyone stood behind him. "Make your lines straight." I don't think he knew how many kafrs were standing behind him, but they all joined the salaat like they'd been doing it for years. Half the Muslims were drunk anyway. But when he said Allahu Akbar each and every last soul in the room put his or her hands to their ears. We hadn't put any rugs down. The floor was cold and grimy and wet from snow melting off our feet. The stage lights switched up. Red, blue, yellow, green. When we sat up from our first sujdah I noticed Umar a couple of rows ahead. I was sure he loved these guys.

After the prayer Bilal's Boulder played one song. They had spent most of their allotted time on the salat. The song was okay. The vocals were loud and hyper and nobody could tell what he was saying, so they enjoyed the empty aggression and rocked out.

After their set Bilal's Boulder stood in the crowd. They didn't seem too involved in any of the following bands. When slam dancers flew their way, they shoved them back and went back to the crossed-arms tough-guy stance. The Mutaweens did their song "Ahmed Deedat's Dead" and we all laughed.

Then came One Trip Abroad. Dee Dee Ali had it, whatever

you call the *it* that separates born performers from the not-quites. He immediately bonded with everyone in the room, with the probable exception of Bilal's Boulder.

"Alright kids," said Dee Dee towards the end of their set, "you've been great. And we got one more treat for you, a song from the Man himself, the guy who put all this shit together… JEHANGIR TABARI!" The crowd cheered in love for the drunk. He came out from backstage and Dee Dee put a hand on his shoulder, whispered something in his ear. Jehangir shook his head. Dee Dee pleaded. Without knowing what was said, I could tell that Jehangir conceded. He said something to the band.

"Fuck this guy," spat Jehangir, gesturing to Dee Dee Ali. Everyone laughed. "I'm so fuckin' wasted right now." Everyone cheered. "Okay, this song is called 'I Killed a Cat.'" Then the band jumped right into it and Jehangir covered Sid's cover of Frank Sinatra's "My Way." Creatures in the audience slammed into each other. I could have sworn I saw a member of Bilal's Boulder punch somebody but everything happened too fast to see. Jehangir screamed the lyrics. *And now, the end is near / and so I face the final curtain / you cunt, I'm not a queer / I'll state my case, of which I'm certain / I've lived a life that's full / and traveled each and every highway / and more, much more than this / I did it my way.*

I found myself in the pit getting thrown and hit every which way and I did only what I could do to avoid ending up on the floor. *Regrets, I've had a few / but then again, too few to mention / I did what I had to do / and saw it through without exception / I've planned each giant course / each careful step along the highway / and more, much more than this / I did it my way.*

Jehangir looked like he belonged up there, maybe even more than Dee Dee Ali. I don't know. Too much was going on. I couldn't really get more than a parting glance at him. *There were times, I'm sure you knew / when there was fuck, fuck else to do / but through it all, when there was doubt / I shot it up or kicked it down / I fought them all / and did it my way.*

I saw the Infibulateds' singer in the crowd, her tits still out, holding her own in an onslaught of rowdy slam dancers. Some guy who struck me as a storytelling punk elder shook up a beer bottle with his thumb over the hole and sprayed it everywhere. Then I saw Rabeya by the stage. Fasiq climbed up and danced around Jehangir. *Knocked out in bed last night / I've had my fill, my share of looting / and now, the tears subside / I find it all so amusing / to think I killed a cat / and may I say, oh no not their way / but no, no not me / I did it my way.*

Fasiq threw his fists in the air. I observed hard words said between Bilal's Boulder and the Infibulateds' singer. Then somebody knocked into me hard and I grabbed somebody to stay on my feet. He turned around and shoved me backwards into the first guy who hit me. At one point I felt like I was whitewater rafting, though I had no raft and the raging rapids were people. Rabeya was standing on the stage. I didn't know why or when she got up there. Didn't have time to think about it. *For what is a brat, what has he got? / he finds out that he cannot / say the things he truly feels / but only the words, not what he feels / the record shows, I've got no clothes / and did it my way.*

The melee ended with the song. Exhausted, Jehangir's head cocked back and his eyes aimed up at the lights. We screamed our approval. I wondered if his stomach hurt, if he had suffered for our sake.

Rabeya fell to her knees before Fasiq. From where I stood I couldn't see her face when she lifted the niqab. She let the cloth fall back over the intersection of his penis and her mouth. Then she bobbed back and forth with almost athletic power as the audience took a second to realize what was happening, then burst into a roar of enthusiastic disbelief. It couldn't even register to me what I was seeing, what Rabeya was doing and where she was doing it. Fasiq beamed with the proud smile of a natural iconoclast, the giant white Star of David on his blue shirt stealing attention like a second face. Jehangir just stood there laughing with no idea what to do. Fasiq gently palmed the back of her burqa'd head as it smashed repeatedly into his pelvis, her hands braced on his hips. Somebody handed him a beer and the scene was complete: punk rocker with a Zionist t-shirt and Budweiser in his hand getting blown by a girl in full purdah while two hundred drunk punks looked on. Fasiq's body stiffened and his smile disappeared.

"The Moment of Truth," someone said next to me. Rabeya pulled away, Fasiq's penis emerging from the fabric. It was pointed to the ground, slowly going flaccid, with a trail of saliva hanging from the tip. He let it hang as though yet unaware that it was time to zip up. Rabeya rose to her feet and turned to the crowd. She lifted her niqab—again I couldn't see her face, but they did—and with a violent motion of her neck let it fly. The white ropes of semen twirled like Australian bolos in the air before landing in the direction of Bilal's Boulder. The crowd popped. Even people standing near Bilal's Boulder cheered though the projectile sperms could have easily hit *them*. The general reaction was that Rabeya's onstage blowjob might have been the most Punk Rawk thing any of them had ever seen—if not the blowjob itself, the act of spitting semen at spectators.

Noticeably wary of what could happen, Jehangir started up a fast hard song that had everyone slamming into each other. Hopefully the moment would be forgotten in a thrash-riot. It wasn't. The Bilal's Boulder guys got mean hitting everyone around them with forearms and elbows and kicking their knees up high like the assholes you sometimes see at shows. They were out to hurt people. One kid protested and found himself in a reverse chinlock. The band worked him over in a straight lynching. Jehangir saw it and yelled into the microphone. Bilal's Boulder kept going. Jehangir yelled again. People around the fight made nervous attempts to pull them off. Jehangir yelled again. Then he looked at One Trip Abroad, then back at the fight, then—I could be wrong, but I swear he did—at me. And he flew off the stage right at them, plunging fast in a storm of punches and kicks and pulling and shoving, mean faces, snarling teeth, eyes both angry and scared at once, mashes of people into each other with stray arms everywhere, nobody caring anymore who they actually hit. Somebody grabbed Jehangir from behind and they all jumped on him. From the other side of the Intercontinental Umar climbed onstage, ran over and jumped in the scene. I felt as though I was watching them both drown, Jehangir and Umar, drowning in people, sinking fast under heavy boots and hands. Umar held his own, fighting Bilal's Boulder at every side. The stage lights continued to rotate colors—they didn't know better. Red, blue, yellow. Last time I ever saw Jehangir Tabari, he and those tearing him apart were all bathed in green. Then he was gone.

CHAPTER X

The lion of this world
seeks a prey and
provision;
the lion of the Lord
seeks freedom
and death.
—Jalaluddin Rumi

Early one morning I woke myself up, saw that it was still dark and rolled out of bed. Went down to the bathroom, turning on the water but not the lights. Washed my hands. My arms up to the elbows. Brought water to my nose and mouth. Washed my face and my ears. Back of the neck. Feet. Walked back to my room. Spread out a towel on the floor and stood on it with feet parallel and pointed at the Bayt. Kept my back straight. Inhaled through my mouth. Felt the air come in cool and go out warm.

"Allahu Akbar," I said. Then I made Fajr.

It had been over a week and we still had Jehangir's ashes in our living room. Nobody had a clue what he might have wanted for himself. Drive out West and scatter them by the Pacific, said Umar through his teeth, his jaw still wired shut. Snort him like Stiv Bator, said Amazing Ayyub. I opened the urn once and touched them. They were harder and stronger than you'd expect, not so much ashes but little chips.

Little chips of man.

And that, in a jar, was Jehangir. Jehangir king of the shaheed stage dive. Jehangir who gave tafsirs to the drunken streets. Jehangir who's up there with the houris in a hollowed pearl sixty miles wide. Jehangir the electric-guitar muezzin drunk and calling us all to stupor-prayer. Jehangir who took my Islam to its perihelion climax. Jehangir the rustlin' and ramblin' cowboy fellaheen. Jehangir star of twenty thousand unborn deens. Jehangir the champ who left us championless like Husain did on those blood-clumped Karbala sands. Jehangir whose heroes were Malcolm X and Johnny Cash. Jehangir the street-punk anarchist who pissed all over his deen but then went and died for it anyway. Jehangir who spoke Urdu, Pashtu, Punjabi, a little Farsi and six dialects of English. Jehangir the new punk laureate after Patti Smith and Jim Carroll. Jehangir the Walt Whitman Iqbal. Jehangir the skinny South Asian golden-skinned and orange-mohawked. Jehangir the walking peak of eloquence. Jehangir the living 69 between death and love, think about it like that! Death with love's dick in his mouth and love with death's dick too. Jehangir who went as Hollywood Hulk Hogan for Halloween. Jehangir with the scowling James Dean look, James Deen, James Deen Jihad though I'm not sure if the struggle was ever Holy or even a War. Jehangir the feminist but still a nonchalant male slut. Jehangir who wore the sad and pained story of fourteen centuries but who practiced Islam like a newborn baby would. Jehangir who drinks with Sid at the Lake-Fount. Jehangir who stole the Shah's car. Jehangir the very last tycoon. Jehangir Oi Oi Oi, Jehangir Roots n' Boots or Shoes n' Booze,

Jehangir American Muslim.

When I remember Jehangir I see him in the boardslide before a marble-pillared backdrop, skateboard precisely angled on the rail, feet sharply poised, perilous stone steps on either side, arms outstretched like an effortless Apollo—I know he can ride that railing no matter how long it goes, even across oceans, even with all of us on his back.

With almost a month left to my winter break I drove home. I brought almost everything I owned, not completely sure I'd come back for spring semester. Left Mustafa's books where they had always been.

At home my religion stayed soft and calm like there was nothing to fight. Without a speck of disrespect to Jehangir and the taqwacores, it was the best feeling in the world.

Jehangir's distorted melodic solo did not represent the majority of American Muslims, but neither did the shaykhs of al-Azar. Most of us fall somewhere in that big gray void between.

I remember the yellow-covered pulp novel Jehangir left in the Rochester masjid. *The Punk*, by Gideon Sams. I wonder who found it and if they gave Gideon a chance. I remember the Imam of Manassas, immortalized at least to Ayyub though Jehangir's traveler tales. I wonder if he actually existed, or if there was even really a masjid in Manassas.

Since New Year's I've only heard the word 'taqwacore' once or twice. It stays out West, living its own life. Bands come and go without my awareness. It's like they're all a universe away. The notion of Muslim Punk feels like an ex-girlfriend to me, or at least how I'd imagine an ex-girlfriend would feel if I had one. I'm glad it's still out there and I hope it's doing well, but to check up on it would just hurt me all over again.

Somehow my email address had circulated its way to the hands of a zine writer in Campbell, California wanting to ask me about Jehangir and 12/21. Apparently Jehangir had become the Kurt Cobain for a whole mess of people. His face had turned into a t-shirt, his name a cliché lyric.

The zine writer interviewed me like I were a Sahaba. Did Jehangir pray, how did he pray, did he do it at the right times or just whenever, did he make wudhu, whose fiqh did he follow, what bands did he like, did he support liwaticore, was he politically active in any way, did he ever sing or put out an album, so on and on. I gave the guy what he wanted and now it's somebody's sunna.

Everything in the body regenerates. You get new skin, new organs, new cells. Quite literally, the person you were seven years ago no longer exists.

If I lived fourteen centuries I would be, give or take, sixty different people.

I'm sure they found someone to take my room. Jehangir's too, for that matter. It's been long enough. Neither of us are going back. Soon the weather will be nice again and Fasiq will climb out that bathroom window with his weed and Qur'an and maybe two new recruits. He'll fill their heads with tales of Jehangir and a mysterious nation of Muslim Punks somewhere out there, toward the far ocean—

And maybe, insha'Allah, Fasiq'll have a story or two about me. I don't know what; maybe just that I was *there* for all of it. I wasn't a crazy punk or holy blasphemer but at least I was *there.* If Lynn's still around he can say that I hooked up with her in what used to be my room. Whatever.

We're gone to the archives: Jehangir, Rude Dawud, prehistoric Mustafa and me. When Umar, Rabeya, Fasiq and Ayyub move out so too goes our memory. It's like we move out twice. It's like that Cordoba cathedral with ayats on the wall and no Moors in sight.

For some reason, to me they were all on the same side of some impassable boundary as Jehangir. The other day I noticed a child's handprint in the sidewalk and immediately envisioned Amazing Ayyub saying that the five outstretched fingers represented the *ahlul-bayt* of Muhammad, Fatima, Ali, Hasan and Husain. I smiled thinking of Ayyub and even laughed; but it never struck me that I could call the house and talk to him, that he remained a full flesh-and-blood human life no matter where I went.

I think of Buffalo whenever my hands get so cold that my fingers hurt. Imagine the desert, Jehangir used to say. He'd close his eyes and tell me that as far as he was concerned he had fled to Karbala.

"Hey there's Andrew Jackson," he'd say with eyes closed. "Andrew Jackson out in Karbala, wow, cool. Riding his white horse, makin' it stand up on its hind legs."

Mark Twain lived in Buffalo. He's buried in Elmira. Jehangir hajj'd there and poured Zamzam water on his grave, but I think this has already been mentioned.

...Jehangir Tabari who passed through the world like a stranger, Jehangir Tabari in Buffalo like Imam Burroughs in Tangiers, Jehangir Tabari the new Hassan bin Sabbah and Jehangir Tabari the only Jehangir Tabari there ever was, Jehangir Tabari Leader of the Youths of Paradise, Jehangir Tabari who'll someday have people whipping themselves for his innocence. Jehangir Tabari, the Sealed Nectar.

...Jehangir Tabari the staggering Sophoclean bicephalic pitbull on creatine, Jehangir the Gutter Dervish.

If Allah's the Beloved, Jehangir shaved his initials in Her pubic hair.

If intoxication's just a Rumi metaphor, Jehangir fucked Allah with a beer bottle.

Buffalo has a mean winter. Even when the snow comes light and fluffy there's just too much and then it piles on like a massive carpet-bombing. By February it starts to wane here and there only to hit you hard just when you think it's let up.

I don't miss that. On weather alone, you can be depressed in Buffalo no matter what you do.

But I miss people.

Muslims, non-Muslims and the sincere tweeners. Damn *al-zariyats*, they tossed me far.

Jehangir's dead and cremated. I'm glad they didn't bury him in the cold Buffalo ground. Maybe his cremating will save him from the Torment of the Grave.

Staghfir'Allah.

If the Rab wanted to He could reassemble Jehangir and torment him all the live-long day, really get him good for all the rotten things he had done. Should that be the Allah that you want, knock yourself out.

It's okay to *watch* cartoons; but if you fear the Fire, limit your drawing to trees and rocks.

I'm talking to a girl on the internet. Her name is Zuhra. She's a freshman at Binghamton University, a little over an hour south of Syracuse on the I-81. She baby-sits part-time for a devout Christian family in the neighboring town of Vestal. Two boys and a girl; sweet kids, she says.

We've never met but I close my eyes and imagine her. An inherent, intangible modesty reads in her eyes. With the Christian kids there's a graceful mom-love to her hands when she band-aids a scraped knee or washes their hair in the tub and makes sure the shampoo stays out of their eyes. The way I imagine her, she always has her straight black hair up in a bandana but when she lets it down she just kills you. It's also rare to see her smile, I mean really really smile when it's not just her showing her teeth but you see the smile in her eyes too as they light up and open wide, a spiritual smile from deep down inside her. When you finally see one of those you're *done.*

Another item from my daydream file: she has one pair of jeans with a substantial tear in the back, high enough on her right thigh that it reveals just a glimpse of her underwear. She wears the jeans with full knowledge and I can't think any less of her for it. Any remotely sexual gesture from the girl comes with such awkwardness and uncertainty that you only sanctify her more. God bless her. I see fifteen-year old girls walking around now with things like *Princess* or *Flirt* emblazoned across the asses of their sweatpants and I don't know what to do with that.

Chances are I'm totally off-base. Like I said, we haven't actually seen each other. She's never mentioned whether there's actually a hole in her jeans. But I do know that Zuhra writes poetry—she told me that much. Nothing she'd show anyone, though. She likes Sylvia Plath and Anne Sexton. She also plays guitar. I told her that Rasullullah said it was better for your body to be filled with pus than poetry and that Allah turns musicians into monkeys and pigs on the Day of Judgment, but I followed that up with a smiley-face emoticon. *LOL,* she replied.

I also know that Zuhra drinks. She drinks to the point that her kafr friends appoint one from their group to look after her whenever they go out, watch her, keep track of how much she has, cut her off when she's done and ward off sleazy guys. She'll drink until she passes out and urinates on herself. Zuhra views her own life in frames of personal tragedy and waning resistance to inevitable self-annihilation as laid out by her heroes. Sylvia Plath and Anne Sexton were both suicides. Zelda Fitzgerald died in a burning mental institution.

I stood watching from the screen, draped in the ihram of pilgrims: two white towels, the *izar* and the *rida.* The izar was wrapped around my waist, the rida over my left shoulder leaving the right shoulder and arm naked. That was how they did it in the time of Prophet Muhammad, peace and blessings be upon him. My bare feet were cold on the spaceship floor. Labbayk Allahumma, Labbayk.

Over the ihram goes a bulky spacesuit required for survival in Earth's poisonous atmosphere. As I pulled it on I wondered what it might have been like to visit the Holy City when it actually existed—when there was a Ka'ba, Zamzam well, stations of Abraham and Shaytans to pelt with stones; back before Mecca and Tokyo and New York and Paris were all identically matching holes in the dirt. The Holy City is now as it was the day baby Ismail cried of thirst and his mother ran desperately between those two hills.

Goodnight, Islam. Don't let the bed bugs bite.

—Abu Afak, *Ten Million Miles Home*

Not a bad book. It gets cornball but charmingly so. I ordered it online.

Sometimes I think of Jehangir as an Islamic Rob Van Dam with all these amazing moves that nobody's ever seen before, flip-flying his way to the big wow finish Five Star Frog after which he always holds his ribs like it killed him. Then I reconsider. Maybe Jehangir was only an apostate, a bum, a lazy slob alcoholic with the maturity of an ejaculating eleven-year-old. Maybe it doesn't matter either way.

If he left me with anything, it's this simple idea:

I can answer my own question.

Fuck the local imam, fuck the PhDs at al-Madina al-Munawwara, fuck Siraj Wahhaj, fuck Cat Stevens. Fuck the traditionalists and fuck the apostates too—fuck Ibn Warraq, fuck Anwar Sheikh, fuck Ali Sina, fuck them all, let me puke out every book I've consumed, give me the Islam of starry-night cornfields with wind rustling through my shirt and reckless *fisabilillah* make-out sprees that won't lead to anything but hurt. Knee-deep in a creek is where I'll find my kitab. If Allah wants to say anything to me He'll do so on the faces of my brothers and sisters. If there's any Law that I need to follow, I'll find it out there in the world.

Jehangir had said he came to Buffalo for his brother. I didn't know what that meant because he had no brother. He always used to talk about how, with the exception of his uncle, his whole upbringing had been overrun with women.

Now I know what he meant.

Jehangir's uncle was a truck driver and one summer took him up and down and left and right across this continent, seeing it all—all people, all ways. Texas, Mississippi, New York, D.C., Montana, the Dakotas, Oregon. Mexico and Canada. It's hard for me to imagine Jehangir Tabari as a child, figuring he didn't have the mohawk, but it felt right to picture him adventuring and tasting life and living in a tractor-trailer cab. Anyway when he was out in California with the taqwacores, Jehangir remembered us out here and figured he had found something that we, his *brothers*, could use. So he brought it like missionaries from across the ocean or Muhammad coming down Hira. Brought it East to cold Buffalo, preached his new Sufism and left us.

Umar used to have one of those Torso Bob things. It was basically a punching bag designed to look like an armless guy from the waist up. Umar's Torso Bob looked pretty mean. If he was a real guy, and had arms, I wouldn't have messed with him.

One day Jehangir convicted Torso Bob of apostasy—"I heard him sing the Qur'an!"—and sawed his head off. It was pretty funny. Jehangir made a big show of it, all ceremonial Protection of Virtue style. Umar still used the headless torso. The head was used in a game of 'flaming dodgeball.' Fasiq dabbed rubber cement all over the head, then lit it. We had fun tossing fireballs at each other until Ayyub burned his leg.

When I left Buffalo I took the head with me. I didn't think anyone would mind. It's just a piece of that era, a relic from previous chapters reminding me that it all actually happened.

I have a mess of artifacts from the house, keep them all in a cardboard box in my closet. Dog-eared Abu Afak paperbacks, some CDs, a t-shirt for some band I had never heard of, an empty beer bottle. And the burqa, which I wore once. Just in my bedroom with the door closed but I wore it. I sat on my bed unable to see right or left, only directly ahead. Felt like a horse with those shields on its eyes. For no particular reason I was completely naked underneath. My cock grew and poked up the cloth. Looking at it I finally understood the term "pitch a tent." That's what it looked like. I grabbed it. The fabric made my hand almost feel like someone else. I slid off the bed and rested on my knees, still stroking. With my left hand I lifted the niqab, exposing my mouth for Fasiq's imaginary dick.

I don't know why this happened. I don't know what it means that I spunked in the burqa. Insha'Allah, it doesn't mean anything. When you think about sex all the time and exhaust your possibilities, eventually—given the proper circumstances—you'll entertain a different perspective. Just because I thought about that doesn't mean I wanted to do it. I was probably turned on by the concept of the blowjob. It'd be nice getting one, as far as I can imagine. Maybe I'll find out if this thing with Zuhra picks up (insha'Allah).

So there you have it. As a Muslim I dropped the ball. But I'm pretty sure that I'm still a human being.

Sulayman hiya hatta matla ill Fajr.